HOT LIKE FIRE

∽✤∾

SHERRICE THOMAS

AWAKENED VITALITY
PATASKALA, OH

HOT LIKE FIRE

For information about special discounts for bulk purchases, please contact Awakened Vitality, Inc. Special Sales at (614) 496-1143 or visit our website at www.awakenedvitality.com.

Library of Congress Cataloging-in-Publication Data

Thomas, Sherrice
Hot Like Fire: a novel/Sherrice Thomas
Visionary and Metaphysical-Fiction.I.Title

  ISBN-13: 978-0982672716
  ISBN-10: 0982672713

Printed in the United States of America

སྐ ᘒᑕ

I dedicate this book to the creator's righteous women who are seeking the truth for themselves. The chains of religion, racism, and patriarchy can't confine you. Know God for yourself.

HOT LIKE FIRE

ONE

"A PSYCHIC? Let me get this straight. You want me . . . to go with you . . . to see a psychic?" Lillie Corven stopped jogging and gulped down deep breaths of the fresh sea air. She turned to see her friend face to face. "I believe this California heat has fried your brain."

"No, my brain is working better than ever, silly. It's just that vacations shouldn't be boring, right?"

Grace Kendall raised her hands and shrugged her shoulders. Lillie slapped her own thigh and sniggered at her friend's silly declaration. Sweat dripped down her face like a leaky faucet enticing her to long for the nearby ocean where the palm trees blew in the wind. Despite her state of shock, she welcomed the invasive odor of salt water into her nostrils.

"Boring is one thing. Wasting time is another. And your idea is a huge waste of my precious time."

Grace winked her right eye in her best friends direction and wolfed down water from her magenta bottle. Henna red kinky-curly hair framed her heart shaped face perfectly, emphasizing the coyness of her radiant smile.

"Look. We're here on vacation to relax. There's no time to entertain your silly new age fetish."

With Lillie's hectic work schedule, she rarely had time to wind down, so she decided to take full advantage of this opportunity. She'd planned water excursions, massages, and other luxurious adventures for this vacation. Supernatural visitations from the dark side weren't part of the plan.

"Hey! Don't hate me because I'm open to the spirit world."

Grace, the quintessential flower child and free spirit, drove Lillie bananas. She placed her hand on her cocked hip and retorted, "Whatever. Let's finish this run so we can shower and get ready for our massages."

"Not so fast, sister. Sage does readings in the comfort of her own home, which is just a little further down the beach."

"Sage?" Lillie screamed and as her mouth dropped, her eyeballs bulged out. "Humph! Only you would be on a first name basis with a clairvoyant beach bum. I bet you planned this all along."

"Well, not exactly." Grace reached to scratch her nose and diverted her attention to the ground. At that point, Lillie knew she was lying.

"I've heard her visions are ninety-five percent accurate and since we're close to her home—"

"Shut the front door," Lillie exclaimed. "She actually keeps track of how many of her visions come to fruition?"

As an entrepreneur, Lillie understood the power of metrics. When used in the correct manner, statistics could be weaved together to tell a story for current and potential clients. Presenting a scorecard with strong measurements separated her company from the others bidding on the same contracts. Sage did work out of her home, so technically, she could be considered an entrepreneur too. The combination of the mystic appeal and tracking success stories probably kept her in business. She'd almost convinced herself that Sage's practice was normal, and then she came back to her senses. She'd seen too many exposés on psychics and wasn't about to fall for this mess. Several years ago, Miss Cleo, from the Psychic Friends Network, took the world by storm with her infomercials. Thank goodness droves of people exposed her plethora of lies before she could rip anyone else off for her own financial gain.

Lillie zeroed in on Grace, looked her dead square in the eye, and shouted, "Do you really believe in this stuff?"

"Oh, so just because her business isn't as straight laced as yours, it's not real?" Grace challenged.

Lillie took pride in the fact of being open to the perspective of others without compromising her own beliefs. At the same time, she couldn't believe Grace had the nerve to compare her legitimate business to Sage's fake shenanigans.

"You know what? I'll go with you, just to prove your Sage is a fraud and a charlatan."

"Maybe you'll convince her to get saved, sanctified, and filled with the Holy Ghost. Oh I forgot, you're barely saved yourself," Grace jested, as she dropped her head towards the ground and bucked her hips in the air, faking a church lady shout.

"Humph! We'll see."

"Her place is right by the flimsy looking T-shirt shack."

Grace's eyes brightened as she pointed in the direction of their destination. Lillie followed her friend's optical target and couldn't help but notice crooked palm trees surrounding the home, an odd sight for such a pristine beach.

"Down there by those crooked palm trees?"

"Umm hmm. I'm sure of it. In fact, I'll race you there."

Before Lillie could respond, Grace took off running with a powerful, cheetah-like stride that caught the attention of several onlookers. Standing in Grace's trail of sand, Lillie's jaw dropped. Without hesitation, she jolted into action, pumping her arms and legs with gazelle like intensity. Lillie executed each stride with precision and speed. She welcomed the taste of victory as she increased the pace.

Grace floated through the salt-flavored air like a slinky grey-hound sniffing out the finish line. At the foot of her friend's heel, Lillie continued to press towards the mark. At that moment, Grace lengthened her stride and released an exponential dose of nitro, almost crashing into Sage's gate just to beat Lillie by one stride.

"Hah! Top that!"

Lillie swallowed the nasty taste of defeat while Grace danced circles around her, belting out, "I am the champion! I am the champion!"

Onlookers who watched the race applauded and cheered while Lillie stomped the ground, causing morsels of sand to invade her eyes. She rubbed them with vigor, but the sandpapery feeling clouded her vision for a moment.

"You know I would have won if you were woman enough to race me fair and square."

Now, they were face to face with Sage's tiny beach house. Lillie couldn't help but take notice of the tide rolling away while the seagulls dove through the cloudless sky. She wondered if the briny oceanic scent attracted them to the sandy haven. Just then, a shimmery chill filled the air in the midst of the California heat and the hair on Lillie's back rose. Her feet rooted to the ground as her confidence faded and an ominous fear took over her psyche.

"Do you feel that?"

Grace didn't respond so Lillie whipped her head around to see Grace's chest heave up and down to an erratic rhythm. Ironically, their capricious heart palpitations seemed to be in harmony. Thump, thump! Thump! Thump, thump, thump! Both women shivered, despite the fact they were in the midst of ninety-degree heat. New beads of sweat formed on Lillie's forehead and trickled down into her ears.

As her anticipation grew, Lillie tried to shift her focus from her emotional reaction to the tangible surroundings. To Lillie's surprise, no neon lights or marketing signs let those passing by know this was the home of a psychic. Blue paint peeled off the wood that had given way to the abuse of the corrosive sea air. Wild, unkempt trees with uneven branches and dried leaves surrounded the perimeter of the home. The weed infested flower garden revealed the heart of plants crying out for tender love and care. A beach house was supposed to be synonymous with relaxation. This one didn't meet that criterion.

Grace sauntered onto the porch and quickly rang the doorbell. Who Lillie imagined would answer didn't appear. Before her stood a portly older woman, not the exotic strumpet she'd expected. She'd even envisioned Sage wearing a purple hip scarf with gold coins dangling from the cloth. Instead, this so-called psychic had all the trappings of an Amish grandmother.

"Hi. I'm Sage. I've been expecting you two."

Her voice rang sweetly like an old church mother who gave out peppermints and hugs. Sage flashed a smile revealing a dental disaster that could have been the catalyst for the war in Iraq. Tiny pieces of meat stuck in between her tartar-encrusted teeth, dingy brown in color. When Sage opened her mouth to speak, the stench almost knocked Lillie off her feet. She convulsed as she felt bile in her stomach rise. The lethal stench that emanated from Sage's orifice was definitely a secret weapon for world domination. Disgusted, Lillie turned away from Sage and focused on the disaster called a living room, filled with a plethora of hideous, dated furniture full of holes. This money pit was a far cry from the psychedelic shack Lillie imagined for the beach diviner. In fact, the room was void of any overt display of mystic paraphernalia. Despite the need for a good old-fashioned cleaning, Lillie saw one redeeming quality—the comfort of a cool sea breeze wafting through the unscreened windows.

Sage gestured for Lillie and Grace to follow her down the hall. When they entered her workplace, the beach-filled aroma from the other room transitioned to one of mothballs and cedar pine blocks. Grace immediately turned her nose up in disgust. Unlike the entry room, this one reeked of the typical paraphernalia she expected to see—tarot cards, crystals, candles, statues of angels, and herbs. Dust rose into the air when Sage plopped her bottom down on a chair to light a murky green candle. The chemical reaction from the flame meeting the wax emitted a vaguely familiar scent.

Sage welcomed her guests to sit in front of her workstation. She pulled out a translucent crystal ball and gently set it on an ornate silver stand fashioned out of entwined red-eyed cobras. Lillie prayed silently for divine protection when she thought she saw their eyes shift. Sage closed her eyes for a brief moment then reopened them to stare at some imaginary item over Lillie's shoulder. From the look of things, she appeared to be in a trance. Without warning, her eyes moved in swift little circles then rolled back into her head.

Caught up in Sage's web of deception, Grace twisted her fingertips. Not as receptive to Sage's mystical antics, Lillie crossed her arms and lodged her feet in the ground like a tree planted by the rivers of water. She wanted nothing to do with this pathetic charade. Without warning, Sage hummed like a Buddhist monk, then, she blurted out, "You. Young lady, what's your name?"

If you're a real psychic, shouldn't you know it already?

An exasperated sigh escaped from Sage's lips as she tapped her fingers on the desk, waiting for a response. The resounding echo resembled ominous claps of thunder on a stormy summer night; an audio cacophony created to make even the fiercest linebacker to run for cover. Lillie's initial level of confidence dropped, as she tasted the salty beads of sweat slowly dribbling down her face.

"My. Name. Is. . . . Lil . . . Lillie."

The tremors in her voice shook like a six point earthquake on the Richter scale. Unable to control her own body, she shifted from one side of the chair to the other. Lillie noticed the tiny hair on her arms rising. She rubbed her arms for comfort, only to feel the formation of tiny goose bumps. Fear ran rampant and Lillie didn't know how to catch it, so she closed her eyes and scrunched up her cheeks. Sage cackled, reminding Lillie of a crazy witch flying across the sky on a shabby broom. Then she spoke sweetly, "Ah, a lily. What a deceptive flower. So delicate, its beauty is often mistaken as weakness." Sage stopped for a moment and looked in Lillie's eyes. "As I observe your aura, I see . . ."

"My what?" Lillie squirmed as a gust of cold air sent chills down her spine. She vehemently shook her head and narrowed her glinting stare, leaning in towards Sage's bizarre presence. Sage sighed and rolled her eyes, placing her hand over her forehead and shaking it vigorously.

"Your aura. You know, your energy field. Your life force. The color around you that's not visible to the carnal eye. Yours is indigo, or a deep blue. You have visions, right?"

Grace's mouth dropped as she stared at Lillie in disbelief. Even though she and Grace were close, Lillie had never revealed this to her friend. Plus, indigo was her favorite color. She couldn't believe this crazy psychic would be privy to such information. Then she remembered. God give some gifts prior to repentance.

"You don't have to answer, Sage already knows," she purred, like a black cat on Halloween.

Why is she talking about herself in third person?

Even her sarcastic thoughts couldn't distract her from her fate. Electric pulsations surged through Lillie's body, forcing her to lurch forward into Sage's embrace. At that moment, she became intrinsically aware of Sage's soul-piercing power. The depth of her scrutinizing gape was unbearable, so Lillie looked at the ground to avoid further eye contact. Still unable to get comfortable, she shuffled her feet back and forth. She grabbed her water bottle from her hip and took a huge gulp.

"Well, the eyes are the windows to the soul. Even though you're trying to block me, I've seen enough, so hold on for the ride. You'll marry and bear children with a powerful and influential man. The two of you will work together in some capacity. Are you involved in church ministry?"

Lillie choked on the water and spit the excess contents of her mouth all over Sage's grubby, linoleum floor. This overwhelming psychic prophecy seemed sacrilegious. Without warning, the room began to shake and Sage chanted in an eerie, foreign language.

Grace buried her head in her lap and released a muffled scream. The odor from the scented candle that initially assaulted Lillie's nostrils grew more pungent by the minute. It reminded her of the spice her mother used when she seasoned her famous baked chicken—sage. Just as quickly as it started, the room stopped shaking and everything went back to normal. Almost like the spine-chilling events never happened in the first place.

Sage opened her eyes and lifted her head to meet Lillie's eyes again. She narrowed her own and curled up her lips. Just as Sage's eyebrows rose, she blurted out, "Wait a minute, there's more. Um, let me see your palm, please. I need to be sure."

Grace finally came up for air and laughed like a crazy hyena. Lillie kicked her friend under the table to no avail. Sage reached for Lillie's hand and a young girl skipped out of the adjacent room, adorned in a dingy gingham dress with a crusty looking mock apron. Her deep-set grey cat eyes caught Lillie's attention as she played in her stringy dishwater blond hair. Lillie cringed when she heard the young girl butchering the notes of a familiar nursery rhyme.

"Hickory Dickory Dock. The mouse ran up the clock. The clock struck one. The mouse ran down. Hickory—"

The juvenile stopped in her tracks and drew in a lung full of air for all to hear when she laid eyes on Lillie. "Get away from here, you . . . you . . . you . . ." She released a blood-curling scream and sprinted full speed out of the room leaving an ethereal white cloud of smoke behind.

The piercing sound led Lillie to clamp her hands over her ears. Offended by the child's actions, she demanded of Sage, "What's wrong with her?"

Sage shot Lillie an irritated glare and then let out a sinister howl that shook Lillie deep down within her soul. Grace plopped her head back down in her lap again and let out the same muffled scream as before. Lillie couldn't help but jump in her seat when Sage let out a witchlike cackle and slammed her fist on the table with tumultuous force.

"There's nothing wrong with her. She just confirmed what I thought. The spirit of death is chasing you and you can't outrun it no matter how hard you try."

Overwhelmed by the strange revelation, Lillie tried to stand to her feet. She had every intention of grabbing her friend and running as far from this place as possible. On the contrary, she found herself unable to control her own body and fell to the ground in a catatonic state. Against her better judgment, Lillie surrendered to the void of her subconscious mind and in moments, everything went . . . black.

TWO

As Lillie glided through Flow's entrance, she absorbed the ethereal energy radiating from the crowd. The purple and silver décor showered a glittery ambiance throughout the place that exuded a heavenly aura. Lillie thanked her lucky stars for the VIP seating at the oval table adjacent to center stage. When she settled on a comfy seat with an overstuffed cushion, she reveled in the proximity to the artists. In fact, she could literally reach out and touch them as they performed.

The owner, Elaina Martin, hopped on stage to greet her star performer who also happened to be Lillie's best friend, Theo Smith. By day, he served as a prominent civil rights attorney, next in line to make partner at his firm. By night, an acclaimed spoken word artist known for his ability to make words flow like the seemingly effortless power of a tropical waterfall. Calliope may be the muse of poetry, but Theo was the master of lyrical excellence. As he approached the stage, his tongue traveled slowly around the base of his succulent lips with tantalizing precision. Lillie blushed when she recalled the first time she'd seen Theo work this sexy gesture in high school. Once he noticed how women swooned over him, it became his signature mannerism.

A handsome man with smooth, blemish-free dark chocolate skin, Theo's white teeth rivaled a crisp winter snowfall. Memories of the fresh lime Shea butter he used to groom his locs to perfection rushed Lillie's psyche, stirring her inner prowess. His 6'3" muscular frame added cream to the crop. The women at Flow weren't just starving for pastries or thirsty for herbal tea. The lecherous beam in their googly eyes exuded lust for Theo and they didn't even bother to hide it. Theo's knack to work his God-given charisma made every woman he encountered feel special. Sometimes, he cursed the talent because on more than one occasion, some woman misinterpreted feelings of mutual attraction. Little did they know, Theo only had eyes for one woman and her name was Lillie Corven.

An uber handsome man strolled up to the stage with a black guitar case covered with music notes. He sat in the chair next to Theo, who held the microphone in a seductive stance as he began to flow.

My Lady in Waiting

As I close my eyes, I see the beauty of my lady in waiting
So succulent but virtuous, and even though I'm not dating her,
We're connected in the spirit realm. Far apart, yet in tune in our hearts
Ready to live for her, excited about providing for her, willing to die for her
Can't stop thinking about her, overjoyed about the potential thought of seeing her
Imagining what she's doing at this very moment in time
As pure white snow makes a smooth blanket on the ground
My lady in waiting moves to the rhythmic sound
Keeping it tight, making sure it's right, for the moment we unite, in holy matrimony
My lady in waiting, I hear you, see you, smell you, feel you, I love you
Thanking God for you before I actually set eyes on your beautiful face,
In adoration of your beauty and grace, my beautiful lady in waiting

The audience went wild, especially the women. Some clapped and a few snapped their fingers. Others verbally expressed their appreciation of the artist.

"You go, boy!"

"Yeah, baby!"

"Um! I'll be your lady in waiting."

"Alright, my brother!"

Theo pointed upward and positioned his manicured hands in a gesture of prayer. Mesmerized by his tattoos, Lillie couldn't even clap. His right arm displayed the word SALVATION inked in smooth calligraphy. REDEMPTION covered his left arm in the same royal font. The tasteful artistry exuded perfection with not one drop of ink out of place. With a smooth James Bond swoop, he jumped off the stage. Theo made a beeline to Lillie and gently caressed her hand.

"Happy Birthday, Lady Bug."

Lillie plopped her hands on her cocked hips and jerked her neck. She hated when Theo used her childhood nickname in public.

". . . You look amazing tonight. This just confirms what I believe . . . you're my lady in waiting."

Lillie threw frustration to the wind and beamed from ear-to-ear, pleased he'd noticed. A pink sleeveless sundress clung to her bosom and flowed as she moved. Her butterfly necklace shined bright, calling attention to the matching earrings that dangled from her ears. Theo's frozen gaze showed his appreciation for the designer sandals that accentuated the shapeliness of her calves. Lillie rocked a two-strand twist style, compliments of her stylist Lisa Keyes at Keyes to Style. Not one strand out of place. She pinned a pink flower in her hair just like her godmother, Diana, used to wear. Just a dab of eyeliner, eye shadow, and lip-gloss graced her face, yet it seemed to add just the right touch.

Lillie chuckled as Theo bent down to hug her. Last week, she'd chided him for making her stand on her toes to return his affection. Her 5'4" frame was nowhere near equivalent to his 6'3" height, yet the electrifying hug sent icy chills down her spine. Regaining her composure, she pulled away and in a playful gesture, punched him in the arm.

"That wasn't the greeting I've dreamed about." Theo grimaced.

Steamy tension embraced the atmosphere like a bear hug, so Lillie wanted to be careful with their interactions. Despite the fact she'd been madly in love with him since fifth grade, she didn't want to ruin their friendship.

"Well, I need a date for a client dinner Friday night. Are you free? I left you a voice message about it last week. Did you get it?" Theo cocked his head to the side, anticipating Lillie's response.

"Uh, yeah . . . about that. I'm not sure if I can make it. Plus, I need someone to watch CoCo Chanel." Lillie blinked quickly and turned her head away to avoid eye contact.

"Come on, now. That's a lame excuse."

Theo's intense stare made her squirm in her seat. Since he was a skilled attorney, she could never win a debate with him, especially if he was passionate about the subject.

"Plus, CoCo is litter trained." Theo chuckled. "Who ever heard of a dog being litter trained anyway?"

"Whatever! My dog has class. It's not an excuse. I just don't feel like dealing with a bunch of people getting their hopes up for healings and stuff that will never happen." Lillie turned her nose up in the air.

Theo scrunched his forehead and shook his head. "How can you say that?" He handed her a gift box wrapped in blue paper. When Lillie opened it, she was surprised to find a Tiffany's bracelet. He reached down to place the bracelet on her arm. When he finished, she jumped out of her seat and shrieked, "Oh my goodness! Thank you. This was the bracelet I've been looking at. How did you know?"

Theo winked at Lillie and she melted. Just then, Theo's phone rang. He looked at the screen and said, "Hey, I gotta take this call. It's the office. I'll be right back."

When Theo left, Lillie signaled the server and ordered a hot cup of Jade Oolong tea and a pumpkin scone. While she waited on her order, she tried not to think about Theo and continued to enjoy the poetry performances. The audience applauded for the next poet when Lillie saw a handsome man walking in her direction from the kitchen. He carried a cup of tea and a plate in his hand. He sported a white shirt and tie underneath his checkered apron. Tall, fit, and well groomed, with a smile that could break hearts from California to New York. His wavy hair and hazel eyes were the perfect complement to his butter cream complexion. When he arrived at the table, he gently set her order down and she inhaled his mesmerizing scent.

"Your tea, Miss."

Mr. Carmel Latte Dream flashed his pearly whites, and Lillie couldn't help but admire this man, a true work of art, handcrafted by the creator.

"Um . . . yeah . . . thanks."

Lillie's beet red cheeks kindled, revealing her embarrassment. She tried to speak and found herself fumbling words in front of this living and breathing version of Adonis.

"You ordered an exquisite blend. Do you like teas from Taiwan better than all the others?"

His voice. It's so . . . sexy. Wow! Who is this man? Perfection at its best and he knows about tea. This mere fact simultaneously piqued Lillie's mental and physical interest. Caught up in the handsome man's spell, she stared with her mouth agape.

"Miss?"

"Oh, thank you. Yes, I love oolong teas. I'm also a fan of Indian chai teas," Lillie answered with an awkward grin.

This man, by far, was one of the finest she'd ever seen. It didn't help that Theo was eyeing her from across the room.

"Miss … what's your name, by the way?"

My name's Mrs. Caramel Latte Dream; I mean . . . "My name's Lillie, and yours?"

"Adam."

The flirtatious way the name rolled off his tongue drove Lillie wild. With a quick glance at his left hand, she saw a ring-less finger, even though there seemed to be a faint tan mark. She couldn't be sure, without making it obvious.

"I just started working here this week. Do you come often?"

"Yes. I come here quite often and I've never seen you before."

Adam flashed Lillie a smile, revealing a full mouth of brilliant, shiny white teeth. His smile was blinding.

I wonder if he bleaches his teeth.

"You're right. I have to admit, when I saw you place the order, I put on an apron and asked the server to allow me to bring it to you. I'm the new event promotions manager so I come up with the creative ideas to get people in the door."

Okay, he's interested in me. What happens next? "Great, it's nice to know that I can get that type of service around here. When you have some time, maybe you can share more about your position here at Flow."

"Sure, I'd be glad to. Being new in town, I don't know many people. I sure do miss my church back home. I do know Elaina's pastor quite well, though. In fact, he and my father . . . well, that's not what I came over here to talk to you about. As I was saying before, I've been attending the early service at his church on Sundays. Have your heard of Radical Faith Church?"

"Yes," Lillie exclaimed. "All of my friends go there, so I attend from time to time. I prefer the later service, though."

Adam hesitated then said, "I've been talking to Pastor Andrews about joining his minister's class. It will be a review since I was ordained at my home church, New Bethel, in Chillicothe. I preached every fifth Sunday there. You know, my dad was the pastor there before . . . well, I won't bore you with that."

Lillie chuckled as she listened to Adam talk about his church. He stood proud and tall with an authoritative stance, letting the world know he was royalty without even saying a word. He'd starched his white button down collar shirt to a crisp, complimenting his sculpted fade that rocked waves in his hair like the ocean. His tie matched the ensemble he sported. Lillie admired his smooth butterscotch skin, flawless as a baby's bottom, without a blemish or a scar. The sexy gleam in his hazel eyes sent Lillie soaring to higher highs of excitement.

"Sorry to interrupt. Just wanted to make sure I introduced myself to your new friend." Theo's voice dripped with jealousy and sarcasm. His actions didn't shock Lillie since he made his presence known to all Lillie's male suitors. Theo extended his pompous hand to Adam, who shook it with a firm hold. Impressed that he didn't back down, Lillie's scale on the attraction meter went up a few notches.

"I'm Theo Smith and Lillie's a special friend of mine."

"Nice to meet you," Adam responded, his eyes fixed on his adversary's. "I'm Adam Johnson, the new event promotions manager. It's good to know someone as beautiful as Lillie has a bodyguard."

Silence filled the air like smoke from a kitchen grease fire. If Theo's eyes were lasers, his intense stare could bore a hole in Adam's head. After a few moments, Theo broke the awkward silence.

"Since when do event promotions managers wear aprons?"

Lillie almost choked on her tea. "Theo, that's enough." She cut her eyes at him for effect then turned her attention to Mr. Caramel Latte Dream. "Adam, it was nice to meet you."

Adam took Lillie's hand in his and brushed his lips across it in a gentle kiss. Lillie closed her eyes to savor the seductive gesture as he turned to walk away. Unfortunately, Theo ruined her momentary taste of ecstasy with his jealous banter.

"What's going on with you and Mr. Tea Scone King?"

"You have no right coming to my table to interrupt my conversation."

"I took it easy on this one. He should be thankful."

Theo grabbed one of Lillie's Matcha scones and munched while she talked.

"I'm going to ignore the fact you didn't ask to eat that."

"Well, the man makes a mean scone. Maybe he can be your chef."

Lillie wrinkled her nose. "You're despicable!"

Not wanting to attract attention to their table, Lillie pulled Theo to the back of the building in Elaina's office. When she closed the door, she gave him a piece of her mind.

"I guess Adam should just bow down and thank you for attempting to humiliate him at his place of employment, in front of me, a woman he wants to get to know."

"Humph! Who does he think he is coming in here with that sneaky glint in his eye?"

"Whatever! You need to stop."

"I'm not going to stand back and let him have you."

Lillie threw her head back and laughed hysterically.

"Oh wow! You can't be serious. All these women in here would die to be with you, and you won't give them the time of day."

"No disrespect, but they're not the real deal, and I refuse to settle, unlike you," Theo reasoned. "My lady is in waiting. When she figures it out, we can make this thing happen. I'm talking about getting married, having a few babies, and leaving a legacy for our future. What do you know about that?"

She knew Theo was referring to her, but she's made a decision a long time ago that she valued his friendship far too much to take a chance on getting involved romantically. What if it didn't work out? Where would that leave her? Mr. Caramel Latte Dream, on the other hand, was a different story. Something about him intrigued and beckoned Lillie in the deep recesses of her soul. She wanted to pursue that something, whatever it was.

"Listen, you can't stop me from seeing other men, Theo. You're not my boyfriend."

"Oh really?" Theo planted his feet in a defensive stance and crossed his arms. A tingly sensation surged through Lillie's body. Theo's frustration with her both irritated and turned her on at the same time.

"You're not my daddy, Theo."

Her wavering tone must not have been convincing because Theo cuddled up to Lillie and whispered in her ear, "I'm not trying to be your daddy. Would your daddy do this?" He caressed her face and nibbled on her ear. Lillie caught her breath and almost slipped to the ground. Once she recovered, she pulled away.

Theo walked over to where Lillie stood and before she knew it, he was kissing her with unadulterated passion. Her anger dissipated as he gently caressed the small of her back. The sweet mint flavor of his breath intoxicated Lillie into a state of wooziness. Theo stopped kissing her long enough to look her in the eye causing her to melt with love.

"So, do you still want to get to know this man, or are you going to take your rightful place as my queen?"

THREE

MIXED EMOTIONS plagued Lillie's conscience as she lay on the couch continually playing out the decision in her mind. The all-white décor of her luxurious condominium coupled with gold accents and green plants provided the sanctuary she needed to make complex moral decisions. Since she'd turned Theo down for the dinner date, she promised to go to the revival at Radical Faith. Now, she wished she'd accepted his original request.

The mere thought of attending a revival perplexed Lillie's analytical psyche. She remembered how her godmother, Diana, used to complain about how the church mothers treated her at her first revival. She and Uncle Bruce were dating at the time and he invited her to the revival at the church he pastored. She chose to wear a form-fitting white dress and her trademark accessory—a beautiful lily in her hair. The Corven's didn't want to name their daughter Diana so instead, they named her Lillie to represent the beauty, style, and flair Diana possessed.

When her aunt walked in the church, holding her young son, Alvin's, hand, the keyboard player struck a few off key chords that sent a cognitive dissonance into the atmosphere. The shouting church mothers cut some serious steps but when the drummer missed a beat, they looked up and stared daggers in Aunt Diana's direction. Not only was she strikingly beautiful, she had the nerve to be confident about it. Immediately, the church mothers turned up their noses as the usher escorted her to the seat the pastor had designated for her on the front row. Her dress must have been too short because they handed her an embroidered lap cloth the moment she sat down.

Several months later, Uncle Bruce announced that he and Aunt Diana were going to get married. For the next six months, the old church biddies did everything in their power to prevent the union. They conducted a full-fledged investigation. What they couldn't find they made up. Despite their catty antics, he married her anyway.

Once they established their new home with expensive antique furniture and the finest appliances money could buy, they thought they would live happily ever after. Unfortunately, reality set in. Aunt Diana was used to Columbus, and the southern Ohio town she now called home was a drab. The church members hated her for some reason she couldn't put her finger on. Plus, Uncle Bruce spent all of his time taking pasturing and neglected the emotional needs of his family. To make up for it, he lavished her and Alvin with gifts and a credit card with no limit.

Lillie benefited greatly from this allowance and remembered asking, "Aunt Diana. Where's Uncle Bruce?"

Her aunt would smile and say, "Obviously, he's where he wants to be."

Lillie didn't know him well, because she only saw him when she stayed with them for weekends and Aunt Diana would take her to church. He was pleasant enough because he'd give her handfuls of peppermint candy to put in her pocket. Uncle Bruce's perfectly sculpted Afro and chocolate skin just made his shiny smile even better. Now that Lillie was older, she wondered if he was a player. Her Aunt Diana constantly complained about her husband putting all his time into the congregation. Maybe he was really spending his time inside the sugar walls of various members of the congregation.

Tears welled up in Lillie's eyes as she recalled her aunt's beautiful presence. She'd been dead for over twelve years and Lillie was still struggling with accepting it. She made a point to keep in contact with her god brother, Alvin. He'd enlisted in the army after his mother's death and rarely came to town to visit. For this reason, Lillie and her friends took frequent trips to wherever he was stationed. Her parents also visited him quite frequently, as well. Alvin may not have been her blood brother, but they were as close as any true siblings could be.

Because of her godmother's experience, she'd never been to a revival before and didn't know what to expect. She never thought highly of the church because people tended to do things that they preached against. Especially those in leadership. Last night, she'd fallen asleep watching television and awoke to the horrific preaching of some hair-brained evangelist. What a spiritual atrocity! If the one at Radical Faith Church was anything like this, she planned to walk out without looking back.

The evangelist preached to the syncopated rhythm of an imaginary song, which made his message seem contrived. To make matters worse, a flock of women, whom he referred to as disciples, took turns holding up his long, flowing purple robe. These austere looking women followed his every move as if he were God reincarnate. Sweat poured from his body as he continued the charade. One of the disciples held up a golden goblet to his lips, gazing to his eyes like a girl lost in love. Lillie fought the urge to slap the girl into next week then remembered it was on television.

Out of nowhere, an elderly woman popped up at the altar. Her tear-stained cheeks revealed a distraught state. An owl-like screech bellowed from the preacher man's mouth as he placed his forceful hand on her belly. The woman stumbled like a drunken vagrant and fell back with her eyes closed. Before she hit the ground, an extremely overweight "disciple" caught her, guided her to the floor, and covered her with a white sheet. Then, the woman shrieked like a banshee, bucking all over the ground. It was a pointless covering because Lillie could see the lace trim of the woman's thigh high stockings.

The remaining "disciples" encircled the woman and yelled out words in a foreign tongue.

"Eee tay shay oma notta say," cried one.

"Roka sheatta ratta rook so," screamed another.

Lillie chuckled to herself as she recalled the lyrics to the famous Labelle song, "Lady Marmalade." The women sounded like they were speaking the same French as in the song.

"Ke at ta roko so," sang the other one as she clapped her hands in the woman's face.

To Lillie's dismay, white foam dripped out of the woman's mouth. She couldn't believe a network had the audacity to allow this on their channel.

I guess if you pay to get it on, they'll put it on.

The "head disciple" held a Bible in one hand and a cross in the other. A woman with a white shawl, that had to outweigh her by at least twenty pounds, flicked liquid from an ornate flask on anyone within spitting distance. A third woman poured oil from a clean vial into her hands and touched the flailing woman on the ground on her forehead, then smacked the palms of her hands so loudly; Lillie heard it above the irritating Hammond B-5 organ. Sickened by this comedic display, Lillie turned the channel to the latest housewives drama show. At least they admitted to being drama infested. Grace would cringe if she knew what Lillie was watching. She didn't own a TV because she felt the networks only aired shows that lower ones vibration.

Earlier in the day, Theo called three times to make sure she still planned to attend the revival. He even volunteered to pick her up, just in case she decided to chicken out. Right when the most boisterous housewives cold conked the real troublemaker in the face, Lillie heard her front door open. Grace bounced in the living room, singing one of her favorite neo-soul tunes.

"The universe surrounds me with your love. My heart is like quicksand, pulling you with magnetism of the earth," she sang.

Lillie's Yorkichon, CoCo Chanel, jumped, begging Grace to pick her up. She was no bigger than a minute, yet she barked as if she didn't know it.

"CoCo, you're the only dog I can tolerate on this earth," Grace said as she hugged the canine. "Lillie, you better watch out. I just might give her a new home."

"Whatever! She'd come back. CoCo has it too good here. You can't even water a plant regularly; so I know you'd forget to feed her." Grace playfully punched Lillie in the arm and they laughed hard, causing the dog to start barking.

"Girl, I heard you on the phone. Is that fine Theo coming over here?"

Even though Lillie decided against a relationship with him, she couldn't help but feel a twinge of jealousy when it came to other women in his life.

"Oh, my goodness. When did all of this Theo talk come about? I know he's a great catch, but he's not even your type."

Grace's natural beauty and enchanting feminine wiles drove men crazy. She tended to fall for the earthy, Rastafarian, guitar-strumming, vegan heroes. Theo's "distinguished gentleman from the hood" persona didn't align at all. In the past, Grace interacted with Theo in a buddy manner. Since they returned from the California trip, she had started flirting with him.

"Whatever!" Grace placed her hand on her cocked hip and stepped back. "Is Theo coming, or what? Why should I drive when we're all going the same place? Maybe we can reduce our carbon footprint by riding together more."

Lillie couldn't believe Grace was using her "Earth Goddess Save the Planet" card to catch a ride just to see Theo. She knew her friend hated extreme evangelism, revivals, and healing services just as much as she did. She couldn't believe Grace was even going let alone planning to carpool.

"Hope you ladies are decent," Theo called out from the foyer. CoCo barked and jumped in the air when he entered the room.

"Hey, CoCo," Theo greeted her and playfully grabbed her mouth. CoCo pulled away, growled, and came back for more.

"You forgot how to knock again, I see," Lillie teased. Theo embraced her then gave Grace a quick hug.

"Lady Bug, when are you going to get it? I'm not going to knock on your door. I was just talking to your god brother and he said—"

"Don't try to change the subject. You need to give me the same respect I give you, buster. I knock on your door." Lillie stopped as Theo and Grace both arched an eyebrow, to show their skepticism. "I do sometimes. Whatever! I mean, I could be walking around here naked, and you can't just—"

Grace snuggled up to Theo as she cut off Lillie's statement. "Yeah, Theo, maybe we should go to my place and talk since it's not quite time to go, yet."

Too disgusted to watch the interaction, Lillie put CoCo in the cage.

"No thank you, Grace." Theo gently brushed her away and turned towards Lillie who chuckled on the inside at his polite rejection.

"We need to get going." Theo took Lillie's arm and escorted her out the door.

"Wait for me," Grace yelled.

FOUR

W HAT DO people do at these revivals anyway? I hope it's not like the one I saw on TV last night."

Theo leaned back as he gripped the steering wheel to make a right turn. "Just relax and trust me. You are in for a treat. I promise."

"Yeah! Stop stressing and just go with the flow," Grace chimed in.

What qualifies Grace, the new age queen, to give me advice about a revival? She was no more or less a Christian than Lillie. In fact, she stll believed in the power of angels, crystals, chakras, and Jesus Christ.

"I struggle with these revivals. The spirit realm is real, I know that first hand, but there are so many revivalists who are out there just for the money and the relative fame."

"I agree with you wholeheartedly on that one. You know conquerors used organized religion to keep people in line. That's why I believe Jesus isn't the only way to God."

Theo choked and swerved to the right, barely missing the cars in the other lane.

"You know what, you're right. That's because he is God. You don't need a way when you know The Way."

Theo sounded like an old black preacher marching in the Civil Rights movement. All he needed to do was break out singing "We Shall Overcome" to complete the package. "Humph! Then tell me why these so-called pastors take pride in pimping their poor congregation while they drive the finest cars and fly in their own planes? What does a pastor need a plane for?" By now, Grace's cheeks were beet red as she expressed her thoughts with a fiery passion. "Tell me why the church is full of single women waiting on God to send them a man and they keep getting fatter and fatter. The ones who aren't overweight are bitter. Frankly, I'm sick of it."

Lillie cracked open the bottled water in her purse, anticipating a good battle between her friends. She took a swig and turned to Theo, awaiting his response.

"Oh, so you say pastors are swindling people but you're willing to play around in psychic land and let Sage take your money?"

Lillie choked on her water and spit it out. Water covered Theo's dashboard and windshield. He didn't miss a beat as he grabbed a towel from his console and wiped away the contents of Lillie's mouth. Grace crossed her arms and stared daggers out of the window.

"Don't think that the gifts are only limited to the church. Just because Sage isn't a tithe paying, holy-ghost filled, foot stomping, hand clapping fake doesn't mean her predictions aren't accurate."

"Whatever! She's the fake, not our church members. Thank God Pastor Andrews is the real deal," Theo testified. "He's grounded in the word and not caught up with luxuries."

Lillie smirked because as much as she loved Pastor Andrews, she knew one thing—he was human. As long as humanity came into the picture, he was doomed to not measure up. She enjoyed the fellowship at Radical Faith but after her Aunt Diana's experience, she refused to get involved. Even though, she'd seen some really handsome pastors along the way. She had a secret crush on Uncle Bruce when she was little. Even though she knew of most of their reputations, there was something about a man of the cloth that intrigued her.

Theo whipped his vehicle into the church parking lot with ease. He placed the car in a close spot and jumped out to open the door for the ladies. As the trio walked towards the building, Ms. Blakey popped up out of nowhere, looking like she'd just sucked on a basket of lemons. No one would believe they all knew her since grade school since she exhibited such a curt attitude towards them. Her husband died last year, and ever since she'd become a mean, bitter old woman. Not wanting to ensue her wrath, Lillie and her friends typically stayed as far away as possible. Unfortunately, her close presence wouldn't afford that opportunity today.

"Hi, Ms. Blakey," they said in unison.

"Humph," she grunted, turning up her nose, looking them up and down. "I can't believe you're coming up in the Lord's house in jeans and T-shirts. Why don't you have any respect for Jesus? All this worldliness up in the church."

"Worldly?" Theo questioned. Ms. Blakey ignored him and continued her ranting and raving. Then just as quickly as she started, she transitioned to another topic. Her entire demeanor changed.

"How's your parents doing, Lady Bug?" Trying to work through the quick mood transition, Lillie couldn't help but wonder if she should offer some Black Cohash and Dong Quai to the obviously menopausal woman.

"They're doing fine. Mom is still growing her herbal garden and making remedies for all of us. Maybe you should call her to see what she's got for you." Lillie regretted letting those words slip out.

"Oh really? Humph! I just might call your mama. She's so sweet. That daddy of yours on the other hand . . . You tell him I said, go to hell."

"Ms. Blakey!" Lillie shouted.

"Humph!"

Lillie's father didn't care for Ms. Blakey and since she lived right across the street, he didn't have a problem letting her know it. Their age old battle used to be entertainment for all the neighborhood children. In the summer, her father grew his special crop in the backyard amongst her mother's herbs. One day, he walked outside and his specific patch was chopped down to the ground. He came in the house screaming that that old biddy across the street better not be getting high off the stolen supply. Her mother had to talk him out of knocking on Ms. Blakey's door and demanding that she return the stolen goods. The neighborhood children knew she was the culprit because they could smell the herbal surprise from her bedroom window every Sunday night.

"I thought she was a Christian!" Lillie's father would yell at the top of his lungs. "Humph! Even the Bible Thumpers know I grow some good stuff."

Lillie's mother just shook her head and continued mixing her concoctions. Ms. Blakey's next trick jerked Lillie out of her reminiscent state.

"And you, with the zodiac T-shirt. You oughtta be ashamed wearing that mess to church. What's your name, baby?" Ms. Blakey asked, changing her tone from bitter to sweet.

"Grace."

Lillie didn't understand why Ms. Blakey asked the question. She had babysat Grace after school every day for five years when they were children.

Switching back to her nasty tone, she said, "Grace, when are you going to stop living a lie? You ain't fooling anybody but your friends. I've been on this earth a long time, and I know what I see."

Grace stomped toward Ms. Blakey with fury. Before she could do any damage to the elderly church mother, Theo picked her up and carried her into the church, while she screamed and hollered. Pastor Andrews and Bianca Davis ran out of his office.

"Hi, Pastor Andrews," Lillie said. "Everything is okay. Grace is just having a moment."

"Hey, baby girl." Pastor Andrews reserved this term of endearment for his favorite parishioners, and everyone knew Lillie had a special place in his heart. Her nonchalant attitude about church seemed to intrigue him. "It's good to see you here tonight," Pastor Andrews said as he shook his head in disbelief.

"Pastor," Grace's whiny voice took on shrill tone, "Ms. Blakey . . ."

Pastor flashed his Mandingo smile and Grace relaxed her shoulders. She took a deep breath and Pastor Andrews gave her a fatherly hug then stroked her shoulders.

"Y'all know she's going through the change of life and plus, she's mourning the death of her husband. Just be patient with her."

Grace shook her head and turned her attention to Theo who was chatting with Bianca.

"Bianca, I didn't know you were coming tonight. Where's my man, Todd?" Theo asked.

"Um, yeah. I had a change of plans," she answered nervously. "I was, uh, meeting with Pastor, about, um, a secretarial position. You know that Todd's been laid off for quite some time and we need the money."

"Sorry to hear that, sis," Theo sympathized. "God has a way of providing for his own."

"Yes, he does," said Pastor Andrews who winked at Bianca and flashed a bright smile revealing the most beautiful teeth Lillie had ever seen. She was amazed when she looked in Bianca's direction and saw her blush.

Okay, what's really going on here?

FIVE

AND THE Lord has called each one of us to the ministry of reconciliation. Consider this. If we're supposed to reconcile people to the Kingdom of God, why are we always fighting amongst ourselves?" Pastor Andrews preached with fire in his heart.

"Alright, Doc," a spectator yelled from the congregation.

"Jesus said unbelievers would know we're Christians by the way we love one another. If we can't love each other in the body of Christ, then how can we be a beacon of light shining in the community?"

"Preach, brother," one of the parishioners hollered words of encouragement.

As she listened to the rest of the soul stirring, prolific dissertation, she was thankful that she came to the revival. Pastor Andrews was preaching up a storm and the congregation seemed to love it. In fact, most of them stood on their feet to clap and cheer him on.

"I'm here to tell you folks that today, right here at Radical Faith Church, there's room at the pool for you. All of you who are burdened and heavy laden, come on up here to the altar. Jesus wants to trade his yoke and burden for yours. He told us in his word that his yoke is easy and his burden is light. Come on to the altar to trade your sorrows and pain for the joy of the Lord. Those of you who already have that joy, I need you to worship him in spirit and in truth. Speak and sing in the spirit so that we can invoke Heaven on the behalf of our brothers and sisters who need deliverance from that heavy yoke and that even heavier burden."

All of a sudden, people started practically running to the altar and falling on their knees. Prayer warriors surrounded them with love and tissues to dry their weeping eyes. Others stayed at their seats and worshipped, just as the pastor had asked. It was a beautiful sight and it touched Lillie's heart like never before. She found herself falling to the ground and laying prostrate. Without warning, Lillie felt a connection with God in her spirit and found herself caught up in an open vision. In awe, she watched as the figure of an illuminated being emerged before her, skimming specks out of a great pot full of gold. Each time the being skimmed the filth, the precious metal became more evident. Eventually, the consistent effort resulted in the visible revelation of the gold in its most pure state. Just when she thought it was over, she heard the voice of the Lord.

"Lillie, you'll be tried by the fire, but you're coming out gold."

Just as the vision dissipated, Lillie caught a glimpse of Adam, the gorgeous man she'd met at Flow. Surprised to see him, she turned away just for a second. When she turned back around, he was gone. *Now, that's strange. I know that was Adam.*

After the service, while people were greeting one another, Adam walked in Lillie's direction. He winked and his eyes danced seductively as he took in the view. Lillie giggled in anticipation of his closeness. He gently embraced her causing Lillie to experience a warm and fuzzy feeling. Her cheeks burned with redness. Lillie noticed Theo cringing as he watched their interaction.

"It's good to see you, Mr. Caramel . . . I mean, Adam."

"Hey. I didn't expect to see you here." Adam flashed a bright smile that invoked a longing in Lillie's soul. Her breast tingled and she felt warm surges in all the forbidden places. Lillie was surprised at her body's uncontrollable response. She'd never felt this way about a man she hardly knew before. Then again, she'd never met a man as visually appealing as Adam.

"I met with Pastor this morning, and I'll be joining his minister's training class next week."

To Lillie's surprise, Theo stepped up to her side and grabbed her hand.

"Hey, Adam. I'll take it from here. Lillie's my date tonight."

"Date?" Adam questioned. "Who brings a date to a revival?"

"I do. And I'd prefer that you stay away from her, if you know what's good for you."

"Are you threatening me?" Adam spoke through clenched teeth. He changed his posture to a defensive stance, planting his feet in the ground right in front of Theo.

"No. I don't make threats; however, I do make promises." Theo snarled and returned the defensive stance. "And Lillie can vouch for the fact I never break a promise."

Lillie couldn't believe the interaction unfolding right before her very eyes. Despite Theo's threatening words, Adam smiled smugly and shook his head in disbelief. "It's Theo, right?"

"Don't act like you don't remember my name. You might make Lillie laugh with all that foolishness, but it's not funny to me." Theo balled his fists and invaded Adam's space.

Adam gawked at Theo for a brief moment and then gained his composure to respond. "I'm going to ignore your Neanderthal behavior since we're in the house of the Lord, in case you forgot." The tension in the air thickened as their testosterone levels elevated. Lillie could smell danger in the atmosphere. Theo stepped closer to Adam and stared him dead square in the eye. Lillie had to admit that as immature as it seemed, it was flattering to have two men battling for her love. Adam didn't move an inch.

Instead, he fortified his stance, and matched Theo's glare without as much as a flinch.

"Oh, I know where we are and you need to quit perpetrating this ridiculous holier than thou act," Theo spat with venom, clinching his jaws with extreme aggression. The two men stood so close, Lillie wondered if they could smell each other's breath. The poison must have hit home because Adam grimaced. Tired of the banter, Lillie backed away from the altercation, trying to hold her composure together.

"Stop it. Both of you." She curled her lips in distaste.

Sensitive to Lillie's discomfort, Adam put a halt to the heated discussion. "Check this out. We can fight all day long, and it won't matter, because Lillie's a grown woman who's capable of making her own decisions. We'll just see what she has to say about this."

Both men gleamed at Lillie, waiting for her response. Lillie pursed her lips in aversion to their barbaric behavior. She was growing tired of their display of machismo.

"Theo, you're my best friend, but I do have a life outside of you. I really wish you'd stop acting like my daddy. If I want to spend time with Adam, I will. And guess what? I don't need your permission."

Theo's eyes grew as big as saucers, and then he stomped away from Lillie grumbling, "Fine, ruin your life with this trash."

Ignoring Theo's temper tantrum, Lillie turned her attention to Adam. "As for you, Theo is my best friend and plays a significant role in my life. He's always been overly protective of me, so if you want to be in my life, the two of you will have to work something out."

Adam smiled and Lillie noticed his dimples. She exhaled to release the tension caused by the altercation. Adam chuckled and his demeanor transformed from charged to the victor who won the spoils in a war.

"It's okay, Lillie. You must be something special for him to stand up for you like that. His possessiveness just makes me want to get to know you even more."

Just then, Lillie remembered the psychic reading in California. Maybe Adam was the man to which Sage referred. It certainly couldn't be Theo.

Before Lillie could imagine any further, Grace interrupted their discussion. "Hey, Lillie. I hate to bother you, but Theo's in the car waiting for us. You may want to make this quick." Grace started to walk away and Lillie waved goodbye to Adam.

"Adam, it was good seeing you here. I need to go right now," Lillie shared. To her surprise, he grabbed her hand and kissed it gently, taking Lillie's breath away and stopping Grace in her tracks.

"Will I see you on Sunday?"

Lillie blushed and responded, "You sure will if you come to the mid-day service."

"Goodbye, Lillie."

Adam embraced Lillie sending an unfamiliar charge of energy through her body. Heat rose from the soles of her feet to a forbidden place, causing Lillie to be aroused. The sensation was overpowering to the point she almost forgot she was in the church. Breaking from the hug, neither one of them spoke a word. Lillie walked briskly to catch up with her friend. She threw her hair over her shoulder and gave Adam one last glimpse as she caught up with Grace.

"Go 'head, Lillie," Grace teased. "I don't know why Theo chases after you when you clearly don't want him." Grace studied her non-verbal response as if trying to gauge a reaction. Lillie stared in the opposite direction, avoiding eye contact.

"Or do you?" Grace's eyes bulged in anticipation of Lillie's answer.

Clearly in denial, she answered, "No, Grace, I don't! I just don't think you and Theo are a match made in Heaven, that's all."

Not wanting to see how her words stung, Lillie continued to avoid eye contact. Grace smirked and shook her head.

"Oh, so you think you can have your cake and eat it, too? You can't have Adam and police Theo, too."

"No one's trying to police Theo. That's absurd."

"Absurd? Oh really? You know it's true. And, you have the nerve to act like you don't want him, but you can't keep your nose out of his business. Tell that lie to someone who doesn't have a clue."

"I don't want him, but he's still my best friend and so are you. I will always care about who both of you date."

Grace pointed at Lillie and accused, "You're full of it and so selfish!"

"Selfish? Girl, please," Lillie rebuffed as she jerked her neck and rolled her eyes at Grace.

"Yes. Selfish. I didn't stutter, did I?" Grace stood her ground.

Lillie brushed off the accusation and went in for the kill. "Let's get down to brass tax. Why are you interested in Theo? He's not even your type, and you know it."

Lillie couldn't see Grace's new age fetish in competition with Theo's devout Christian worldview. Grace believed in the loving power of Christ just as much as she adored the Hindu goddess Kali and mimicked the antics of Ashe, the Yoruba warrior goddess. Theo, on the other hand, represented Jesus, ride or die.

Grace didn't give Lillie the pleasure of answering the question. Instead, she went for the jugular.

"If you want Theo out of your love life, why are you all in his?" Grace's suspicious tone couldn't be mistaken.

Lillie wondered the same thing, even though she'd never admit it. Being his best friend typically put her in the position for women to seek advice on how to win his heart. These situations made Lillie feel awkward, just as Grace was making her feel today.

"Grace, my friendship with Theo is complicated. If you plan to pursue him, know that I'll ask questions about your intentions to make sure you're the right one for him. Because you're my best friend, too, I'll be questioning him as well."

Grace rolled her eyes and shouted, "You're such a hypocrite."

Before Lillie could respond, Theo honked the horn.

"We'll continue this later."

"Yeah, yeah, whatever!" Grace responded as they walked to the car. "Are you still coming to my Brazilian funk class tomorrow or what?"

SIX

"HELLO?"

"Is this the beautiful Miss Lillie Corven?"

Who in the world is calling my phone with this deep voice?

Lillie hesitated before answering, "Yes, this is she."

"I bet you didn't expect to hear from me, did you?"

"It would help if I knew who you were. I don't give my number out to just anyone."

Lillie knew this meant someone must have given this person her number. She wasn't listed and she hadn't given her number out in ages, especially not to a man.

"Are you trying to break a good man's heart? I can't believe you don't recognize my voice." The caller sounded hurt. His voice was familiar to Lillie, almost like her god brother Alvin's. Then suddenly, it dawned on her.

It's Mr. Caramel Latte Dream!

"Adam? Is that you?"

Oh no! I'm not ready for this.

"Not to be rude, Mr. Carmel, I mean, Adam. But how did you get my number?"

"Mr. Carmel what? Okay, I'm going to let that slide. How did I get your number?" He chuckled, igniting the flames of Lillie's heart. "Ancient Chinese secret."

Lillie's heart fluttered, leaving her breathless. She thanked God no one could see here blushing like a schoolgirl.

Mesmerized by his deep, sexy voice, Lillie was at a loss for words. She had to get off the phone to catch her breath and pull herself together. "Let me call you right back. I believe your number registered on my caller ID."

"Yeah, I won't keep you. I'm calling to invite you and any of your unmarried friends to a single's gathering at Flow."

Already, Adam's initiative left a strong impression on Lillie. He'd only worked at Flow a short period of time and was already showing the characteristics of strong leadership. Lillie liked a man who could take charge to make things happen.

"Wow, that's great, Adam. I have something in the oven that needs to come out right now," she lied. "I can call you back, though."

"Not a problem. Goodbye." Her name slid off his tongue in such a tantalizing way that made her want to cry, 'Mercy!'

"Goodbye."

Lillie hung up the phone before she lost control, and then rushed over to Grace's condo with CoCo Chanel nipping at her heels, yapping loudly. She let herself in and walked into the peaceful atmosphere set by Grace's eclectic décor. The shades of sunset colors relaxed even the most perplexed spirit in a room full of plush brown couches, Moroccan silk throws, red sheer curtains, indigenous artwork, and curved Henna lamps. Lillie resisted the urge to plop down on the silky floor cushions.

Grace's tranquil, silky sarong flowed in sync with her effortless movements in the kitchen. The exotic smell of savory coconut, vegetables, and fruit filled Lillie's nostrils. Ever since she'd met this Hawaiian guy at Flow, she'd started experimenting with tropical cuisine.

Grace smoothed out the colorful sarong as she walked out of the kitchen to greet CoCo, then hugged Lillie.

"What's cracking, Lil?" Grace had recently started teaching Hip Hop aerobics to a community youth group. Despite her suburban upbringing, she picked up their slang to make her conversation more relevant.

"You'll never guess what just happened to me?" Excited, Lillie jumped up and down like an innocent schoolgirl and Grace modeled Lillie's behavior. Every time she jumped, CoCo jumped. Knowing that Grace was mocking her enthusiasm, Lillie rolled her eyes and stood still.

"You're right. I won't, so just tell me. "

"Adam called me!"

"Girl, that man is fine! I mean, he's not my type, though. Too clean cut."

"Oh, he's perfect for me." Lillie gazed into the sky, illusory and romantic.

"Adam must be something special, because I haven't seen you like this, except when I catch you checking out Theo on the sly. You passed up a good thing in him, you know."

"If you say so," Lillie shrugged her shoulders.

"Since you're goo goo over Adam, it gives Theo time to come to his senses and get with me."

Grace wasn't teasing and Lillie knew it. The thought of Theo with another woman was disturbing, but she knew it was inevitable. She just didn't want it to be Grace. That was a little too close to home. Instead of worrying about it, she changed the subject back to Adam's call and shared the information about the invite.

"Sounds lovely. Don't worry, I'll talk Theo into coming because you know he'll fight you on it."

Lillie chuckled because she knew Grace was right.

"Thanks, Grace. It sure does smell good in here. What are you making?"

"Quinoa mixed with sweet potatoes and coconut, sautéed spinach with sundried tomatoes, and Hawaiian fruit salad."

"What a tropical delight! Are you entertaining the Hawaiian guy? What about your undying love you keep declaring for Theo?"

"No way! Island man is cute, but I'm on a mission to get my man." Grace swayed her ample hips from side to side giving Lillie her best rendition of a seductive hula dance and CoCo tried to join in. "I plan to live in that phat house on the hill, overlooking the river, and popping out Theo's babies like a real queen should."

Lillie's temples flared thinking about Grace with Theo. She knew that sooner or later, she'd have to come to terms with her friend's intentions. If Theo decided to take Grace's bait, she'd just have to accept their relationship.

"Yeah, yeah, yeah. Why are you cooking all this food again?"

"Nothing special. Just Masseri's first day back from California. To celebrate, I thought I'd make her dinner. Plus, Elaina is bringing her grandbabies. I offered to watch them while she and Adam go to a client meeting for Flow."

"I didn't know she was back in town."

Then Lillie thought about the slew of messages on her unchecked voice mail. Unless she actually answered the phone, it was hard to get in contact with her. She had her crazy work schedule for that. Masseri had been on tour promoting her new Brazilian funk aerobics DVD. Avid physical fitness enthusiasts, Lillie and Grace met Masseri Jennings in college while recuperating in the Oval after jogging five miles. They introduced her to Theo and the four became fast friends. When Masseri started teaching aerobics, Lillie and Grace were her first students. Over the years, she amassed a following that afforded her the opportunity to quit her job as a physical therapist and teach her class all over the country.

Grace pulled out her cell phone to show Lillie a picture of Masseri in all her California glory. She left Ohio with butterscotch colored skin, but the California sun blessed her with a new tone that put Masseri in the redbone category. The constant workouts and strict diet afforded her a sleek, muscular physique. Since she was a fitness profession by trade, Masseri sported a short, curly, sun-bleached hairstyle for a wash and go style. Men and women alike were in awe of her alluring beauty.

"Wow! She's even more beautiful now than when she left. Does this girl ever age?"

"Not at all, huh?"

Grace and Masseri were the proud owners of Power Moves, a group fitness studio in the Clintonville area. They dreamed of this in college and made it come to fruition after graduation. Their degrees in Exercise Science and Nutrition definitely weren't going to waste.

"Make sure you come to our class in the morning. We're co-teaching. I know you have to be tired of walking on that treadmill every morning."

"Maybe I will. Just the smell of this food makes me feel like I've gained ten pounds. What time will it be ready?" Lillie smiled as she thought of the lie she'd told to get Adam off the phone. There was no food in her oven, but there was a great deal of food in Grace's.

"If you get your crazy dog out of my kitchen, I can finish up."

"I guess my dog and I aren't welcome. Come on, CoCo. Let's go call Mr. Caramel Latte Dream back." Lillie picked up the canine and whimsically sauntered towards the front door.

ဆ ભ

"Now, that's creative. Getting single people together in an environment outside of the church or
the club is an excellent idea."

Adam laughed hysterically then cleared his throat. "I'm glad you decided to call back and I'm glad you and your friends can make it. Speaking of your friends, is Theo going to really be alright with me being in the same room with you?"

Lillie burst out laughing.

"I mean, he's really protective of you. What's up with that?"

"Theo and I have been best friends since fifth grade. When I moved to the neighborhood, he took on the role of my personal tour guide and protector. We even went to the same high school and college; as you can imagine, the protector part hasn't changed." Lillie paused to reflect. "He's special to me; but, as you stated on our first day of class, I am a grown woman. If Theo plans to be in my life, he'll just have to get over it and stay out of my relationships. I mean, it's not like he and I are involved or anything."

"Whatever you say, I'm here to tell you you're in a relationship with him. You're the only one who doesn't see it," Adam jested.

Shocked by the bold nature of his comment, Lillie changed the subject. "What makes you so passionate about preaching, Adam?"

"Funny. No one's ever asked me that. Of course, I enjoy sharing the word of God with anyone who will listen. Plus it makes me feel closer to my father. I remember listening to his sermons and being proud to call him my dad. I've always wanted to be just like him."

"I bet. That's not unusual. Most men want to be like their father. Especially if he left that kind of impression."

"Lillie, if you only knew. I love my father with all my heart, but at this point in my life, I'm still striving to be even half the man he was."

"I guess perfection can't be duplicated, right?"

"That's right."

She was impressed with Adam's admiration for his father. Not sure what to say next, Lillie felt it was best to end the conversation.

"Adam, I look forward to this dinner. It's a brilliant idea. Just what I need right now," Lillie said as she kicked back on the couch and twisted her hair around her fingers.

"Yeah, it will be just what you need. I promise you that." Lillie enjoyed how Adam inadvertently allured her with his words. She sighed, falling under his charismatic spell.

"I hate to rush you off the phone, but I have a meeting with Elaina and her new investors. Duty calls."

They lingered on the phone for a few moments, neither one of them speaking a word, just breathing and enjoying the moment. Then, they both hung up. Still in a daze from the conversation, Lillie decided to take a nap before she crashed Grace's dinner party. CoCo Chanel jumped on the bed and snuggled up next to her. Rubbing the canine's belly, she fell asleep instantly with visions of her new love interest, Mr. Caramel Latte Dream.

SEVEN

L ILLIE CONTEMPLATED her escape from Theo's vehicle and walking to Flow as she listened to him go on and on about why he didn't want to go to this dinner.

I knew I should have driven my own car!

Grace's "carbon footprint reduction" excuse was getting old. She didn't know what was worse – Grace making stupid googly eyes at Theo or listening to him spew his negative energy. She ignored her friends and thought about the brilliant changes Adam had made at Flow. He'd convinced Elaina to remodel the basement and rent it out for meetings, gatherings, and other events to generate additional revenue. Adam's business mind never ceased to amaze Lillie.

Of course, Theo's constant complaining interrupted her thoughts. His behavior appalled Lillie to the extent that she was beginning to warm up to the idea of Grace pursuing him just to keep him out of her hair. Lillie took deep breaths as they pulled up to Flow. The anticipation of seeing Adam again caused her heart to flutter incessantly and she didn't know what to do or say. Sharing this with Grace when Theo was present wasn't a good idea, so she decided not to speak at all.

"Theo. Before we get out of the car, I'd like to ask if you could do me a big favor." Grace batted her fake eyelashes. They were the perfect length and thickness, giving her a mysterious and sexy look. Lillie had no idea what she was about to ask Theo, but with this dramatic production, it had to be good.

"Depends."

Well, at least he's honest, Lillie thought. Even though she was frustrated with Theo, she couldn't help but get warm and fuzzy inside about his jealous rants. Attraction to Adam wasn't magically turning off her love for Theo.

"Tonight is about having fun, learning something, and making connections, right?" Grace flashed Theo a bright smile.

"Yeah, that's my understanding," Theo grunted as if he knew what her next question would be. Lillie didn't dare speak one word.

"Good. I'm glad we have a common understanding of the purpose. So, can you lay off of Adam?"

Lillie caught her breath as she held back a snicker. She couldn't wait to hear Theo's response.

"Look, Grace. I'm not going to make any promises, but I will say this. If he doesn't start, neither will I."

"We'll take it." Grace wiped the sweat from her forehead with an exaggerated move of her arm. Lillie couldn't help but notice that Theo grunted again.

The trio exited the vehicle and walked into the building. Masseri met them at the door, still clad in her sleek magenta t-shirt, branded with her Brazilian funk aerobics logo. Black yoga pants hugged her tiny frame like a glove. As she walked, the click of her designer flip-flops revealed her every move. The sunshine revealed the healthy gloss of her short curly hair donned with cute metallic clips that matched her t-shirt.

"What's shaking, bacon?" Masseri had a strange tendency to great her friends with food names.

"Nothing much. And you know you don't eat bacon," Theo grunted.

Lillie and Grace simultaneously shook their heads at Theo's antics. The four friends exchanged hugs and headed down the stairs. As they entered the basement, Adam greeted them, shook Theo's hand, and gave hugs to Lillie, Grace, and Masseri. When he hugged Lillie, he held her longer than was customary. Intoxicated by his aura and the alluring aroma of his cologne, she floated to another world.

As Adam fixed the collar of his blue polo shirt and smoothed his khaki pants, Lillie couldn't help but notice his muscular physique. She allowed her imagination to roam to a high definition visual of what his toned buns were like underneath his clothing. As if he read her thoughts, Adam tilted his head slightly to the side and winked in her direction. Theo turned up his lips in disgust, oozing disapproval. Adam ignored him and focused on starting the meeting.

"I'm glad you all were able to make it to our first singles dinner. Please give the owner, Elaina Martin, a hand for allowing us to use these wonderful facilities, free of charge. Now that I've greeted you, fix your plates and we'll get started with the games in about fifteen minutes."

As Lillie scanned the room, she noticed a spread of lasagna, tossed salad, garlic bread, beverages, and desserts. Her stomach growled loudly reminding her she hadn't eaten since breakfast. Normally, she would've asked a million questions about who'd prepared what; because Lillie didn't eat just anyone's cooking. But today, she dropped her idiosyncrasies and allowed her inhibitions to take over. Plus, the meal was probably catered by the staff at Flow or one of Pastor Andrews many restaurants. She piled her plate high and sat down. The others followed Lillie's lead. She closed her eyes to savor the flavor as she took her first bite of the lasagna.

Oh, my goodness. This lasagna is to die for! Wait a minute, it's vegetarian. Even better!

Suddenly, Adam appeared out of nowhere. "I see you're enjoying my masterpiece."

"Are you serious? You cooked this? A guy like you doesn't strike me as the kitchen type. I mean . . ."

"I'll have you know. My father taught me all of the family's secret recipes. As a child, I can remember him and my mother cooked together almost every night. It was their way of bonding."

"Now, that sounds like true love. How sweet," Lillie cooed.

"That true love blossomed into some great meals. Then they passed those culinary skills on to me. Once they inducted me into the fold, the variety of gourmet meals increased exponentially at the Johnson family household."

Before Lillie could respond, Theo appeared.

"Adam, the food was great. Kudos to the caterer." Lillie was surprised at Theo's sincerity. Then she remembered Grace had pleaded with him to be cordial. Smiling as if they shared a secret, neither Adam nor Lillie said a word about the identity of the chef.

"Thanks, man."

"You and Elaina have done a great job with the décor in here," Grace chimed in.

"I appreciate your compliment."

Pastor Andrews walked in and went to the front of the room. Since Adam invited people from single's ministries at various churches, he mentioned that Pastor Andrews would be stopping by to greet people. Bianca followed slightly behind him carrying a yellow steno pad and shiny leather briefcase. Her green button down shirt clung to her curves. Lillie almost choked when she noticed the shirt buttoned down to her visible cleavage. To make matters worse, Bianca's pencil skirt stuck to her ample behind like glue. This wardrobe selection was definitely out of her norm. Loose spiral locks of honey-blonde hair fell to frame her fully made up face as she'd pulled it into a jeweled clip. Lillie wondered what had brought about this change in their friend's appearance.

"I just wanted to take a moment to thank you all for coming out. As you know, I think highly of Adam's father, Pastor Johnson, and it's my honor to take his son under my wing while he's away from their home church in Chillicothe."

Everyone gave Adam a round of applause and even stood in his honor. Once the applause subsided, Pastor Andrews continued to speak.

"When Adam expressed the interest to lead our single's ministry, he assured me that he would include fellowship activities with other churches. I thought it was a great idea and wanted you to know that each of your pastors is on board with this venture. Who knows what it could turn out to be? With no further ado, I'm going to get out of your way and let Adam lead you tonight."

After Pastor gave his brief speech, Bianca fixed a plate for him, wrapped it in aluminum foil, and they made their exit.

"She's taking her assistant role quite serious, don't you think?" Masseri sneered. She was never one to hold her tongue. For some strange reason, she'd never been fond of Bianca and didn't mind sharing her distaste with the world.

"Hush!" Grace ordered.

"Humph, you all think to highly of her. One day, you'll see her stuff stinks just like everyone else's." Masseri rolled her neck and dipped her garlic bread in the sauce.

Bianca waved at Lillie from the hallway. As she waved back, Lillie reflected on Masseri's observation. It was strange for Bianca to be there since the pastor's former assistant rarely accompanied him to events.

Adam divided the singles into three teams and assigned a stereotype about single Christians to each. Then he directed them to elect a leader who would help facilitate a discussion around the stereotype. To Lillie's surprise, she and Adam ended up on the same team, along with two other people named Sharon and Kenny. His charisma and enthusiasm when sharing his perspective commanded their attention.

"I believe that too many single women think Jesus is their boyfriend. I even read a book where one shared how she set up romantic evenings with him. Who does that?" Lillie tried to hold back her disgust when sharing this with the group.

"I do." This comment came from Sharon, a young lady from Acts of Faith. "I light candles and everything. Humph! I can worship my Lord instead of sitting around lonely while I'm waiting for the Lord to send my king."

Adam chuckled and responded, "We're not expecting anyone to sit around lonely; however, let's look at it from a different perspective. How would you feel about a single man doing the same thing?"

"Worship is one thing, but the date part, that's just plain old nasty." Kenny snarled in response. He was from New Manna Christian Ministries. "I'm just saying. If Jesus is God in the flesh and God is a spirit, then God literally placed his spirit in a human body so he could be his own sacrifice for our sins. Why would we set up a date with a spirit who's our father? That's like incest."

"Brother Kenny has a good point here. Oftentimes, single women get so caught up in the idea of waiting on God that they miss the man he sends their way." Adam shared his philosophy with ease.

Lillie was having a great time until she noticed Theo watching her out of the corner of his eye. She picked up her cell phone and sent him a text message.

> Lillie: *Shouldn't u be focusing on ur group's conversation?*
> Theo: *No, Lady Bug. Rt now I want 2 focus on u.*
> Lillie: *Hmmmm. We'll talk.*
> Theo: *Yes, we will.*

When Lillie finished reading the message, she heard a familiar buzzing noise. She looked all around the room yet couldn't determine its source.

Bzzzzzzzzzz! Bzzzzzzzzzz! Bzzzzzzzzzz!

The people in their table groups were chatting incessantly almost as if they didn't hear the same sound.

Bzzzzzzzzzz! Bzzzzzzzzzz! Bzzzzzzzzzz!

When she looked in Theo's direction, a golden light illuminated the space around his body.

Bzzzzzzzzz! Bzzzzzzzzz! Bzzzzzzzzz!

Lillie almost peed her pants when three life-sized honeybees flew in the room carrying a crystal jar filled with an amber-like substance. They placed it right in front of Theo and a beam of light shot out of the slide in Lillie's direction. She jumped up from her seat to avoid the ray and then . . .

"Lillie, I know you're not sending text messages while Adam is dropping this serious knowledge," Kenny scolded.

No stranger to experiencing open visions, Lillie knew to play it off because no one else would even know what she was talking about, since they couldn't see it. So, she smiled at Kenny and placed her phone in her purse. The rest of the discussion was a blur because she couldn't take her mind off the vision.

It was getting late, so Adam wrapped up the dinner with an exciting close. Who knew a praying man could exude such fiery passion and sexiness all at the same time? A few of the members hugged him and complimented the success of the evening.

As soon as the line thinned out, he made a beeline to Lillie and whispered in her ear, "Do you like jazz?" His sweet breath was hot and damp in her ear, giving her the shivers.

This man is crazy sexy!

"Love it."

"Great. I'd love to take you to Nirvana to check out some great talent. I can pick you up around seven tomorrow, if that's okay with you. That way, you won't have to set up dates with the Holy Spirit like your girl Sharon." Lillie playfully punched Adam on the shoulder and tossed her head back in laughter.

"So, I'll see you tomorrow?"

"See her where?" Theo interrupted as he, Grace, and Masseri approached.

Lillie grabbed Theo's arm and dragged him out the door while Grace and Masseri waved and followed behind.

"See ya, Adam," Lillie called out and Theo sneered.

Theo fussed the entire way to the car and Lillie tried her best to ignore him. Feeling the tension, Grace announced she was riding home with Masseri. As Theo drove to Lillie's place, he continuously shifted in his seat from one side to the other.

"Did you enjoy dinner?" Lillie asked, trying to lighten the mood.

"It was alright for what it was," Theo responded in a grumpy tone.

Theo's extra tight grip on the steering wheel revealed his heightened level of angst. Extremely irritated by his behavior, Lillie decided to give him a piece of her mind.

"Don't you get it? I need you to stay out of my dating life. I support the fact that Grace is interested in you. What's the problem with you supporting Adam's interest in me?"

"Grace is fine, but she's not you. I'm tired of playing this game. I want you, and I need you in my life. I dreamt about you before I even laid eyes on you. I hear in my spirit that you're my wife, so why do you fight it?"

Theo's wet tongue caressed his lips and Lillie couldn't deny his sexiness.

"Lillie, I love you. You're my rib." She was breathless, speechless, not sure how to respond. Tears stroked her cheeks gently so Theo handed her a tissue.

"I love you, too, Theo," Lillie shared in between sobs. "But you know this wouldn't work."

Theo sighed and took several deep breaths to keep his cool. They rode the rest of the way home in silence. Lillie knew pursuing Adam would be a turning point in her relationship with Theo. When they pulled up to her condo, she turned toward him to say goodbye, and without warning, he kissed her. Surprised, yet pleased, she returned his kiss with unbridled passion. Their lips locked and Theo quickly slipped his tongue in her mouth. He gently darted it back and forth, then round and round, beckoning Lillie to join the rhythm. Giving into her feelings, she wrapped her arms around Theo and caressed him as they turned up the heat. A surge of electric energy shot through Lillie's torso, causing her to connect with Theo's body. When she couldn't take anymore, Lillie broke their embrace. She was so confused.

Wow! I really do love this man and he makes me feel so . . .

"I can feel you, and you feel me too because we're meant to be together." He kissed her again. "Don't throw this away over curiosity and a lusty thrill." He leaned in and kissed her on the lips again. "We're destined to be together and you know it. You've always known it."

To seal his statement, he kissed her on the forehead. All Lillie could do was gaze into his eyes, more confused than ever. Would she choose Theo or Adam? Lillie played the question continuously in her head until she arrived at a clear decision. She exhaled, opened the car door, and sauntered into her condo.

EIGHT

TONIGHT WAS the night. Lillie's first date with Mr. Caramel Latte Dream. She was lounging in the relaxation room at Keyes to Style waiting for her appointment. This was Lillie's favorite part of the experience. Lightly scented candles, Zen music, soft and natural lighting from lamps made from Washi paper provided a tranquil setting for clients to relax and refresh.

She'd just finished getting a massage, manicure, pedicure, and facial. Once her stylist finished her hair, she'd get her makeup done for the finishing touch. Lisa walked in the room and gave Lillie a hug.

"Hey, Lillie. What's going on with you?" Lisa's jet black, spiked hair was a perfect match for her sassy personality.

"This is a special night, and I'm counting on you to make me even more beautiful than I already am." Lillie flipped her hair, pursed her lips, and snapped her fingers in a zigzag pattern for effect.

Lisa laughed at Lillie's dramatic request as they walked into the styling room. She draped a black cape around Lillie's neck and they proceeded to the shampoo bowl. The smell of mangos and coconut filled the room as Lisa lathered Lillie's hair with luxurious shampoo. After the conditioning treatment, they returned to the styling room.

"What's the special occasion? You haven't spent this much time here in ages."

"You read me like a book." Lillie bounced into the chair and smiled from ear to ear, while Lisa elevated it to just the right level.

"I met this guy who works for Elaina at Flow," Lillie shared as Lisa combed through her hair.

"Girl, I thought you were going to come in here to tell me that you finally came to your senses and got with Theo," Lisa sassed.

Reflecting back on the passionate kisses she shared with Theo, Lillie's conflicted heart screamed for his touch. Of course, she'd never let anyone else know. "Um . . . no. That's not going to happen and you know it." Lillie crossed her arms and poked out her lips.

Lisa quickly spun Lillie's chair around, "Okay, well it's Adam then. Elaina told me about him and from what I hear, girl, that man is fine!"

"Yes, he is and he's been the perfect gentlemen." Lillie gloated.

"So, where is he taking you?" Lisa inquired.

"To a jazz club called Nirvana. It's my first time ever going there."

Lisa laughed heartily and then said, "It's good that you'll experience something for the first time with him. This will help build a relationship if you two decide to go that far."

"What do you mean?"

"Well, my husband likes it when he can show me something I've never seen before. It makes him feel special." Lisa smoothed mousse on Lillie's wet hair, and then wrapped it in a circle.

"That makes sense. I'm just glad to meet a man like him. Outside of Theo, most of the men who are interested in me don't seem to have any class."

"Oh yeah. I remember the guy who kept coming here to see you. What was his name? Tank? Tom?"

"It was Tone. In fact, his family and close friends called him Big Tone." A handsome, educated man focused more on his Greek life than dating. He lived and breathed his fraternity.

"Being a successful black woman makes it hard in the dating world," Lisa explained. "It seems that most of the cultured black men date outside of their race." She worked hard to secure the paper strips around Lillie's wrapped hair.

"I've noticed that, too. In fact, I think more black woman should be open to men of other cultures. Heck! We're all God's children at the end of the day, right?"

"I know that's right. But I have to admit, I love my husband's brown skin. There's just something about it that I don't think I'm willing to trade in for another color." Lisa led Lillie to the hot dryer.

"You like what you like and you can't help that," Lillie teased. "You know I'm going to fall asleep under this dryer, right?"

As Lisa escorted her to the dryer, Lillie's phone rang. When she answered it, Alvin sang out a hearty greeting.

"Don't try to sing like Brian McKnight when you know you're wrong for not calling me!"

Alvin continued to sing and Lillie continued to fume at her god brother's inconsideration. He only called on holidays and birthdays even though she reached out to him much more frequently.

"Come on, Lady Bug. If I called you all of the time, you wouldn't miss me. Plus, the phone's not my thing. I'd rather see you in person and we both know that Hawaii is a long way from Ohio. Anyway, how's my little sis doing?"

Lillie plopped down on the seat of the dryer Lisa prepared for her and continued to chat with the hot air blowing on her wet scalp. Alvin always had stories to share about the crazy women he seemed to attract. His mother used to tell him he was handsome just like his daddy and he had the same problem.

"So when are you coming to see me?"

Alvin's pregnant pause gave Lillie the answer she wanted to know. "Lillie, you know I can't come back home. I just can't after all that's happened."

Knowing better than to talk about the issue, Lillie decided to try another approach. "Better yet, I would love to come out to Hawaii. I've been everywhere else you were stationed except there. You know Theo and Grace will travel at the drop of a dime. Oh yeah, we'd bring our friend Masseri, too. Do you remember her from my OSU days?"

"Heck yeah! That girl is fine. Yeah, bring her with you when you come. I've got plenty of room. Maybe you and Theo could have your wedding here."

Lillie held the phone up and looked at it in shock. "Wedding. Who's wedding? I keep telling you that we're just friends."

"Umm hmm."

"Shut up, Alvin!"

"Have you ever been here before?" Adam asked as he opened Lillie's car door.

⁎ ∾

She couldn't help but notice that he'd pressed his dress shirt and slacks to perfection and the waves in his hair were even tighter than the last time she saw him. Lillie stepped out of the car, holding on to the door handle for leverage.

"I've only driven by this place. The funny thing is I've always wanted to stop in. Now, being a minister, is it okay for you to listen to jazz?"

Adam's eyes lit up as he smiled at Lillie. He locked his arm in hers as they stepped onto the walkway. "Listening to jazz has never sent anyone to hell. Only Ms. Blakey would say that. My father was an anointed man of God who loved the Lord and listened to Miles Davis, as well. Don't get me wrong, he had issues just like anyone else, but I'm sure listening to jazz wasn't the source. So, I tend to ignore hypocrites like her."

"She's special; yet, I do see her point," Lillie replied. "I've known Ms. Blakey since I was a child and I've heard her say holy living doesn't appeal to most Christians. As far as she's concerned, either you're in or out. There's no compromise."

Before she could analyze the situation any further, the maître de seated them to the right of the stage. Instead of the standard chairs, plush red and black couches surrounded the table.

"How do you like it?" Adam flashed a bright smile.

Lillie was enthralled with the sexy waves in his hair, accentuated by the lighting.

"Umm, yeah. I love it." Lillie gave an awkward response as she surveyed the room. Artistic sketches of jazz greats adorned the red walls. Some of them held microphones, while others embraced instruments. Eclectic chandeliers hung from the black ceiling over each table, providing just the right amount of soft, natural light. It was different from the décor at Flow, with its blend of purple, blue, green, white, and black. The ambiance of this place was melancholy, yet quite comforting.

The strum of the guitar, pluck the bass, and blow the saxophone mesmerized the audience. After the second song, a voluptuous woman in a tight dress grabbed the microphone and belted out the strongest "Bop, bop, bop, bop, skiddily, boo, bop" Lillie had ever heard. Adam's eyes grew as big as saucers, as if he'd seen a ghost.

"Hey, are you okay, Adam?"

"Uh . . . yeah. I mean . . ." He coughed to clear his throat. When he regained his composure, he shared, "I thought that Soul Derivative was performing tonight. I wonder what happened. You would have loved to see them perform. Their lead singer is phenomenal."

"Janeen Holmes? Yes! Her voice is phenomenal."

"Hey, didn't the woman on the stage win some sort of musical competition?"

"Yeah. She won a recording contract that has taken her quite far in the jazz realm."

"What in the heck is she doing back in Columbus?"

"That's a good question. I'd like to know the same thing."

An erotic force accumulated momentum with each sway of the songstress's hips. She sashayed to Adam's side of the stage and bent down, giving him a clear view of her ample breasts. Then, she sang to him. "Your bedroom eyes see right through me. I'm dreaming of the love you'll make to me." Adam's faced turned beet red and he wiggled in his seat. As she rose, she threw her head back and laughed in syncopation with the song. Then, she had the nerve to shake her hips and thighs in a hedonistic motion that sent the men in the audience into a catcalling frenzy. Lillie didn't know whether to ignore her or punch her lights out.

"What was that all about?" Lillie snapped, her blood pressure at the boiling point.

"She's on top of the world right now and she knows it. Of course, she likes to give the men in the audience a show." Adam shrugged, blowing off Lillie's concern like it was no big deal. "You know how singers can be."

"I have to admit, I don't know. This is the first time I've been here, remember?"

Adam eased her frustration when he moved in closer and wrapped his strong arms around her. Typically, Lillie shied away from public displays of affection, but with Adam, if seemed so right.

"I'm glad you saved the first time for me. In fact, I hope we have many more first times together." Lillie melted at the sound of Adam's deep, sultry, and seductive voice. Immediately, she thought about what Lisa shared about first experiences with a man and she couldn't help but chuckle.

"You're exposing me to new things. That's what I like about you." She surprised herself when she returned Adam's flirtatious comments by speaking what she was thinking aloud, "We'll definitely have many more first times together. But I have to admit, I'm still a little nervous. Wondering, if a minister should be sitting up in this club like this. I mean, what if someone from the church sees you?"

"Like I said before, there's nothing wrong with me going to a jazz club to get to know you better. Plus, if someone from the church sees me here, they're here, too, right?"

Adam had a valid point. She didn't want to ruin their first date with incessant worrying, so she took a deep breath, sat back in the comfy couch, and exhaled.

ᘓ ᘔ

Basking in the glow of like, Lillie drank of Adam's energy as she gazed into his eyes. He looked good, smelled good, and felt good. The table was the best in the house, and their meal was superb. The servers seemed to be delighted to wait on them. The couple couldn't talk much, though, since the music was so loud. Instead, they depended upon expressions to convey their feelings for one another. Lillie was mesmerized, captivated, and under Adam's spell. Just as the song ended, the songstress gave shout outs to the crowd.

Lillie almost choked on her drink when she heard, "I want to say a great big 'thank you' to an old friend, Adam Johnson." The audience applauded. "He went and got saved; now, he's a minister."

Adam stood and waved. The crowd erupted into thunderous applause. The singer leaned with a yearning towards Adam's direction. Her energy was definitely more intense than feelings of brotherly love. It was one of longing and desire.

"You worked here?" No wonder the maître de seated them at the best spot in the house. Before Lillie could ask another question, a busty woman handed her a dozen red roses and gave Adam a strong bear hug.

"Lillie. This is Deena and the burly man at the bar, that's her husband, Bill. They are the proud owners of this wonderful establishment."

"Oh, Adam. You're too kind." She kissed him on the cheek and turned to Lillie. "Girl, you've got a hot commodity here. Make sure you take care of my Adam."

Lillie smiled and hugged Deena. As she scooted to the bar, a few others patrons came to the table to greet them.

"Now that you know I'm a celebrity here, may I have this dance?" Adam extended his hand to Lillie and she willingly took it. He gently kissed her hand as he led her to the dance floor. While the songstress belted out the Etta James tune "At Last" Lillie and Adam moved across the floor. Despite Lillie's awkward movements, he danced with precision and excellence, not missing a beat.

"Adam, you took dance lessons, didn't you?" Lillie teased.

Shrugging his shoulders, Adam laughed and said, "Sure did. Then, I got a job teaching dance lessons. The schedule was flexible and it paid the bills while I attended college."

"Where did you go?" Lillie inquired. She was pleased to know that Adam was educated.

"To start out, I attended the Ohio University branch in Chillicothe. Then, I transferred to the main campus in Athens."

"You're a Bearcat?" Lillie spewed then pretended to gag.

Adam smiled, showing his pearly whites that Lillie was beginning to love. "Only a Buckeye would ask that question. Yes, I'm a Bearcat. I graduated top of my class with a degree in marketing," Adam postured. "How about you?"

"I graduated with honors from The Ohio State University with a degree in business management." Lillie caught her breath as Adam dipped, lifted, and spun her around. All this pleasurable movement excited her sensory nerves.

"You know, I used to slow dance with my dad as a child. I specifically remember dancing with him at Father Daughter dances." Being in Adam's arms caused intense feelings to rise in Lillie. The sensation was so electrifying and new.

"Oh, so you're a daddy's girl?" Adam teased.

"Yes, sir and I'm proud of it," Lillie said with a smug grin on her face.

Adam responded by pulling Lillie closer, yielding a mutual excitement between the two. Once the song ended, he kissed Lillie on the hand and led her back to their seats, where she continued to enjoy the ambiance and Adam's company.

"Lillie, I'm not the type of guy who beats around the bush. I'm into you, and I want to know if you feel the same way."

"Wow. You know how to shock a lady," Lillie responded in amazement. "To answer your question, yes, I do."

Adam flashed a bright smile and said, "Great! I want to know more about you. Like where do you work? Do you have children? Do you like dogs? What's your favorite color? Then I expect we'll be seeing more of each other, right?"

Lillie laughed as she responded, "I own a human resources consulting firm called Mosaic Talent. We provide diverse staffing solutions for a variety of organizations across the state. I don't have any children and since I'm an only child, no nieces or nephews. I do have a god brother who's in the army. He calls every once in a while, but that's about it. I love dogs. In fact, my dog's name is CoCo Chanel. She's a Yorkichon who thinks she's human. Right now, she's probably upset because she's in her cage while you and I are out on this great date. My favorite color is indigo, and yes, I want to see more of you. Now, it's your turn."

"You know the answer to the first question. Like you, I'm an only child. I've always wanted a big brother, though. I have two children from a previous relationship," Adam shared.

"Oh. You have children?" His revelation surprised Lillie, but she loved children, so it was definitely not a deal breaker.

"Yes. Most men our age do. I'm not sure how I'll get along with CoCo Chanel since I love big dogs, and my favorite color is black."

"That's cool." Lillie envisioned them walking hand in hand at the Ohio State Fair in matching black outfits.

"I also want to let you know that my children have a great mother. She lives in Chillicothe and we share the responsibilities. It works out perfectly." Adam shrugged his shoulders and continued to groove to the music, then asked, "What's your favorite dish? I'm just dying to cook for you."

Just as she was about to respond, her phone vibrated. She picked it up and took it out of the case. It was a text message from Theo. Not wanting to appear rude, she excused herself and went to the ladies room. The shocking red décor took Lillie's breath way. Even in all its beauty, the color seemed out of place for a restroom. Lillie plopped into a plush red chair as she read and responded to the message.

Theo: *Enjoying ur date w/ Mr. Caramel Whatever?*
Lillie: *Yep*
Theo: *SMH!*
Lillie: *U can't be serious.*

Theo had always been her protector, but he'd never acted like this.

Lillie: *Y r u hating?*
Theo: *Whatever! Don't let him walk u 2 the door. Hug him in the car & end it there.*
Lillie: *We'll see. Stay out of my biz.*
Theo: *Love u. Goodnight.*
Lillie: *Love u, too. Still, stay out of my biz.*

Theo has lost his mind! Now, he was trying to control her dating life through text messages. Lillie tossed the phone into her purse, and then smiled in the mirror as she refreshed her lipstick and powder.

"That must have been an interesting text. You had to leave the table to answer it," Adam observed. Lillie jumped like a grasshopper when she heard Adam's voice.

"What in the heck are you doing in here?" Lillie screamed.

Adam pointed to the sign on the door and Lillie couldn't believe her eyes. This was a coed bathroom.

"Yeah, it shocks most people. So, what about that text?"

"I can't talk to you in here."

Without hesitation, Adam grabbed her hand and they headed back to the table. Once they were seated, she answered Adam's question.

"The text? Oh, it's nothing," Lillie lied.

"Uh huh. I bet it's your wannabe man, Theo," Adam cajoled. "I can't say that I blame him, though." His smile was mesmerizing, taking her mind off Theo for the moment. It was definitely time to change the subject. Just then, she remembered that she hadn't responded to Adam's dinner invitation.

"You know what, Adam, I'd be delighted to have you cook for me and I'm anticipating a great meal."

NINE

DINNER WITH Adam turned out to be a delightful treat. He prepared scrumptious chicken Alfredo with a crispy tossed salad and bread sticks with just the right touch of garlic butter. He'd even made Lillie's favorite dessert— lemon cake with lemon icing made from scratch. She couldn't figure out how he knew, but she was sure the dessert choice wasn't happenstance. This meal was even better than what he'd prepared for the single's gathering at Flow.

"Can I help you with the dishes?"

"No way. This evening is all about you. We can't have you doing dishes at our first private dinner."

"Thank goodness. I'm so full I can barely move."

Lillie plopped on Adam's chocolate brown sofa as he cleaned the kitchen with meticulous expertise. She enjoyed watching him move through the kitchen with minimal effort. Rubbing her belly, she thought of the yummy treats he'd promised to prepare for her.

A gorgeous, saved man who cooks and cleans! I've hit the jackpot.

Adam's house wasn't the typical bachelor's pad. It was immaculate and organized, like he'd prepared for a spot on Home and Garden TV. Even the canned goods in his cabinet were in alphabetical order. His decorating skills were impeccable; however, he didn't live in the best neighborhood. The surrounding slumlords didn't take care of their property, which made his beautiful home seem out of place. Lillie had to admit this quaint, urban two-story home didn't compare to Theo's lavish, custom home in the suburbs, overlooking the Olentangy River.

"I could get used to this royal treatment. Promise to spoil me like this and you'll never get rid of me," Lillie teased.

"Go on and make that casual covenant."

"Casual covenant? What's that?" Lillie asked as she walked back into the kitchen.

"When you put a statement like the one you made into the atmosphere, the universe sets a course of action into motion. Our words have power." Adam was dropping knowledge that heightened Lillie's curiosity.

"I've never heard that before. Tell me more." Adam's understanding of the spiritual realm intrigued her. He could break down complex spiritual concepts with expertise, whether it was in the form of a sermon or in casual conversation.

"Think of it this way: have you ever said, 'I'm sick and tired', and then felt sick and tired?" Adam questioned Lillie.

"Yeah, but I thought it was just happenstance. I've never connected making that kind of statement with it actually occurring."

"Gotcha. Here's another example. Most stalkers make comments like 'You will never leave me' or 'Over my dead body,' then we end up watching them being convicted of murder on the six o'clock news." Even though this was a scary observation, it was realistic.

"What if I say something like 'You'll cook dinner for me every night.' Will it happen?" She threw the challenge out to see if Adam would bite.

"Of course, dinner for my lady is always in the plan." Adam grabbed Lillie by the waist and sucked gently on her lips. The power of their chemistry blew her away. While she recovered, Adam dimmed the lights and turned on a sultry tune.

"My dear, may I have this dance?" Adam asked in a formal, yet charming manner.

"Why, yes, you may," Lillie responded. He took her by the hand and led her in a seductive slow dance. Enthralled by his suave movements, she fell under Adam's seductive spell and they danced the night away.

TEN

O H MY goodness! Are you serious?"
Lillie jumped up and down like a child in a candy store.
Once she regained her composure, she thanked God the
person on the other end of the phone couldn't see her outburst.

"Yes, I just thought I'd call to let you know. We'll send you an invitation to the banquet with additional details by the end of the week."

She ended the call and kicked back in her plush reclining chair.
A prestigious client nominated her for the Human Resources
Innovator of the Year award. Accepting the nomination created
the potential for Mosaic Talent to attract new accounts, which
of course meant more work. Despite her young age, Lillie had
built quite a career for herself, starting with working for a human
resources firm right out of college. When the owner announced
his plan to retire, he selected Lillie as his protégé and groomed her
to take over. This entrepreneurial opportunity came with a price,
so she often worked sixty to seventy hours per week. Once clients
started pouring in, she moved the office from Upper Arlington

to a plush spot in the Easton District with its trendy restaurants and eclectic stores.

This had to be her lucky day. In addition to the news about the nomination, Adam asked Lillie to have dinner at his child-hood home. She propped out her chest with assurance since this invitation evidenced the progression of their relationship in the right direction. For the past few months, she and Adam had been inseparable. He even helped her with her caseload to secure their time together. In turn, she spent more time at Flow. When they weren't working, they walked in the park, danced the night away at Nirvana, or attended one of his many speaking engagements.

Lillie jolted back to reality when she heard her office manager, Rosa, chatting at the front desk. When she recognized Theo's voice, she skipped out of her office to greet him and almost collided with the indigo vase full of calla lilies.

"Look who brought Miss Lillie her favorite flowers," Rosa purred in her baritone voice. A voluptuous down-home woman from Louisiana, no one believed she had twelve grandchildren. She moved to Columbus to live with her daughter when she'd lost her husband and her home to Hurricane Katrina. For some reason, she'd taken a liking to Theo and convinced herself he was Lillie's future husband.

"What a great surprise!" Lillie just loved calla lilies. Even though she appreciated Theo's gesture, she had mixed emotions about him lavishing her with such wonderful gifts while she was involved with Adam.

"One of my clients told me about your nomination so I thought I'd stop by and congratulate you in person." Lillie walked back to-ward her office, and he followed. Theo set the vase on her desk and pulled out a box of her favorite Godiva chocolate turtles.

"I'm meeting Masseri, Grace, Bianca, and Elaina for lunch. How about joining us?"

"Oh, Theo. I can't. I'm going to Chillicothe to meet Adam's parents this evening, which means I'll have to work through lunch. Maybe some other time?"

"He's not wasting any time, I see. Isn't it too soon for that?"

Lillie smirked at Theo's question and decided not to respond.

Theo frowned and walked toward the door. "Oh yeah," he shouted over his shoulder. "Are we still on for dinner at your parents' house? Your mom told me she's making the shrimp dish we all like. You know your dad is excited since he always has the munchies."

Lillie threw her head back as laughter exceedingly flowed from her throat. "Don't crack on my daddy's herbal activities. You know it's medicinal or at least that's what he tells everyone."

"Yeah right," Theo teased.

For years, Theo maintained contact with Lillie's parents. He served as their legal counsel and managed their retirement funds. Plus, Lillie's mother needed help with the accounting for her home business. She decided that retirement bored her to death, so she started selling her homemade body care products. Her father named the business Charmed Essentials because he swore his wife placed some sort of spell on the products that made people fall in love with them. Lillie loved watching her mother proudly stamp her labels with the words "All organic" and "No genetically modified ingredients." In fact, most of them came from her garden, a local health and wellness store, and a farm in the neighboring town. She's always made lotions and potions but never sold them to the public. It started with her bridge club members. She gave them free samples and they loved them so much, they became loyal customers and spread the word.

Just remembering the commitment, Lillie replied, "Sure. I'm starving just thinking about it."

"Thanks for the flowers and the candy. You know they're my favorite."

Theo hesitated, then walked back into Lillie's office. "Before I go, can I ask you one question? What is it about him? You've never acted like this before." Theo's voice escalated several octaves, making his displeasure evident. "We hardly ever see you unless you're at church or at Flow with him."

"That's what happens when you fall in love with—"

Theo banged his fist on the wall and flashed a glare at Lillie.

"In love? Yeah right. You barely know him. I find that hard to believe."

Theo gently reached for Lillie and caressed her shoulder. His warm touch sparked a fire in her belly. Her internal conflict heightened as she fought the natural urge to return his genuine affection. Lillie resistance melted like hot butter when his tongue traveled slowly around his lips and he cocked his head to the side.

"I'm your best friend and you know we're destined to be to-gether. How can you kiss me the way you did in the car that night and claim to love him? Like I said, I don't believe you."

Theo's accurate intuition led Lillie to take a more direct approach.

"If I was your girlfriend and Adam brought me calla lilies and chocolate, how would you want me to respond?" Always a man of integrity, Lillie knew this statement struck a chord with him.

"Okay, I get it. I promise not to undermine your relationship with your little boyfriend." Theo's so-called apology dripped a sarcastic price tag, and she wasn't buying it.

With her eyes on Theo's handsome face, Lillie's words flowed in slow syncopation. "As I've told you before, Adam and I are growing closer, and if you want to continue to be a part of my life, you need to accept that." Lillie turned to face Theo again. "Okay?"

"Okay," he agreed with reluctance. "Only because I know you'll be mine sooner than later. You can't deny your one true love for too long. We're destined to be together, and you know it."

Instead of facing the truth of Theo's words, Lillie made a strategic move that would send Theo packing even though she didn't want him to go.

"Speaking of Adam, he's also joining us for dinner. He's dying to try Mom's home cooking."

Theo stood in the doorway, shaking his head. "Are you serious? It's bad enough I have to share you with Mister Caramel what-ever, but not my food. That's where I draw the line."

Lillie glided to the doorway and gave Theo a customary hug to get him out of her hair. To her surprise, he embraced her just a little longer than usual. Then he brushed his full lips against her forehead. Lillie's desire to get him out of her office went out the door. She folded her body into his arms, then he grabbed her face with a seductive force and kissed her with a powerful passion. Even more surprising, his touch made her tingle on the inside and she couldn't deny their chemistry. It was so innocent and sweet yet tantalizing at the same time. Confused and caught up in the moment, Lillie couldn't help but return his kiss and the heat of their hearts connected and set ablaze. Just as quickly as she surrendered, she thought about her relationship with Adam. Lillie jerked away from Theo and began twisting her hair.

"I know you felt that spark, too."

Still hot and bothered, Lillie twisted random strands of her hair, playing the coquettish role. Theo had such a way with words.

"You're twisting your hair because you're nervous. I know you like the back of my hand. You've done that since we were little kids." Theo chuckled. "I don't think you like Mr. Caramel Latte Dream as much as you say, let alone love him. In fact, I believe he's a distraction because you're scared to get with me. Just know I won't be waiting around for too long," Theo promised as he walked out of her office.

"Goodbye, Rosa," he called out.

"Take care, baby," Rosa returned his departing salutation and walked into Lillie's office.

"Rosa, please hold all my calls. I'm going to get some work done so I can get out of here on time to meet Adam."

Rosa sighed so loud, Lillie stopped in her tracks.

"Yes, ma'am?" Rosa might be Lillie's employee, but she understood the concept of respecting her elders all too well.

"Baby, I've been in this world a long time and I only want the best for you. That other young man is nice, but he's not the one for you."

"What makes you say that?" Lillie inquired leaning in to Rosa's space.

"With you and Adam, I see a mere infatuation that won't last. It's new and fresh, so it's fun. You and Theo, on the other hand, have a deep love for one another on top of a great friendship. What you have with Theo is real, lasting. It can stand the test of time. What you have with Adam is temporary bliss ignited with a twist of lust." Rosa massaged Lillie's shoulders to ease the tension. "How long are you going to keep playing games with these men?"

Lillie snipped at Rosa, "I'm not playing games with them. Adam's everything Theo's not." Lillie wasn't sure whether she was trying to convince herself or Rosa. "I enjoy spending time with him, and we happen to have a lot in common. I love the way he looks, the way he smells, and Rosa, the way he moves is so darn sexy. Plus, he's intelligent, too!"

"Okay, then even with all that, it's obvious you're with Adam because you're scared to be in a relationship with someone you've known for so long. You're afraid that it may not work out and you'll lose him forever, right?" When Lillie didn't respond, she gave Rosa the ammunition she needed to continue.

"Aha, just what I thought. Now look me in the eyes and tell me you don't love Theo." Much to Lillie's dismay, she couldn't honor Rosa's challenge.

"I'm not surprised. You love Theo and you know it."

Unexpected tears streamed down Lillie's face as she listened to the elderly woman's words. With such rich experience, most people didn't ignore her words of wisdom; yet Lillie chose to do her own thing instead.

ELEVEN

AUTUMN LEAVES blessed Lillie's eyes with rustic shades of yellow, orange, and red on the back road to Chillicothe. This route took a little longer than the direct one; however, the sites made it a worthwhile time investment.

"Hon, I'm so excited about meeting your parents. I feel like this is a big step in our relationship," Lillie said with enthusiasm, amazed by Adam's ability to keep his eyes on the road while making eye contact with her.

"My mother has been dying to meet the woman I've been talking about non-stop. She even invited some friends from her church."

"From church? Oh, heck no. They're setting me up for the great inquisition. I know this one inside out, because we do it to Theo's female friends all the time." Lillie squared her shoulders with confidence, not about to let some old church biddies get the best of her.

"You're exaggerating. Don't be silly," Adam said. "By the way, do you remember the singer from Nirvana?"

"Oh yeah. How could I forget? She wanted to sop you up like gravy on her biscuit." Since they'd been dating, Lillie noticed women attracted to Adam like a moth to a closet full of clothing. This woman employed the most aggressive approach of them all.

"Well, I wanted to let you know she had a death in the family and they asked me to do the eulogy. That's the reason she decided to stay in the city. In fact, she bought a beautiful home here."

"How convenient." Lillie turned up her nose and crossed her arms. She understood Adam's ministerial duties always came first, but she didn't care for that Jezebel. After they pulled up in front of the house, Adam strolled around to her side of the car to open Lillie's door. He bent down and brushed his lips against hers. Lillie closed her eyes to savor the chills going up and down her spine. She stood up to meet his touch, the power of his presence sent her body into a frenzy and she almost fell to her knees.

"You can't kiss me in front of your parent's house, Adam Johnson."

He grinned mischievously and escorted her inside.

Mrs. Johnson embraced Lillie with a tight bear hug and shouted out, "Oh my. You're even more beautiful than the picture Adam sent." Lillie had to admit she was wrong about this crew of women. At first glance, she could tell they were genuine. She looked around expecting to see an older version of Adam somewhere; however, he didn't show his face.

"Mama, Mrs. Daniels, and Ms. Tina, this is Lillie Corven. Isn't she beautiful?"

The ladies shook their head in unison.

"Adam, where are my godchildren?" Mrs. Daniels asked.

"Their mother took them on a trip to visit some relatives in Pennsylvania."

Before Mrs. David could respond, Adam's mother started giving directions. "Let's eat before this food gets too cold." Lillie noted his mother's command and wondered how she compared.

Most men sought women like their mother and surely, Adam was no different.

She followed Adam to the bathroom where they washed their hands. Even on this short walk through the home, Lillie appreciated the royal antique décor. Imperfections in the polished wood revealed what was most likely the original flooring. Even though Adam's mother had covered the furniture in plastic, the relic value shined through.

The immaculate home smelled of homemade food, and Lillie couldn't wait to dig in. She would have to spend extra time on the treadmill tomorrow to burn off those extra calories. The cherry wood table beckoned her to have a seat, so she obliged. The others followed suit and Adam blessed the food. As they enjoyed dinner, Mrs. Johnson drilled Lillie with questions.

"Well, we want to get to know you better, so tell us about your family."

Lillie shared information about her mother and father and answered Ms. Johnson's questions with ease. She and her friends seemed impressed with her answers.

"You know, I wish Alvin could have been here to meet you, but he's no longer with us."

"I'm sorry to hear that, Ms. Johnson." Lillie paused. "You know Alvin is my god brother's name, too."

"How sweet," Ms. Johnson responded in a catty tone that caught Lillie by surprise.

"You mean to tell me you didn't know?" Adam's mother may have questioned Lillie verbally, but she fixated her stern, locked and loaded gaze on Adam.

"Um . . . no. I didn't." Lillie joined Ms. Johnson and flashed Adam a glare.

"Well, it's not exactly dinner conversation, Mother." He turned towards Lillie. "Twelve years ago . . . someone . . . brutally murdered my father." Adam face shook uncontrollably as he held back tears.

"My Lord. You're still hurting, baby? I didn't know. Umm hmm. God rest your daddy's soul." The beam in Ms. Johnson's eye shined brightly as she admired her son.

When Adam asked her to meet his parents, Lillie asked a million questions about the family. She wondered why they didn't name him Alvin, Jr. When she'd asked him, he said his parents told him they wanted him to have his own identity.

After everyone finished their meals, Lillie followed the ladies into the kitchen to help with the dishes. Adam stayed behind to clean the dining room.

"I hear you're a business owner, Lillie. What do you do?" Mrs. Tina asked.

"I run a human resources consulting firm called Mosaic Talent. We offer a variety of solutions to businesses who choose to outsource their HR responsibilities." Lillie popped out her chest in pride as she shared about her business.

"Oh wow. That sounds nice. How's that working for you?" Ms. Johnson inquired.

"Business is flowing in steady," Lillie replied. "Thanks for asking. Adam's been encouraging through this process."

"Speaking of Adam, you know he's called to pastor. Do you know what that would mean if you two decided to marry?"

Ms. Johnson caught Lillie off guard with the quick subject change. This woman didn't beat around the bush. This line of questioning aligned with the inquisition she originally anticipated.

"Yes, ma'am, that's means I'll be his wife. I'll be an HR professional business owner and he'll pastor a church."

Ms. Johnson jerked her neck like rubber. Her coal black eyes pierced Lillie's psyche like an ice pick.

"His father encouraged me in everything I took on, as long as my dreams didn't interfere with what he wanted to do. Adam takes after his father, you know." Lillie detected a hint of sarcasm in Ms. Johnson's tone. Not sure how to respond, she decided to remain silent.

"Hmm. It seems a beautiful and talented young woman like you would have her choice of men."

"Ma'am, I really care for your son. In fact, over the past few months, I've grown to love him." Almost immediately, Lillie regretted sharing her feelings.

"Love? Child, please," Mrs. Daniels sassed.

Ms. Tina shook her head disapprovingly, and then chimed in with her two cents, if it was even worth that. "Are you ready to be a preacher's wife, baby?"

"By the time the proposal comes around, I'll be ready." Lillie shook her head firmly.

They continued to clean the kitchen in silence as Lillie reflected upon the conversation that just took place. She was sure Adam's mother was simply being overprotective, or was she hiding something?

୫୭ ଓଷ

Riding during the night hours robbed Lillie of her sightseeing adventure. Surely, it would have taken her mind off the visit. As much as Lillie enjoyed meeting Adam's mother, she didn't appreciate the overt scrutiny.

"I'm so glad you had the opportunity to go back home with me." Adam's beaming smile showed his pearly white teeth, even in the darkness. It was obvious he wasn't privy to the conversation she had with his mother.

"Yes. It was great," Lillie lied.

"Looks like you hit it off with Mom." Adam nodded his head in Lillie's direction and flashed a smug grin.

Unable to hold back her feelings any longer, Lillie let out a loud, exaggerated sigh.

"What was that all about?" he inquired as he cocked his head and wrinkled his nose.

"You think your mother likes me so much? Well, let me ask you this. When I was helping her with the dishes, she fired off a million questions as if I was the prime suspect in a murder case. What do you think about that?"

Adam swerved to miss a huge buck in the middle of the road, and then slowed down to readjust the car. Just in case there were other deer following the buck, he flashed his bright lights for a few seconds then resumed his speed. Lillie silently thanked the Lord there were no other cars on the road. Yet and still, the distraction wasn't enough to stop her from questioning Adam.

"I asked what do you think about that, Adam?"

"Do you realize we could've been seriously injured if we would've hit that deer?"

"Yes, but thanks to your great maneuverability skills, we're safe," Lillie snapped back in a sarcastic tone. "Now you can answer my freaking question."

"I'm sure she wants to know about the skeletons in your closet. In fact, so do I. What skeletons do you have in your closet, Lillie Corven?" Adam teased.

"Don't try to deflect. Answer the question."

"Girl, you're tripping. I answered your question. This conversation is over."

"Over? Over? I think not. Not to mention you didn't even tell me your father was deceased."

"Come on, Lillie. I explained why I didn't tell you," Adam snapped. "As I said before, this conversation is over."

Once Lillie saw Adam wasn't going to budge on this subject, she pretended to go to sleep. She didn't "wake up" until he pulled into the driveway of her condo.

"You're home," Adam muttered under his breath.

Lillie grabbed her purse from the backseat and waited for Adam to exit and open her door. When they arrived at her doorstep, Adam reached for her hand. Despite her frustration, her heart skipped a beat and she swooned. It only lasted for a moment though. He just had to speak to break the mood.

"Babe, from my perspective, we had a great day. Please don't let my mother's nonsense cause you to be angry with me."

"Nonsense? Are you going to dismiss your mother's concern as nonsense?" Lillie's sarcastic tone hit its target. Adam winced and stared down at the ground before bouncing back into the game.

"Yes, I am. Did it ever dawn on you maybe she's a little lonely? With Dad gone and all, she counts on me so much. Now, she sees me falling in love and maybe she feels threatened."

As much as Lillie hated to admit it, Adam's theory made sense. Of course, Ms. Johnson was simply trying to push her away. She was probably one of those possessive mothers who wanted her son all to herself.

"You're probably right. Promise me you're in this for the long haul, not some short term fling."

"I promise, Lillie. And I'll seal it with a kiss." Caught off guard by Adam's gesture of affection, Lillie's knees buckled when she felt the flood of emotions shoot through her body.

"Good night," Adam whispered as he broke their embrace.

Since she was at a loss for words, Lillie flashed a coquettish smile and waved like Miss America as she walked in the house. He blew a kiss to Lillie and she reached up to catch it, then blew one back. They both giggled and Adam walked back to his car. At that moment, Lillie exhaled and knew she was falling for this man.

TWELVE

"MOM, THIS meal is bangin'! You put your foot in this one." Theo gulped down another bite. "I see why you married her, Dad." Sam Corven slapped Theo's hand to give him a high five.

Lillie stopped in her tracks and placed her hand on her forehead as if she was in pain. Theo was doing everything in his power to make sure Adam knew just how strong his relationship was with her parents.

"Adam. I must say, Sam and I are glad to meet the man who's swept our Lillie off of her feet. You look so familiar to me for some reason. Almost as if we've met before."

"Oh, I'd remember meeting you, Mrs. Corven," Adam flirted. Since high school, Lillie had to put up with her male friends who were awestruck by her mother's mature beauty. Sophia blushed as Sam fumed and mumbled something under his breath about young men being rude, hitting on his wife at his own dinner table. All eyes were glued on him, until Adam broke the silence.

"Mrs. Corven, would you mind sharing the recipe? I enjoy cooking for Lillie from time to time." Adam grinned and squared his shoulders.

Lillie sighed loudly. She couldn't believe they were competing. The room was too small for their increasing testosterone levels.

"Humph!" Sam grunted. He'd barely spoken to Adam after their greeting. His red eyes revealed that he'd partaken in his favorite herbal pleasure before the gathering. When she was younger, she used to be embarrassed. Now, she just loved her dad for who he was.

"Thank you. You know there's more where that came from, and I have a surprise for dessert." Sophia Corven smiled lovingly at Theo and then turned to address Adam. "So, you like to cook?"

"Yes, ma'am. All the men in my family are good cooks. Even my father, who went on to the other side of glory, as my mother says." Adam smiled as he reflected on the memory of his father.

"Oh, Adam. I didn't know. I'm sorry to hear about your father," Sophia replied.

Adam smiled as a tear glistened on his cheek. Touched by his show of emotion, Lillie gently stroked his shoulders. Theo looked away in disgust. It was obvious that he didn't have any sympathy for Adam.

"You know what, baby?" Sophia asked as she strolled to the pantry and grabbed her recipe box and a blank index card. "I'm going to give you that recipe. I don't share that with just anyone, you know, but if my Lillie thinks you're a good cook, I'll take her word for it." Sophia flashed a smile Adam's way. "Now, eat up before your food gets cold."

Sophia loved nothing more than cooking for Lillie and her friends. That's why she made sure to prepare meals for them at least two Sunday's per month. Lillie kissed her mother to show appreciation for putting an end to the tension. Theo must have given in because he stopped glaring at Adam and then gave him a high five. Lillie wondered if he respected the fact that Adam's sympathy ploy won the battle of the egos. She hoped the two of them would learn to get along and make her life so much easier.

As Lillie turned her back towards Adam, she caught Grace and Masseri gazing into each other's eyes. They'd always been close, but this situation differed from the norm.

Grace broke the gaze with her buddy only to find Lillie in her space. She shuddered and cleared her throat as if trying to regain her composure.

"Tell us about your trip to California," Grace said to Masseri who'd just scooped some of the raw vegan pasta dish in her mouth. Since their college days, Sophia always prepared a different dish for Masseri. She'd made this masterpiece using shavings of zucchini as the pasta along with a heap of veggies and marinara sauce. All from non-genetically modified sources, of course. Like clockwork, Adam excused himself to take a phone call in the corridor. For some reason, he and Masseri didn't care for one another.

"Nothing special. Alvin came to visit me, though."

"Alvin? My brother?"

"Yes, Lillie. The one and only."

"What in the heck—"

"Now, Lady Bug," Sophia interrupted. "You know Alvin has always fancied Masseri. Don't get your panties all in a bunch."

"We met an intriguing man from Ethiopia who shared some information about the Queen of Sheba and King Solomon's connection."

Lillie wanted to grill Masseri about the time she spent with Alvin, but she decided to move on for the sake of family peace. In the meantime, she whipped out her cell phone and sent Alvin a text about the situation.

"What's the connection, baby?" Sophia asked, leaning closer to Masseri. Lillie could read her mother like a book. This gesture showed she had a genuine interest in Masseri's revelation. Just then, Lillie's phone buzzed. Alvin responded to her text in all caps, "STAY OUT OF MY BEESWAX." Lillie made a note to grill him about the situation when she had more time and less company.

"Here's the deal, some of the Ethiopian emperors claimed they descended from the lineage of the emperor Menelik, the son of Queen Sheba and King Solomon."

"I've heard that before and I believe it's true. In fact, many people believe it's one of the reasons the various councils who met many moons ago excluded the Ethiopic version of the book of Enoch. You know, the supposed theologians, kings, and clergy who met to determine what books should be included in the Bible," Sophia shared. She and Sam were true scholars who researched historical events to tie in the significance to the supernatural. Before Lillie was born, they'd even been kicked out of several churches due to their controversial teachings. This was probably the reason they didn't go to church while she was growing up. She would go with Theo and his family from time to time, though.

"I guess King Solomon brought the Ark of the Covenant to an Ethiopian orthodox church in a city called Axum. They say it's still there. Let's say their claim is accurate? Do you realize the impact that would have on the church?"

Sophia smirked, waiting for her husband to chime in. Philosophizing was his favorite pastime after smoking a fat joint and eating a scrumptious meal. And he did, right on cue.

"That would change the course of history. It would force those racist clergy members to recognize a few things about what God really intends for his people. The Ark of the Covenant in the hands of black folks, like us. Imagine that!"

Lillie wondered how he could make so much sense in his marijuana-induced state.

"I know, right," Masseri exclaimed. "But that wasn't the most fascinating thing he shared. Let me tell you about the honey church."

Lillie's ears perked up as she jerked her heard in Masseri's direction.

"Honey church?" she and Adam exclaimed simultaneously as he popped his head back in the room and ended his call.

"Oh, so now you're interested."

Masseri had minimal tolerance for organized religion so she treated church like a spiritual social. She had no problem touting the philosophy that "the powers that be" puts pastors in place to stop people from free-thinking. In her mind, the savior mentality extended to pastor worship, which distracts people from connecting with the real God. After the revival she saw on television, she wondered if Masseri has a valid point. Plus, she couldn't stop thinking about the dream she had last night. In the dream, Lillie walked through a pitch-black cavern listening to the lull of the effervescent spring flowing gently on either side of the red dirt path. An eerie buzzing joined in with the flowing waters to create a cacophony of sounds. All of a sudden, the familiar voice of a child singing out of tune ruined the peaceful atmosphere.

"Hickory Dickory Dock . . ."

Oh no, not her again!

With fear in her heart, Lillie took off running from the little California girl in the dingy gingham dress. She looked back continually to make distance remain between her and the devil's spawn. Pain shot through Lillie's legs like a bolt of lightning as she tripped over a huge rock. Right then, a netted hammock fell before her and an unexplainable force gently nudged her on board. A voice spoke to spirit of death. As she lay in an unusual comfort, the contraption rose slowly into the air and a sweet-sticky substance dropped on her lips. Instinctively, she ran her tongue around the perimeter of her lips. Lillie closed her eyes and exhaled to savor the delectable taste. When she opened her eyes, a beam illuminated the darkness to reveal the amber-hued substance dripping down the walls to the floor of the cave. A massive ball of flames floated effortless through the air consuming the drips of honey that Lillie began to crave. Instinctively, she knew if this fire consumed all of the honey, she would die.

Lillie's alarm clock beeped like a freight train, jolting her back into reality. She leapt from her bed, only to trip over the familiar white bedspread that now lay on the floor along with her extra fluffy pillows. She wobbled back and forth as she struggled to find her equilibrium. Remembering her dream, she traced the outline of her lips with her dry morning tongue and to her surprise; she tasted the residue of the sweet-sticky honey from the cave.

Masseri's chatter about the honey church turned out to be quite intriguing. The church is located in an Ethiopian cave infested with honeybee nests. She showed them a video clip of the inside of the cave. Lillie gasped when she saw the deep dark cavern from her dreams.

"What's wrong, babe?" Adam inquired.

Lillie assured him she was fine and encouraged Masseri to continue. Since the honey was made in a church cavern, the natives considered it to be holy. In fact, they had deemed honey wine as their country's natural drink. One of the specific uses of the beverage was in communion service. Masseri went on and on about the healing quality of pure raw honey. She informed them that it's the only edible substance that never spoils. In fact, it's been found in ancient tombs during excavations still intact and edible. Lillie couldn't help but wonder how it tied to her dream.

"Why do they have church in a cave, I wonder," Adam asked.

Masseri snickered, "Oh, Mr. Bible Scholar is asking me that question. Humph. Well, you know people will make anything holy to have a visual representation of God. It's just like the Queen of Sheba trading her ancient God for a Jewish God. I don't buy that story for one minute. I bet she was still worshiping her sun god Ra. People kill me trading one God for another and thinking that there's not a common connection."

Lillie cleared her throat and chimed in, "Girl, stop talking about all that honey and dig into that shrimp." She'd do anything to make sure Adam didn't rip Masseri a new one.

After the meal ended, Lillie gathered the troops in the living room for an old-fashioned game of Monopoly. This had been a tradition in the Corven household since they were in high school.

"So, who's ready to get spanked today?" Theo was so arrogant since he'd won the last game.

Grace, who promised it wouldn't happen again, responded,

"Who's ready to get spanked? Yeah, right! Get ready to take this spanking from me, Theo."

Right before the game started, Adam pulled Lillie to the side. "I can't stay. I promised my daughter I'd pick her up from her aunt's house. She's out of school for a few days, so she's visiting. Ajay decided to stay in Chillicothe with my mother."

"Aw, we'll miss you. I can't wait to meet your children. Looks like I'll meet Aliyah first." Lillie hugged Adam.

"Oh, you'll love her. She's a sweet girl." Adam kissed her and went to the kitchen to tell Lillie's parents goodbye. Soon, Lillie heard the back door close. As she returned to the living room, she heard Theo, Grace, and Masseri whispering about something. They stopped talking when they realized Lillie was in the room.

"I'm so glad he's gone," Theo said to break the ice.

"Really? You can't be serious." Lillie rolled her eyes. "Anyway, I heard your hushed whispers. Umm hmm. Dogging Adam again?"

Masseri and Grace looked dead at Theo who rose to face Lillie and rested his hand on her shoulder.

"If you must know, your caramel dream man is cheating on you."

Theo's smug grin made Lillie want to slap the taste out of his mouth. Instead, she pushed his hand off her shoulder.

"What? You've got to be kidding me," Lillie screeched.

"I knew it. He ain't the one, Lady Bug. Listen to that boy," her dad shouted from the kitchen. Since they were young children, he enjoyed sitting in the kitchen, dipping into their conversations. He periodically chimed in when he felt compelled. Lillie wished he'd go smoke a joint and get out of her business.

"I saw him at Easton the same day I brought the flowers for you, by the fountain, all hugged up with some big, cute girl. Looking all good like Jordin Sparks before she lost weight. I almost asked her to sing that song you like, Lillie."

"What song?"

"You know. The one about love being a battlefield."

Lillie glared at Theo and shook her head.

"I want to hear more about this . . . betrayal. Is Adam really a player or is Theo just hating, as usual," Grace chided.

"Yeah, Theo. That's a serious accusation. Are you sure? I don't care for preacher man but he could've just been greeting an old friend. You shouldn't assume," Masseri offered.

"At least someone is in my corner. Even though she's been dating my brother behind my back."

"Well, I'm not exactly in your corner. I don't see how you can date the pastor type when you're not even all that into church. He's probably a player just like the rest of them." Theo gave Masseri a high five. "And I'm a grown woman. I don't need your permission to see Alvin."

"Whatever, Masseri. And you," Lillie turned her gaze to Theo, "you just can't let me be happy. Trying to ruin my relationship."

"From my vantage point, it was ruined from the start. You better drop that zero and get with my boy here," her dad shouted from the kitchen, chuckling like an old man giving advice in front of a corner store. He must have been listening to rap music again while he visited Herbal Space. That's what Alvin called her dad's garden where he grew and smoked his marijuana. He had an external garden in the warm months and an internal one when it was cold. Her dad was serious about his weed.

"Who does that? Maybe you should go outside and see if Ms. Blakey is messing with your herbs again."

"I can't stand that old bat. Plus, this is my house, baby girl. If you want privacy, go home." Sam teased his daughter.

Lillie's facial muscles tightened and her cheeks flushed in embarrassment as her friends laughed silently and pointed at her in jest.

"Theo, if I find out you're lying, this will be the end of our friendship," Lillie threatened.

"Lillie, that's harsh. It could be a misinterpretation versus a lie," Grace interjected.

"Whatever you want to call it, I guess you better get ready to keep me around for a long time. Just as sure as my name is Theodore Aaron Smith, your man is shady. You need to listen to your pops."

"Umm hmm," her dad said loudly.

"Whatever!" Lillie retorted under her breath and rolled the dice.

THIRTEEN

AFTER LEAVING her parent's home, Lillie decided to take a ride in the country, a Sunday evening ritual she'd adopted back in high school. Relaxing sounds flowed from the CD player as she listened to the CD Adam purchased for her at Nirvana. Ohio was beautiful this time of year. Hickory smoke from country bonfires filled the air as Lillie cruised along the back roads of New Albany. The towering trees full of red, orange, and yellow leaves reminded her of the trip to Chillicothe she'd taken with Adam.

Lillie turned onto Morse Road and stopped at the local store. New Albany had consistent standards for the appearance of each building in town, so the carryout resembled a brick general store from back in the day. A few of the other suburbs and small towns that surrounded the Columbus metropolitan area had taken on this same concept. It was strange to see a McDonald's with hidden golden arches or a Wendy's where they downplayed the sign that showcased a young girl with red pigtails. Sometimes consistency took away from the very brand that made the business work.

As she exited the store, she recognized Adam's car.

Hmmmmm. I wonder what brings him out this far.

Lillie also noticed two additional heads peeking out of the window snickering at one another. When he exited the vehicle, Lillie called out to him, "Hey good looking!"

The sound of Lillie's voice must have startled Adam because he jumped.

"I . . . um . . . didn't expect to see you . . . um . . . all the way out here," Adam stuttered.

"New Albany's not that far from my place. I've been driving out here on Sunday evenings since my high school days."

Just then, one of the little girls opened the door and said, "Hi. What's your name?"

"My name is Miss Lillie," she responded to the feminine version of Adam. "And you must be Aliyah. I talked to you on the phone a few days ago." Lillie smiled and gave the little girl a hug.

Dressed in denim jeans, an Aeropostle T-shirt, and matching flip-flops, Lillie sensed the girl's carefree spirit. Aliyah unbraided her long red pigtails, as she smacked on a large piece of pink bubble gum. Her hazel eyes sparkled in the sunlight as she blew bubbles. The other little girl opened the car door and jumped onto the concrete surface.

"Who's your friend?" Lillie asked Aliyah.

"Oh, yeah. This is Deidra. She's—" Aliyah started to respond, but Adam cut her off.

"Such a sweet young lady. Her mother and I used to work together and these two formed a fast friendship. We're headed out to the orchard off Highway 310 to pick some apples." Adam's response was a little too smooth, almost practiced. Lillie made a note to remember this little girl's face for future reference.

"Hi, Deidra," she greeted. "I'm Miss Lillie."

"Hi, Miss Lillie."

Impressed with the young girl's manners, Lillie extended her arms to give her a hug. Deidra returned Lillie's embrace and then held her hand.

"Are you Mr. Adam's friend?"

Adam spoke before Lillie could respond to the inquisitive young lady.

"You know, these kids will ask you nine million questions if you let them. We better get to the orchard before it's too late,"

"Yeah, Mr. Adam. My mom should—"

"Okay, kids. Here's some money. Go get your snacks from the store." Adam abrupt interruption didn't stop the children from grabbing the cash. "Tell Miss Lillie goodbye."

"Goodbye, Miss Lillie," the girls chimed in unison.

Now that she'd met Aliyah face to face, she knew it was time to start spending some time with Adam's children.

"Why don't you bring Aliyah by tomorrow after school?"

"Really? Well, sure. We'll stop by your office around four o'clock."

"Sounds like a plan. See you then and have fun with the girls."

"I love you." Adam quickly brushed lips with Lillie.

"Love you, too, hon," Lillie responded. Adam opened her car door, like a gentleman should.

FOURTEEN

"ISS LILLIE! I'm here!" Aliyah skipped right past Rosa's desk into Lillie's office.

"Little girl. Did you forget to speak to me?" Rosa reprimanded. Whether it was the first or the fiftieth time she saw a child, she expected a proper greeting.

"Aliyah. You know better," Adam chided as he entered the office.

She ran back to Rosa's desk and said, "Hello, ma'am. My name is Aliyah. What's yours?"

Lillie grinned as she remembered Aliyah greeting her the same way yesterday. As a reward for good behavior, Rosa gave Aliyah a gigantic cherry lollipop. She looked in dad's direction, awaited his nod of approval. Before he could nod his head twice, she ripped open the delectable treat and popped it in her mouth. When Lillie walked out of her office into the foyer, Adam and Aliyah attacked her with a group hug.

"So, what's on your agenda this afternoon?" Adam inquired.

"I thought we'd go shopping and out to dinner. What do you think about that, munchkin?"

"Oh! Can we go to Aeropostle?" Aliyah's long red pigtails bounced as she jumped up and down. Her sun-kissed skin was the color of butter. Just like her father's, her hazel eyes beamed with joy.

"I noticed your T-shirt yesterday. It was cute. How old are you? Nine, right? Too young to like that store. It's more for teens, right?" It amazed Lillie how fast children gravitated to items designed for teens. Then she recalled that Rosa's five-year old granddaughter liked Hannah Montana and Justin Bieber, who were almost adults now.

"You have a point," Adam agreed. "It's hard to watch my baby girl become a little lady."

"Well, Dad. Kiss your baby and tell her goodbye. I'll bring her home after dinner," Lillie promised.

Adam scooped up Aliyah like a sack of potatoes and swung her around over and over again, as she threw her head back and laughed.

"Bye, Daddy."

Watching the father/daughter interaction touched Lillie's heart and made her look forward to a future with them. At the same time, she wondered how it would be to start a family from scratch with Theo. Adam's soft kiss distracted Lillie from her thoughts then he hurried out the door.

"Wait out here with Ms. Rosa while I grab my purse and jacket."

"Okay," Aliyah responded as she plopped on the fluffy chair in the waiting area.

When Lillie grabbed her purse, her cell phone rang. The caller ID revealed it was her father's cell phone number.

"Hey, Dad," Lillie greeted.

"Hi, baby. Just called to check on you. Are you stopping by here on your way home? We need you to help us talk to Alvin on that Skype thing." She could tell by his jolly tone that he'd just finished blazing up a joint. He must have decided to smoke early as he promised Lillie he'd quit doing it when she came over.

"Sure. Aliyah and I are going shopping and out to dinner, then we'll be right over."

"Aliyah? Is that Adam's little girl?"

"Yes, sir. You and Mom will love her."

Sam Corven's pregnant pause made Lillie a little jittery. "So just how many children does this man have?"

"He has two, Dad. Ajay and Aliyah."

"I don't know about this, baby. Are you ready to just add water?" Lillie pulled the phone away from her ear in shock.

"You need to quit smoking all that marijuana. Just add water? What does that mean?"

"You're the water, Lillie. An instant family. I always thought you'd want to be the only mother of your future husband's children. Are you sure Adam is the one and not Theo?" Lillie wondered how he knew what she'd been thinking earlier.

"Come on, Dad!"

"Hey. I'm just asking. I'm supposed to look out for your best interest, remember?"

"I know, Dad, but you raised me to not be judgmental." The tone of her father's sarcastic chuckle made Lillie second-guess her decision. Being a daddy's girl, she'd always sought his approval. This would be the first time she defied his advice.

"Well, not judging someone doesn't mean you have to get involved with him. And don't spend all your money on his kids. You've worked too hard to lose all of your earnings. What's Alvin got to say about this?"

"Are you serious, Dad? He's not my dad and even though you are, I'm an adult."

"I know you think I'm old fashioned, but there's a certain way real men do things. A respectable man would give you money to take his daughter shopping and out to dinner."

Lillie reflected on her father's statement for a moment, then responded, "I know what I'm doing, believe it or not. If I need your advice, I'll ask. I need to go now. I love you, Daddy and turn out that hydro light. You don't want Mom fussing about that electric bill again." Her dad refused to buy marijuana from drug dealers so he grew his own stash in the garden. Recently, he'd planted some in the house. "I'll see you tonight."

Before he could respond, Lillie ended the call and went to the lobby to get Aliyah. The conversation with her father enlightened her, but at the same time, she didn't mind taking Aliyah shopping. If they were going to be a family, they would share their money anyway. That's what married couples do. Then Lillie remembered . . . she wasn't Adam's wife.

"Miss Lillie." Aliyah handed Lillie a stack of cash. "My dad told me to give this to you."

Lillie beamed from ear to ear because Adam did just what her dad said a good man should. She'd make sure to call him and let him know that his suspicions were unwarranted. If only Adam knew how much this added to Lillie's love bank. With deposits like this, his account could remain open forever.

FIFTEEN

HYPERACTIVE CHILDREN stormed Lillie's neighborhood sporting their mystical Halloween gear. Their disguises ranged from witches to ghouls and angels to biblical heroes. She wondered what Aliyah and Ajay wore for the festive occasion. Since they had school the next morning, it only made sense for them to spend the holiday in Chillicothe with their mother.

"Trick or treat!" an adorable toddler screamed while pulling on his brother's bright red, fuzzy Elmo costume. His excitement paid off because Lillie piled a load of Hershey's Kisses in his ghost-covered sack. She caught a glimpse of herself in the glass screen door that almost took her breath away. Lillie couldn't help but admire the shimmery white belly-dancing get-up she and Grace purchased from Spirit Halloween yesterday. The color offered a perfect contrast to the glittery purple Grace selected. Ever since Yankee Trader closed, this seasonal outlet of horror increased in popularity. Lisa almost flipped her corkscrew when Lillie told her they were going to this store.

"Who goes to that store anyway? Don't you know that's demonic?"

"Come on, Lisa. You believe in that crap?"

"Humph! You better stop playing with the devil. He doesn't play fair and your faith's not strong enough to win the hand."

Lillie experienced the demonic spirit realm first hand during the California psychic adventure. A candy/costume holiday just didn't seem to compare to the real deal. People celebrated the harvest in the old days and now, kids knocked on doors to get candy. She saw Spirit Halloween as a marketing ploy to get people to spend money just like other stores did for Christmas and Easter. What could be the harm? Lisa would pass out and die if she knew about the Harvest Celebration at the church.

Adam volunteered to run the game booths at the church and Masseri went on a mystery trip that she wouldn't discuss with anyone. Lillie knew that meant she and Alvin were hooking up at some undisclosed destination. Theo also was missing in action, which was unusual as well. Left to hang out alone, she and Grace decided to forgo the kosher event at the church and head out to Zydeco on High for some grown folks fun. She couldn't wait to tear into some gumbo from this New Orleans bistro in the Brewery District.

The smooth sounds of Soul Derivative welcomed them upon entering the building. Neon purple lights shined bright on the white furniture to create an effervescent atmosphere. Designer scone-shaped light fixtures illuminated the nightclub, projecting funky designs on the walls. Antique, circular shaped mirrors crafted of wood added another level of flavor to the trendy design. Lillie greedily inhaled the aroma of down home, bayou cuisine that promised to gratify her growling stomach.

Lillie popped her fingers to the sensual rhythms as she stood with Grace in the reception area waiting to be seated. The shining lights changed direction and she caught site of a man-sized vase sitting on the low counter. The intricate design intrigued Lillie so she studied it with intensity. Just then, a tiny woman dressed as a little girl diverted Lillie's attention as she skipped through the front door.

What an interesting costume to wear to such a mystical place.

Then, Lillie realized the identity of the so-called child. The Golden State demon child with the dirty gingham dress! She had the nerve to hop around the foyer humming a child-like song as if she belonged even though no one seemed to notice her at all.

This can't be real!

The filthy, sneaky brat skipped to the stage and screeched out her signature ditty as she glared a hole through Lillie's forehead, her mind control retractor beam locked and loaded.

"Hickory Dickory Dock . . ."

The audience still swayed to the funky beat of Soul Derivative's tune. No one even noticed this spawn of Satan trying to cause a ruckus. Not able to take it any longer, Lillie belted out a heinous scream and almost every club patron raced to her side. Then all of a sudden . . .

Crash!

Thank goodness for her athletic ability. She managed to make a gazelle-like leap over a chair to avoid the man-sized vase that feel from the counter. The tiny hairs on her body rose and her teeth chattered uncontrollably. She covered her ears and closed her eyes to escape the piercing scream that filled the room. Lillie tried hard to focus on her new mission—to stop the shrieking cries. Then she realized the screams were her own.

"Who did this?" Lillie accused the people standing around her as she slowly regained her composure. The crowd looked from one person to the other, all hunching their shoulders and shaking their heads. The maître de stepped forward with his reservation book in hand.

"Ma'am. We're not sure how this happened. The owner glued that vase to the counter with an industrial strength product quite some time ago."

Grace plopped her hand on her cocked hip and demanded, "So how did it fall then? I mean it almost killed my friend, here."

"Um . . . I don't know, ma'am. I just don't know."

SIXTEEN

LATE SATURDAY evening, Lillie decided to drop in unannounced to surprise Adam. She wanted to see how he'd react and to get to the bottom of the alleged mall incident. Since church folks tended to be free with hugs, whether they are genuine or not, she didn't want to make any unwarranted assumptions. When it came down to Theo's track record, Lillie had to admit he never lied, however, jealousy could have caused him to exaggerate just a little. Plus, if the shoe were on the other foot, she would want Adam to give her the benefit of the doubt.

She closed her eyes to inhale the sweet smell of fresh strawberries dipped in Godiva chocolate she'd just purchased at the Easton store. She planned to feed them to him as part of the surprise, if Theo's story proved to be untrue. She'd also picked up CoCo Chanel, a romantic movie, and a couple of patchouli and ylang ylang-scented beeswax candles. As she parked her car in front of his house, she sighed and put her head on the steering wheel. Lillie sashayed her way to the porch when a nervous energy overtook her; butterflies in her stomach fluttered like they were trying to break out of a cocoon.

Happy to find the door ajar, she let herself in and crooned, "Adam, it's me."

He strutted out of the kitchen, standing tall and proud like a modern day Adonis. Without warning, he picked her up and twirled her around in circles. When he returned her to the ground, CoCo jumped into the cradle of Lillie's arms to stake her claim. Adam ignored the growling and snapped his dishtowel at the dog, causing her to jump recklessly out of Lillie's arms and release fiery yaps at Adam. Embarrassed by the outburst, Lillie scolded her pet, and CoCo cried out while burying her head at her owner's feet.

"Hey, hon. I didn't expect to see you, but I'm glad you were able to stop by. I heard about what happened last night at Zydeco."

"Yeah. I'd rather not talk about that, okay?"

"Sure. So to what do I owe this honor?"

She swooned at Adam's reaction. His favorable response added cool points to his stats. Based upon her experience, men who cheated didn't take kindly to surprise visits. "I just wanted to spend some time with you, so I picked up a movie and some snacks." Lillie smiled brightly as Adam reached to embrace her. She snuggled into his arms and took in his scent. Adam always smelled so great, and Lillie loved that about him.

"That sounds like a plan. The kids are staying at my mom's place this weekend so I'm here all alone." Adam took the movie from Lillie and led her into the family room. He placed it in the DVD player and went to the kitchen to prepare their beverages. Adam joined Lillie on the couch and they cuddled as the movie began.

Snuggled like two beans in a burrito, he squeezed her tightly. "Have I ever told you that being close to you is intoxicating?"

Lillie checked Adam's eyes to see if they matched the sincerity she heard in his words. They did.

"Um, you did, but say it again, babe. I've been thinking about this all day." Lillie wanted to ask Adam a corny question, but she wasn't sure how he'd respond. So instead, she continued to watch the movie until she built up the courage to share her thoughts.

"I have a question for you, and I don't want you to think I'm crazy when I ask it." Lillie shifted out of Adam's embrace and turned to face him. Her irregular breathing and the increased amount of saliva made it hard to talk.

"You know you can ask me anything," he assured her.

"Uh . . . do you . . . believe in . . . soul mates?" Lillie asked. "Huh? Well, kind of. I'd like to hear your perspective, though."

Lillie explained Grace's theory that twin flames are derived from a soul that splits in two. Just like a mother's egg splits to form identical twin babies, the soul splits to form two whole beings called twin flames. One twin possesses female energy while the other possesses male energy. These twin flames separate, go experience life, and come back together at a later date. They incarnate over and over again across many lifetimes to get this experience. When they reunite, their union balances their male and female energy. She added that this reunion would most likely occur in their last lifetimes so they could ascend together.

Adam turned up his lips and scrunched his forehead. "Here's what I believe: God places us here on earth and gives us free will. He allows us to make choices, even though he knows what choices we're going to make." He paused for a moment, giving Lillie time to digest his response.

"Okay, so how does that play into my question, Pastor Adam," Lillie jested.

"You see our mate is designed specifically for us. You're my helpmate. Since God designed us for one another, we complement one another's strengths and weaknesses. I complete you, just as you complete me."

Lillie closed her eyes to savor Adam's sumptuous words that infused a sweet essence to satisfy the love hunger deep within her soul. His knowledge of the Bible intrigued her.

"I like this whole completion thing. Still sounds similar to the twin flame soul mater theory if you ask me." She giggled and kissed him on his lips, then his nose, eyes, and went back to his lips. He snuggled closer to Lillie and held her hands.

"No, I wouldn't say that. I'd never heard of a twin flame until today. In fact, I've always been taught that the soul mate concept is based upon a Greek myth. They say our ancestors originally had two heads and four arms."

Lillie threw her head back, laughing hysterically. "When we were kids, there was a song about freakazoids. Remember that?"

"Yeah. That was my jam." Adam snapped his fingers to an imaginary beat and broke up in a dance step doing the Snake.

"According to this silly myth, it sounds like our ancestors were freakazoids," Adam joked as Lillie rolled her eyes. "Okay, babe, I'm sorry. Finish your story, please."

"As I was saying before the comments from the peanut gallery, our ancestors offended some god so they were punished by being split in half. Some Greeks believe this is how human beings were created."

"Really? Seems to be a consistent story about a split no matter what your belief system may be."

"Humph! My God created me through intelligent design. He formed the original Adam with his hands. I know that because my mother showed me the scripture at a young age, since my name is Adam."

"Yeah, yeah, yeah, silly. It's just a myth. You can't criticize other people for their beliefs just because yours are different." Lillie pouted as Adam waved his hand at her, dismissing her perspective.

"Back to my story. According to this myth, we spend our whole lives searching for our soul mates, and that's why we feel incomplete until we find this person. That's why I believe in the helpmeet theory from the Bible. So, Lillian Michelle Corven, you're my helpmeet. Once we get married, of course."

Adam embraced her tightly as he shared his revelation. Of course, his words were music to her ears, and Lillie melted in his embrace.

"On another note, how'd you like that letter I wrote you the other day?" Adam asked, sticking his chest out and nodding his head with a smug smile.

She responded with a juicy French kiss. Adam wrote Lillie love letters with beautiful poems quite frequently. This was one thing he and Theo had in common. Even though Adam and Theo were different, their appreciation for artistic expression was quite similar. Trying to get Theo out of her mind, she focused on being more creative with the kiss. She gently started to suck on Adam's tongue, which shocked him. He quickly recovered and returned her affection. So caught up in the moment, Lillie almost forgot she was a saved woman. Conviction set in and she pulled away from Adam, turning her attention back to the movie. To ensure their hormones had time to calm down, Lillie changed the subject.

"Thanks for bringing Aliyah to the office. She really liked our shopping spree." Lillie's time with Aliyah was quite a success. The young child was quite a handful but quite intelligent. Lillie enjoyed the challenge.

"You're a good mother, Lillie."

Lillie was a little shocked. CoCo yapped as if she understood her owner's confused state of mind. She was not exactly fond of Adam, for some reason.

"Mother?" She scooted over, putting more space between the two of them, and Adam followed, closing the gap.

"Any woman who's going to be in my life has to consider the fact that I already have a family. When my children aren't with their mother, they're not just with me, but you too. So yes, it's important for me to know that you're comfortable taking on the role of their mother."

Lillie wasn't sure how she felt about Adam's expectations. The thought of taking care of children who weren't hers biologically made the idea of being with Theo look appealing. Even so, he needed to stay in his place as a friend. Especially considering what Theo had shared about Adam and his supposed date. Not wanting to deal with the mother issue, Lillie thought this would be a good time to change the subject and bring up the inevitable question.

"Speaking of our relationship, I'd like to clarify something, Adam."

"Clarify? Oh snap! I must be in trouble." Adam laughed playfully.

"Okay, enough with the jokes. I'm really serious." Lillie paused and pursed her lips. Adam patiently waited while she carefully formed her next words.

"We're seeing one another exclusively, right?" she asked.

Adam paused, and his calm demeanor immediately changed to sheer aggravation. "In addition to agreeing to take on the mother role for my children, I also need to know that you trust me." He stared deeply into her eyes, as if he could see her soul. "Without trust, we have nothing."

"I concur, Mr. Johnson. I do trust you, yet, the rumor mill says you were at Easton last week with another woman." Feeling empowered, Lillie squared her shoulders as she awaited his response. She gazed intently into Adam's deep hazel eyes, searching for the truth.

Adam laughed. "You know, I've had enough of your boy trying to throw salt in my game."

Surprised at his response, Lillie raised a brow. "So it's true?"

Adam quickly responded, "Not exactly. Do you re-member the singer from Nirvana?" "I knew it! She's what the teens in Grace's youth group call 'thirsty.'" "Thirsty? You shouldn't try to use slang. It's not your style."

"Adam!" Lillie's high-pitched voice rang loudly in the room. "This isn't about me using slang or my conversation style. This is about you and that . . . that woman. So who is she, and why were you two sitting so cozy?"

"Okay, her name is Mallory Roberts. You know that because you saw the commercials about her new found success. She and I are good friends. I met her when I worked at Nirvana."

"I can respect that, but it doesn't explain the closeness at the mall."

"She had a death in her family, so I comforted her. Remember the funeral I had to speak at? Her father died."

"Oh really?" Lillie sassed.

"Here's the program." Adam fidgeted and shifted his posture as he handed the document to her. "Look! I'm not going to sit here and allow Theo to taint my ministerial intentions. I just can't stand to see someone grieving and not provide comfort. Especially with all that happened with Dad."

Adam bowed his head to try to hide the lone tear that streaked down his cheek. Lillie's compassion kicked in and she decided to not press him any further about the hug incident at the mall. It was definitely reasonable to comfort a grieving friend. Theo's jealous spirit probably caused him to read more into it.

"When we visited you mother, you said your father was brutally murdered. What happened, hon?"

Lillie leaned in to hear more of the story that plagued her at the mention of his father's name.

"Well," Adam continued to fight tears. "As you know, my dad was a prominent pastor in southern Ohio. One evening, he took me on his hospital visitation rounds. He knew I would eventually pastor, so he made sure to expose me to all aspects of a pastor's role in the community and the church."

As Adam poured out his heart to Lillie, she responded with non-verbal cues of affirmation to encourage him to continue.

"After we finished the rounds at Adena Medical Center, I begged my father to take me to a place on Bridge Street to get some ice cream. Since I was so helpful at the hospital, he agreed. I remember it was hot outside, so we were a little sweaty as we stood in line to get our cones. A woman walked up to my father and asked him where he'd been. She had a child with her. He was older than me, though. My father said he didn't know what she was talking about but she continued to question him about his whereabouts. When I think back, I can still see her. She was a beautiful woman."

"That's odd. Who was she, and why did she question your father like that?"

"I'd seen her at church a few times, but I really didn't know her. As to why she was yelling at my father, your guess is as good as mine. I mean, I know why she was yelling now, but I didn't know then."

"Sounds fishy to me." Lillie accidentally spoke her thoughts aloud. She decided not to say much more because she wasn't sure how Adam would respond to her speaking so negatively about the man he loved and looked up to.

"We were next in line to get our cones so my father ignored her ranting so that he could order my cone. Then, he dragged me to the car, trying to avoid her. I asked him who she was. He said she was a crazy lady who wouldn't leave him alone."

Adam paused for a moment and took a deep breath.

"A few weeks later, my father was preaching at a church in East Jackson. It was a small, country church that reminded me of churches you see down south. You know, the kind with the graveyard right next to it. This same crazy woman was there sitting next to the pastor of that church. I found out that she was his wife."

"Huh? If she was married to that pastor, what right did she have to be so concerned about your father's whereabouts? Oh . . . I . . .get it."

"Yeah. It took me awhile, but after watching her stalk my father, fight with my mother, and many other stupid antics, oh, I got it. She and my father were having an affair and he broke it off."

"I'm so sorry, hon. No child should have to witness that level of drama."

"Well, their break-up didn't last for long. They were on and off for years. Eventually, her pastor/husband figured it out. When my father wouldn't leave my mother, the crazy woman decided to take matters into her own hands."

"Wait a minute. Your father . . . he was the pastor shot at point blank range at the holiness church in Portsmouth? Were you there?"

Lillie heard about this heinous crime, but didn't make the connection with Adam's family. No longer able to hold back, Adam's tears flowed like a stream emptying into a river. Lillie reached out to him and took him in her arms to hold him while he convulsed from sadness, hurt, and pain. Nothing else mattered at that moment except taking care of Adam's needs as he recalled events from the most traumatic time of his life. When he was able to speak again, Adam responded to Lillie's question.

"Yes. My mother and I were sitting in the front row so we didn't see her until the last minute. Do you know when she did it, Lillie? During the altar call.! I'm not excusing my father's behavior, but people were giving their lives to Christ and she decided to strut her adulterous behind down the aisle in a white dress with a flower in her hair. She shot my dad as if he were a three-point buck. To make matters worse, she showed little to no remorse about it either. Then, she turned the gun on herself and ended her own life."

Lillie couldn't believe the story Adam was sharing with her. It was one thing to read it in the newspaper. Hearing Adam speak brought it to life. She continued to stroke his back and grabbed the tissues from the coffee table to dry his tears. They sat like this for an hour. Eventually, Adam fell asleep and Lillie followed suit. When Lillie woke up, she found herself being the center of Adam's attention. He stared at her and smiled from ear to ear.

"Thanks so much for being understanding and listening to my story. Most of all, thank you for not judging my father. He was wrong for what he did, but he didn't deserve to die."

"It's okay. I'm so glad you decided to open up and share that with me. No one should have to go through that. I know I wouldn't be able to handle it. I admire that you're still standing. It shows what kind of man you are."

Adam inched closer to Lillie as he looked her in the eye. She jumped in shock, not expecting the forwardness of his all-consuming gaze.

"I'm the kind of man who's committed to you."

He took Lillie's hand and kissed each finger gently, while maintaining intense eye contact.

"The kind of man who's in love with you, and . . ."

As soon as the words flowed from his lips, he kissed her passionately. Caught off guard, Lillie didn't expect to feel the electrical charge that sent a sudden rush of passion through her body. She attempted to gain control, but to no avail; she couldn't harness the urges. Her body shuddered in ecstasy, defying her will.

As they kissed, Lillie's internal longing for Adam consumed her like never before. He caressed her body like a musician tickled the ivories. Before she knew it, she returned each kiss and each touch as if they'd done this a million times. With reckless abandon, they removed their clothes and Adam led the way to his bedroom. Each titillating stroke of his hand sent eruptive explosions through Lillie's body.

Lying completely naked on his bed, Lillie heard Adam whisper, "When you're faced with temptation, God will make a way of escape for you. Make sure you take it or . . ."

"Um . . . I think I should go."

Lillie tried to edge her way off the bed, however, Adam ignored her efforts. He continued to ignite her skin with his fiery kisses. Then his silky smooth hands traveled all over her body to the forbidden place.

"You know, I think we should—"

"Shhh, my love." Adam intercepted Lillie's attempt to bring up protection. "Those things are bad for you." He caressed her face and ran his fingers through her hair. "You're going to be my wife soon," Adam said between hot kisses. "Don't worry, I'll pull out."

As he kissed Lillie's body from head to toe, he guided his tongue to the center of her love and sent her on a wild frenzy of passion. Lillie bucked her body in to the exotic rhythm only love could make. She threw caution to the wind and let the erotic animalism of her physical body take over. Over and over and over again.

SEVENTEEN

THE SWEET love Lillie made with Adam pleasantly overwhelmed her emotions. She'd never dreamed she could feel so relaxed and carefree.

"How's my baby?" Adam kissed Lillie all over as she lay in his arms.

"I never expected our first time to be so wonderful. It couldn't have been more perfect."

"You know we're married now, right?" Adam grinned and nodded his head.

"What? I don't see a ring on this here finger," Lillie shot back. Surely, Adam had lost his mind thinking one night of intimacy classified her as his wife. Even though it did sound kind of nice.

"In the Bible days," Adam shared, "marriages weren't recognized unless they were consummated. In fact, that still comes into play in our legal system today. The ceremony is a manmade phenomenon." With Adam's position in the ministry, his nonchalant attitude about sex outside of marriage made Lille uncomfortable.

"Oh, yeah?" Lillie raised her eyebrow at Adam.

"Yeah. You just tied your soul to mine," Adam joked.

"That sounds so beautiful, hon. But, I still feel like we shouldn't have done this, with your position in the church and all." Lillie wasn't all that into church, but Adam, on the other hand, had committed his life to ministry. In her eyes, the expectations for his conduct were different.

"That's why I love you. Your concern blesses my soul."

Lillie's cheeks flushed with red fire. The fact that Adam could evoke that reaction made her love him even more. She wondered if he had more of a price to pay for what the Bible called a sin. She still couldn't believe that something so beautiful was forbidden outside of marriage.

"Do you think you'll be okay after this, hon? I mean, don't you worry about being forgiven? You're on your way to being a pastor and all. "

"You know the Lord is going to forgive us. He's not some merciless God, and he knows our hearts. Humans have needs and urges, and he knows this."

"But isn't sex outside of marriage one of the worst sins? It seems to be what people preach about all of the time."

"Sin is sin, and this sin is no different than overeating at the buffet after church." Adam's confidence on the matter shook Lillie. She wondered if other ministers shared this perspective about sex behind closed doors. Or did it even matter? For some reason, Grace's idea about the Bible being a history book used to control people rang true. Someone trying to control people would probably want to keep them away from a good thing.

"I have to admit. If tying our souls feels this good, I have no complaints. But what if people see you with me going in and out of your house?" Lillie stood up and started nervously brushing her hair.

"If it will make you feel better, let's pray and ask for forgiveness. We don't have to be sexually involved to be in a relationship. I love you and will honor whatever you decide, because I don't want to lose you."

Adam's puppy dog eyes reached deep into Lillie's psyche, connecting with her on a level she'd never experienced before. Her knees buckled as she struggled to continue standing under such intense feelings. She sat back down on the bed and grabbed Adam's hand. As he began to pray, he firmly squeezed her hand.

"Lord, Lillie and I are coming before you naked, literally, Lord, we're naked. We ask your forgiveness for indulging in what has been one of the most pleasurable moments of our lives."

"Adam, be serious! You don't even sound like you're sorry for what we did." Pulling her hand away, Lillie crossed her arms over her chest and pouted. "This just isn't right, hon."

"Yeah, it's hard to be sorry for what we just experienced, but I'll finish and do it right."

Adam caressed Lillie's shoulder and took a deep breath. Then, he continued the prayer.

"Lord, we're asking for forgiveness and the strength to remain celibate until we're married. In your name, Jesus, we pray. Amen."

Praying with Adam did make Lillie feel a little better, but the guilt loomed like the smell of dirty diapers. CoCo Chanel started doing her "I have to go to the bathroom" dance, so Lillie focused on meeting the canine's needs. Adam jumped up and threw on a pair of shorts. He took CoCo out back to handle her business. When Adam came back in the room, Lillie stood on his California king bed in all her naked glory. Unable to resist, he kissed her legs and caressed her bottom. She touched him all over as he kissed her with an intense urgency.

Forgetting what they'd just prayed about, she yanked off his shorts and he jumped on the bed. He nibbled on her ears and kissed her neck like an expert love maker. She imitated his actions with skillful mastery. Adam's libido was on the rise, and each touch sent Lillie into a manic frenzy. She moaned in ecstasy as she called out his name repeatedly.

Pleased with her response, he threw his head back and shouted, "Let round two begin!"

80 03

The hearty smell of turkey bacon woke Lillie from a sound sleep. CoCo growled as she played with a new toy that resembled a live ferret. Lillie watched intently for a while, and then headed to the plush master bathroom. She grabbed a monogrammed towel and washcloth from the linen closet and jumped in the shower. To her surprise, Adam had her favorite salt scrub, Body Polish from Body by Reeci in the shower. Lillie was amazed at his observance of her habits. The water sprayed from the showerhead, pleasantly massaging Lillie's body. Even though the pressure was strong, the quality of the water was undeniable. It was soft against her skin, causing the experience to be quite enjoyable.

When she climbed out of the shower, Lillie almost tripped over a basket containing Sweet Breeze deodorant balm from Nandi's Naturals. Grace had been bragging about these handmade products since she and Masseri decided to sell them at the studio.

I hit the jackpot! Not only does this man support my business, he supports my friends in their endeavors.

As she sorted through the remaining contents of the basket, a card fell to the ground. Her name was written on the envelope in calligraphy.

The card read: *"Lillie, here's a little something I picked out just for you. Love, Adam."*

Lillie's heart skipped a beat as she hugged the fluffy towel to her skin. The joyous energy of her beaming smile radiated the bathroom. She dried off and walked back into Adam's room to find a larger gift basket with a pair of designer jeans and a beautiful shirt in her size. She was pleased to see an exquisite matching bra and panty set. Lillie caressed the soft lace undergarments and couldn't wait to thank Adam properly.

She slathered the luxurious scented butter from head to toe. CoCo continued to chase the battery operated ferret around the room. Lillie couldn't help but giggle. The clothes Adam purchased fit like a glove. She brushed her long, silky hair into a tight ponytail and made her way to the kitchen, where Adam had prepared a spread fit for a queen.

"Oh, my goodness. All this food? I don't even know where to start," Lillie exclaimed. "Um, you smell good, babe. We can start something right here on this table, if you're game," Adam suggested as he kissed Lillie's neck. Not able to contain her desire, she began to moan. Sliding her jeans and undergarments off, Adam lifted Lillie onto the table and took her right there, while the bacon was frying.

Afterwards, Adam removed the bacon off the range and they both ran to different bathrooms to freshen up. When Lillie returned to the kitchen, Adam strolled over to her, holding a spatula in his hand, and gave her a juicy kiss. She was suddenly weak in the knees. He led her to the newly cleaned table, and CoCo jumped in her lap, hoping to get her scraps.

"That's my girl. I see Adam's taking good care of you."

To Lillie's surprise, CoCo growled. She wasn't sure why CoCo didn't like Adam since he spent so much time taking care of her. Despite her erratic, possessive behavior, she started begging for the food Adam placed before Lillie. This, of course, was pointless since Lillie no longer fed CoCo from the table. The dog was cute, but she was allergic to everything. The allergies didn't stop CoCo from trying to get the forbidden cuisine, though.

"I see you found my gifts. You like?" Adam asked.

"Definitely. You've been planning my overnight stay for quite some time, I see," Lillie accused.

"Not exactly. Those were gifts I was planning to give you, and they just happened to come in handy for today," Adam said smugly. Lillie loved a confident man and his confidence ignited a fiery desire in her loins.

"With all this activity, I wanted to make sure that you had a good breakfast. I like my women with a little more meat on their bones, so we have to fatten you up some," Adam teased.

"You know, if I were at home, I'd be on that treadmill right after this meal. Heck! Who am I kidding? It would have been my first stop before my morning shower." Lillie laughed heartily.

"You don't have to be so uptight. You're with me now, and you can live a little. I plan to show you just how you can be set free from that uppity spirit."

"Adam!"

"What? You know you have that tendency. I love you, anyway, though," he assured her.

While they were enjoying their morning breakfast, "Footsteps in the Dark" by the Isley Brothers filled the air. It was Theo calling Lillie's cell phone. She had assigned him the ring tone because it was one of his favorite oldies but goodies. Before Lillie could grab the phone, Adam answered it and reluctantly handed it to her.

"Hello," she said.

"Now, I know that cat just didn't answer your phone at eight o'clock in the morning, especially since you didn't go home last night."

"Good morning to you, too."

How'd he know?

"I bet you're wondering how I know. Grace was looking for you and thought you were with me, since we were supposed to go to Flow. Do you realize you stood me up?"

"Excuse me? You're spying on me and accusing me of standing you up?" Lillie's allegation piqued Adam's interest and sent Theo into overdrive. Then she remembered she'd made plans with Theo earlier in the week.

"I'm so sorry. Now that I think about it, I did stand you up. How can I make this up to you?"

"Yeah, yeah, yeah. I'm assuming you spent the night with him. Please tell me you didn't. You know what? I don't even want to know." With that, Theo hung up the phone. Lillie's mouth dropped as she heard a series of beeps. She stared at the phone in disbelief until Adam interrupted.

"I'm not going to tolerate this much longer. Check him, or I will." Adam's statement was a declaration that didn't require a response, and Lillie knew it.

As memories of conversations with Theo began to flood her psyche, she felt an unexpected twinge guilt take residence in her abdomen. Now that she'd consummated the relationship with Adam, she wasn't sure what to expect with Theo.

What's a girl in love to do?

EIGHTEEN

"HOW MANY of you have ever done something so terrible you believed the Lord couldn't forgive you?" Adam paused to allow the rhetorical question to sink in. A few parishioners raised their hands or shouted out: "That's me!"

"If you haven't, then good for you. Today, I'm here to talk to the ones who think their sins are unforgivable. Walking around with guilt and shame strapped to their backs like they're paying rent."

Pondering on the sexcapades she'd experienced with Adam for the past few months, Lillie had a hard time watching him preach so passionately. It seemed so sacrilegious and . . . taboo. Especially when he preached powerhouse sermons. In fact, they engaged in a few steamy rounds just before coming to church. Chasing multiple orgasms became her new fascination and Adam more than fulfilled her desires. Lillie worried about not using protection until Adam schooled her on the issues condoms and birth control presented to their health and well-being. Adam simply pulled out prior to ejaculation. He felt guilty for spilling his seed but he didn't want to risk her getting pregnant before their wedding day.

The custom designed suit from Regal Fashions hung just right from his sexy frame. She had to hold herself back from ripping it off in the middle of a hooping holler. Finding it hard to concentrate on the sermon, she found herself daydreaming about their last encounter. As she turned towards the clock, she noticed Ms. Blakey shaking her head in disapproval.

That old hag makes me sick! She needs to mind her own business.

Her heart skipped a beat when she pondered on the thought of being with Adam in holy matrimony, even though he hadn't proposed yet. When she talked to her father about it, he said, "A man won't buy a cow if he can get the milk for free." She wondered if this theory applied to Adam, too. Then she dismissed that idea since she knew her dad loved Theo like his own son. He'd only be happy when Lillie saw the light and accepted him as her husband. Theo definitely would be a good catch, but Lillie just couldn't stand to see their friendship ruined if it didn't work out.

The combination of Adam's good looks, muscular frame, and ability to bring the house down whenever he preached made him a hot commodity with the women at Radical Faith. They made it clear through their letters, phone calls, and fake attempts at getting him alone during counseling sessions that they'd sell their souls to the devil himself for a night in the sack with Adam. With all of the competition, Lillie had to keep it tight, so she worked out like crazy. She also had a standing weekly appointment with Lisa at Keyes to Style. She'd do just about anything to keep Mr. Caramel Latte Dream in her life.

As she continued to reflect, Ms. Blakey glared at her. When Lillie stared back just as intently, the old woman mouthed the words, "I'm telling Pastor." She was always causing some sort of trouble with the members, so Lillie ignored her, turning her attention to Adam's children—Aliyah and Ajay.

"Aliyah, pull your dress down, baby," Lillie whispered. Why is this child such a busybody? Lillie was ready to reach out and touch the young girl when Aliyah defiantly yanked her dress down, almost ripping it at the seams.

"Why does Daddy make me wear dresses, anyway? He's preaching too long!" She pouted, poking her lip out and crossing her arms over her chest.

A rambunctious Ajay punched Aliyah in the arm and she shrieked, "I hate you, you jerk!"

"Ajay! Aliyah! Stop it and sit still," Lillie scolded.

Lillie didn't understand why Adam wouldn't let her send his children to the youth church. Of course, today would have been an exception since he was preaching, but this was the norm. In her experience, it was hard for children to sit through an adult service. Each time she pressed him on it, he responded, "My parents never sent me to a youth church, so why should I send them?"

After his sermon, Lillie took Aliyah and Ajay to the back of the church so that they could all stand next to him while he greeted the members. The pastor typically did this each Sunday, so it was an expectation of the guest speaker, as well. When Pastor Andrews came through the line, he greeted them with hugs and complimented Adam.

"Hey! There's my favorite couple. The Russell and Kimora of Radial Faith!" Lillie almost choked on her saliva when he made that proclamation.

"Umm . . . I . . . I . . . don't preach, Pastor," Lillie responded.

"Keep hanging with this young man and you will. I see it in you, sis. How's everybody doing on this fine day?" Pastor Andrews' joyful spirit was contagious.

"We're doing great, Pastor," Adam responded, matching his high level of energy.

"I've been meaning to call you two. Do you have a few moments to talk with me after you get away from this line?"

Panic shot through Lillie's body as she wondered about the intent of the meeting. *Does he know what we've been doing?*

Grace, who stood in line behind the pastor and first lady, said, "Go ahead, Lillie. I'll take the kids with me. My youth group is having a bake sale and I'm sure they could use some help."

Youth group? When did she start leading a youth group?

Lillie was shocked to see Grace getting involved in the church. The she remembered, it must be all about the pursuit of Theo. Of course, Ajay and Aliyah were delighted. Despite her New Age belief system that conflicted with the tenets of the churches' monotheistic stance, Grace's way with children never ceased to amaze Lillie. Maybe it was because she was a big kid herself.

As Lillie and Adam walked into the foyer of the pastor's office, Adam said, "Oh yeah. I have to talk to you about the kids. Their mother is getting married and I think it would be a good idea for them to move in with me permanently."

"Wow, Adam. That's great." Lillie feigned excitement. As much as she enjoyed having the children around on the weekends, she knew their permanent presence would cut into her time with their father.

"Yeah, that was the point of getting the house, making sure I had a place for my children to live drama free. I'm sure her new man doesn't want someone else's kids running around his house and if he puts his hands on them, I might forget I'm saved."

"What's their mother's name, by the way?"

"Her name is Shannon. She's having a hard time right now, struggling with extreme depression. Of course, her mental state causes her not to make the best relationship choices. I didn't like the men she had around my children and I definitely don't care for her fiancé, so I decided to take matters into my own hands."

Lillie knew several men in the church who had fought for custody of their children, so she knew not all single dads were dead beats. Adam was proud of his children and took pride in the contribution he made to their lives. Even so, the monetary aspect of this new living arrangement concerned her. She knew this decision would affect her finances, if they were to get married. Adam made good money at Flow but it must not be enough to make ends meet because his electric bill was overdue a few weeks ago. Lillie loaned him the money to avoid disconnection. When she asked him what happened, he told her he had to buy some things that Ajay and Aliyah needed and thought he could make payment arrangements for the bill.

Unfortunately, his plan didn't work out. Lillie didn't want the children to be without lights, so she paid the bill for him. He didn't ask, however, she felt it was the right thing to do. His stock increased in her quality man account when he reimbursed her with interest the next week. Lillie hoped the electric situation was a fluke situation and that Adam's integrity would prove her dad's weed-induced prediction wrong. Certainly, her man couldn't be a user. A user wouldn't have paid the money back. Especially when he could induce multiple orgasms in a matter of minutes. With each encounter, her love grew for Adam. His love made her echo the sentiments of Aretha Franklin. She finally knew what it meant for a man to make her feel like a "natural woman."

As they entered Pastor Andrew's office the frown on his face shocked Lillie. She was so used to his jovial mood.

"Have a seat," he commanded. "Since we have an afternoon service, I won't waste time getting to the point. What are your intentions with this beautiful young lady right here?" He extended his arm in Lillie's direction.

Adam spoke up first. "I love Lillie, and I intend to marry her just as soon as I get my finances in order." The mention of marriage made Lillie glow with joy, yet she didn't understand Adam's newfound reluctance. The first night they made love, he'd promised to marry her as soon as possible.

"That's good to know. With that in mind, we need to start the counseling process now. I honor your desire to be one, yet, Adam, you and I both know that we should address issues that could cause problems in a marriage."

Pastor turned his attention to Lillie. "Now, let's talk about what's going on with you. Your lack of experience could also be a catalyst that leads issues to arise."

Adam and Lillie reluctantly nodded their heads in agreement.

"So let's get to the point. Are you two . . . umm . . . intimately involved?" Pastor patiently awaited their answer. Lillie stopped breathing for a few moments. She didn't have to speak because her silence spoke volumes.

Once again, Adam took the lead. "Pastor, we've spent the night at one another's place and have had some close calls, but no, we aren't sleeping together."

Lillie coughed loudly and stared down at the floor in shame. She couldn't believe Adam told a bold-faced lie to Pastor Andrews. She fixated her glance on the lone speck of paper on the floor to avoid eye contact with the Pastor.

What was Adam thinking? I'm sure there's a consequence for lying to the man of God.

"I'm glad to hear that, son, but here's my concern. Ms. Blakey's granddaughter lives across the street from you. She told her grandmother about Lillie's frequent visits and overnight stays. So as your pastor, it's my duty to address this."

Adam remained cool, calm, and collected, as if he'd been through this one hundred times. Lillie's palms sweated profusely. She wished the old biddy and her family would mind their own business. Lillie heard her father's voice calling out to Ms. Blakey from across the street.

Old bat!

She tried to make eye contact with Adam but he stared straight ahead.

"Lillie, do you mind if I talk to Adam alone?" Not sure of the pastor's intentions, she hesitated to respond.

"It's okay, babe." Adam assured her as if he sensed her reluctance. "Please, get the kids and wait for me in the vestibule." He flashed his million-dollar smile and she melted.

Before she got out of the greeting area, she noticed she'd forgotten her purse. Lillie turned around and walked back toward Pastor's office. Just as she rounded the corner, she overheard a part of their conversation.

"Here's the deal. I know you're young, Adam, and you've got your needs. I just ask that you be more discreet. We serve a forgiving God, but these church folks— they'll never let you live it down."

What? He shouldn't be giving this type of guidance.

Then she remembered how Bianca seemed to be around pastor much more than normal lately. Secretary or not, there was definitely something fishy going on between the two. Inside the pastor's office, the two men shared a moment of clarity. As Lillie walked back in, Pastor diverted the focus of the conversation.

"So Adam, are you ready to preach this afternoon?"

Adam's smile brightened the room. He was the first person from the class that Pastor had asked to preach outside of the church in his place. Lillie found it interesting that he'd asked Adam after the conversation they'd just had. She walked casually past them to grab her purse.

"You know there will be some influential men from COMA there."

COMA was the Central Ohio Ministerial Alliance, a group of pastors and ministers who pretty much ran all of the churches in the city. Even though COMA was a strange acronym, this group had power in the community.

"Yes, Pastor," Adam responded coolly, "I am. Thanks for the opportunity."

NINETEEN

THE DECISION to ride to Acts of Faith with Pastor Andrews and his wife paid off. His wife, Lady Abigail, spoke candidly about her feelings on being a pastor's wife and her stories entertained those in the plush Cadillac Escalade. Being in the presence of such a straightforward spiritual woman refreshed Lillie's spirit. At the same time, she couldn't help but wonder how much money the pastors made because First Lady's garb was sophisticated and pricy. She sported a Donna Vinci original two-piece outfit and hat. A long-sleeved canary yellow jacket with an embroidered collar topped a sleeveless dress of the same shade. Her matching hat donned an exquisite silk bow and sparkling rhinestones. A simple string of pearls, pearl drop earrings, and matching satin pumps accented the ensemble.

Lillie's mouth dropped to the floor when she entered Acts of Faith. She was used to the opulent décor of most mega churches; however, none of them were quite to this standard. Strong pillars filled the vestibule to complement the expensive purple clothe draped from the ceiling. Velvet purple walls surrounded the entryway, plush and inviting to the touch. Lillie's feet sank deep into the carpet with each step. Radical Faith Church was a dwarf ministry compared to this.

Pastor Lane and his graceful wife Lady Candace greeted them with hearty hugs. The pastor whisked away Adam and Pastor Andrews to his massive office suite while the first lady took the women and children to her office, which included a private dining room. Lillie's eyes bulged out of her head when she laid eyes on the other first lady's seated at the table. Lillie had never seen such a glamorous, formal dining room in a church and stood with her mouth wide open. Beautiful crystal chandeliers with gold accents hung from the ceiling right above the mahogany dining room table. Before she knew it, the other women noticed her awestruck expression.

"When you have your church built, you can customize it the way you want it. You better get used to this kind of treatment. Your Adam is a rising star, little sis. Ever since the pastors from COMA heard him preach at Pastor Green's church in Chillicothe, they've just been going on and on about getting him on their staff." Lady Candace's ample curves couldn't be hidden under the loose fitting dress deemed appropriate for a first lady. Her thick, wavy hair framed a beautiful, dark chocolate face with skin as smooth as a porcelain baby doll. Motherly ways, a contagious smile, and a hearty laugh, it was easy to love Lady Candace.

"Thank you, Lady Candace." Lillie's cheeks turned rosy as she thought of her beau and his preaching skills. He possessed extraordinary talent, but she had no idea pastors were seeking after him on this level.

"Sister Lillie, you definitely have a good man." Lady Abigail's smile grew serious. She rubbed Lillie's back to show her affection first lady style. "Don't worry. Pastor has decided to take him under his wing. When he gets finished grooming him, you'll be on your way to being the first lady of the next mega church."

Initially, Lillie was fond of Pastor Andrews and felt comfortable knowing that he was taking a shine to Adam. Then she remembered the advice Pastor gave him before they left the church. On second thought, maybe that wouldn't be such a good idea.

Lady Abigail pulled her to the side while the other women continued to chat about Adam's mastery of the Word. "Since our assistant pastor will be the senior pastor at the second Radical Faith campus, Pastor is considering Adam for the position."

Lillie knew she should be jumping for joy, but she couldn't get over how first ladies referred to their husbands as "Pastor" in public. It reminded her of how her mother would call her father "Daddy" in front of her when she was a child. She wondered if wives of doctors called their husbands "Doctor" in public. Did wives of judges call their husbands "esquire"?

"Really? How did he bypass all the other ministers?" Lillie asked, getting her focus back on track.

First Lady went on to explain the beauty of being able to draw a crowd and influence people. She shared that being gifted and called by God wasn't the only requirement for the assistant pastor role. Unfortunately, the other ministers had not developed their abilities in the influence place. Lillie nodded her head as Lady Abigail shared. She gave examples of Adam's ability to coordinate with leaders of singles ministries across the city and the prosperity of Elaina's business since he came on board. The qualifications for ministry equated to those of a CEO for a Fortune 100 company.

Lillie wondered what Lady Abigail would say if she knew about their sexual secrets. Maybe she had the same train of thought as her husband. As long as you're discreet, you can do whatever you want, even though it's against the will of God. Kind of like the military's old Don't Ask Don't Tell policy. Then Lillie remembered that even that questionable legislation had been repealed.

Lady Abigail continued to share with Lillie and then it hit her.

I'm not even all that into church. What would Adam's elevation mean to our relationship?

"So Lady Abigail, how do I fit into this picture?"

The first lady explained that when they marry, Lillie could pay someone else to manage her business. This would give her the ability to support her husband in the ministry, have his children, and be a caregiver in the home. As much as Lillie was excited about marrying Adam, she wasn't fond of giving up her career.

"Three of the most powerful members are in Pastor Lane's office talking to Adam right now. My assignment was to talk to you. Part of the deal is that he would have to get married within the next six to nine months."

"I want to be Adam's wife for the right reasons. Not just so that he can have a prosperous ministry." Lillie was adamant about this point, even though she couldn't help but remember Sage's prediction about her marital status when she and Grace were in California.

Lady Candace strolled over to the duo, sighed loudly, and whispered in Lillie's ear, "Don't be so naïve, girl. You love this man and he loves you. It doesn't matter how you get him to the altar, right?"

For a brief second, Lillie pondered on the question. She knew that Adam loved her and wanted to marry her at some point. Despite this, she couldn't shake the feeling that if he asked her now, he'd only be marrying her so quickly for the sake of his ministry career.

Lady Abigail patted Lillie on the shoulder, interrupting her thoughts. "I know this is a lot to take in right now, so I understand your reluctance. Stick with me, and you'll be a pastor's wife before you know it."

8O G3

Church members jumped out of their seats to cheer for Adam as he preached up a storm. Lillie smoothed out her dress and resumed sitting when she caught a glimpse of all the first ladies seated in her row. Usually, fiancés sat on the second row, so she knew they were treating her special. She looked back to see if any of her friends came to support Adam. There were quite a few members from Radical Faith in the crowd, including Bianca, however, no one else showed up. She waved to Bianca to come sit in the front row with her. Just because she was sleeping with the pastor didn't mean that Lillie wasn't her friend. That's Lady Abigail's problem, not hers.

What kind of friends decides not to support us on a day like this? Adam's preaching at one of the largest churches in the city and they flake out. Interesting!

As she enjoyed the service, Lillie thanked God Lady Abigail had the foresight to tell Adam they were sending the children to the nursery. Their absence allowed Lillie to partake fully in the sermon and relish in the status of being on the arm of the speaker of the hour. No one would have guessed that this awesome man of God brought her to a multiple orgasmic state just the night before. Whenever she questioned him about having sex outside of wedlock in his ministerial role, he referred her to Romans 12. Here, the apostle Paul explained the gift of prophecy, in terms of the ability to speak an inspired message with forthrightness and insight, was a gift given from the Father, without repentance. In other words, he had this gift before he even became a Christian, so why would God take it away over a little sin?

Lillie's face beamed with pride as he preached. "You see, according to John 5, people were sitting by the pool of Bethesda, waiting for the angel to trouble the water. The water wasn't troubled often so only the first person in was guaranteed a healing. These people waited for a long time, taking a chance, hoping to be the lucky person to be set free from infirmities. You and I have more of a chance of winning the lottery than most of them did at being healed in that water. But I'm here to tell you, while they were waiting by that pool, the savior came along and showed them his power. Brothers and sisters, you're going to miss your blessing, waiting on another source. Don't run to the water, run to Jesus. Don't run to that crack cocaine. Run to Jesus. You better not run to the club."

Before Adam could even open his mouth, the congregation shouted out, "Run to Jesus!" Lillie jumped out of her seat and waved her lap cloth in Adam's direction. One of the first ladies gave it to her to cover up her knees since she was sitting on the front row.

"The probability's not slim because he's a sure bet. He specializes in winning all the time. You wanna be healed? You better come on here and . . ."

"Run to Jesus."

People started running to the altar, shouting, and speaking in tongues. The whole church fell out under the power of the Holy Spirit. Lillie couldn't help but think of the Native American Ghost Dances where they would be overwhelmed by the power of the pale visitor they mistook for Jesus. Just when the saints were at the pinnacle of excitement, Adam's tenor voice rose high above all others in his soulful rendition of "We Worship You in the Spirit." The fullness of the song filled the building and the people fell down on their knees to weep and worship. Lady Abigail waved Lillie to the front along with the other altar workers. Lillie couldn't believe that she was actually going to be praying for people when she didn't even know how to pray for herself. Regardless of that fact, she practically tripped over her feet getting to the altar to be closer to Adam's work.

A middle-aged woman with withering skin and a slight limp came to Lillie, asking for prayer for her finances. Lillie followed the pattern she'd seen from the other first ladies. She anointed the woman's head with oil and began praising the Lord for her. This tactic served Lillie well.

I only know the Lord's Prayer, so I guess that's what she'll be getting today.

When Lillie opened her mouth to pray, the woman slumped over and hit the ground and she writhed like a slithery snake. Some sort of unexplainable force held Lillie's mouth in place and drew her eyes to the ceiling. In the white space, she saw a cloudy vision of the woman's contorted face with the words fear written above her head. Out of nowhere, Lillie heard a piercing shriek. Sweat beads rolled down Lillie's back soaking her dress. She looked around to see if others heard the same scream and when she saw no reactions, she knew the truth. No stranger to seeing things that others couldn't, Lillie decided to say the words she'd heard Pastor Andrews say when people were fearful.

"I bind the spirit of fear, in the name of Jesus." Lillie spoke to the demonic presence as she placed her hand over the woman's heart and applied a slight amount of pressure. Even though she mimicked her pastor, she found this technique to be quite effective.

"Go! I command you to leave this woman now," Lillie exclaimed like she actually knew what she was doing.

Overtaken by the power of the Holy Spirit, the frail woman tried to stand but each time, she stumbled. Lillie steadied the woman to prevent her fall as she wept profusely.

Why isn't anyone coming to help me?

Then, she noticed that all eyes, including Adam's, were on her and the traumatized woman. Initially, Lillie gulped with fear then she decided that Adam would love her more if she could set this woman free from the demonic presence. With relentless tenacity, Lillie continued to command the spirit to leave.

To Lillie's surprise, the evil spirit spoke through the woman. The eerie voice loomed out, "Her soul was promised to my father thousands of years ago. I will not leave, for she is rightfully mine."

Just then, the woman fell out jerking on the floor and the altar workers covered her with a white sheet.

Finally, some help!

Lady Abigail came to Lillie's side, descended to the floor, sat alongside the woman, and continued ministering until the evil spirit was completely gone. Lillie assisted her by rubbing the woman's back. When Lillie looked into the woman's eyes, she returned the gaze and cried out," I feel so free! Like a load had been lifted off me."

"Sing a song of deliverance over her," Lady Abigail whispered in Lillie's ear.

Lillie's puzzled look must have cued the first lady into the fact that she was clueless, because she told her which song to sing. She thanked God, it was a typical Radical Faith worship songs. Lillie ministered through song until the woman rose on her own. Her skin was no longer withering and she no longer walked with a limp. The congregation applauded in awe. As the woman danced around the building, Lillie knew her work was complete. Feeling empowered, she moved to the next person. She caught Adam's attention and he raised his thumb at her. His action confirmed what she knew in her heart—they would make a great ministry team.

At the end of the service, Lillie stood next to Adam in the receiving line to greet the congregation. As they exchanges hugs and well wishes, she couldn't believe how much money people slipped in their pockets. After the line had dwindled, a young lady from the praise dance ministry walked up to Lillie. She wore a floor length white skirt and a blouse with long pointed sleeves. The silky material created an ethereal look that set this woman apart from all others. When she reached Lillie, she said, "Woman of God, now that you have labored in the vineyard, the Lord has something for you."

Lillie typically didn't let just anyone prophesy to her, especially after the Sage incident. But this time, she decided to receive the message. The young lady leaned closer and whispered in Lillie's ear. "Deborah was a judge in the Bible. Her name represents the honeybee. You, my sister, are the queen bee. Don't let just any bee join your colony. You don't know how many flowers those bees have pollinated. Your supply will be contaminated if you continue this way. "

Not sure how to take the prophecy, Lillie stared at the woman for a moment.

How does she know about the bees and what does this all mean?

The praise dancer pulled out a purple flag and began to wave it over Lillie. People in the line stood back to watch. With each wave, Lillie felt a mighty gush of wind, so she fell to her knees. Suddenly, the wind began to speak into her spirit and she felt the glory of the Lord surrounding her in a state of perfect peace. Lillie could do nothing but weep as the word of the Lord touched her heart. This went on for several moments, until she felt strong enough to rise. Remembering that she stood in the receiving line, Lillie rose up and straightened out her dress. She gave the woman a quick hug and dismissed her as if the experience never happened. As the woman scooted away, Pastor Lane stepped on the scene to chat with Adam and Lillie.

"Adam, you did a fine job, son. That's the type of preaching that provokes change." Pastor Lane's compliment made Adam grin from ear to ear.

"Thank you, sir. I appreciate the opportunity to minister in your house," Adam responded respectfully.

"This is the house of the Lord, son," Pastor Lane corrected and Adam smiled gingerly.

"This is a lovely young lady you have with you, son. She's like a pit bull on the altar, too. Slaying people in the Holy Ghost like that!"

"Thank you, Pastor Lane." Lillie almost choked on her words.

Sometimes you gotta fake it to make it.

"Oh, you're quite welcome, woman of God. When are you two getting married?" Pastor Lane asked with a jolly spirit. Ironically, Lillie wondered the exact same thing and was interested to see how Adam would answer the question. He pulled Lillie to his side and squeezed her tight enough to show his love for her, yet subtle enough to prevent unnecessary gossip.

"Soon, Pastor Lane. Soon. You can't let someone as fine as Lillie stay single for too long." Adam and Pastor Lane shared a laugh.

"Yeah, you never know. Some man might come in here and sweep me off my feet." Lillie laughed.

"If I was younger and not married to Lady Candace, I'd give you a run for your money," Pastor Lane teased. "On another note, Adam, come to my office before you leave so that I can give you a little something for your time. You can expect to receive many invitations to preach in the future."

He gestured towards Lillie and said, "Make sure you bring her with you. She has a unique anointing for healing and deliverance. Pretty soon, she'll be preaching all over the city."

Lillie gathered Ajay and Aliyah from Children's Church while Adam ventured off with Pastor Lane. Before leaving the church, Lillie noticed Bianca standing in the vestibule chatting with Pastor Andrews and Lady Abigail. Ever since she'd assumed the role of Pastor's administrative assistant, she'd been spending a great deal of her time at the church and was more involved in church related activities. Maybe Pastor's workload had increased. Lillie wasn't sure what to think at this point, so she decided to put it out of her mind for the moment.

On the way home, she and Adam talked about the success of the evening.

"Did you know that over fifty new converts came to the Lord tonight?"

"Wow! It's good to know that what you had to say stirred so many hearts," Lillie exclaimed.

"And the offering was over ten thousand dollars."

Lillie almost stopped breathing when Adam shared the number.

"Guess what? The trustees wrote me a nice check in addition to the money the parishioners handed me in the receiving line. I saw them handing you money, too."

Catching her breath, Lillie responded, "Yeah. It was quite a shock to me. I've never seen anything like it. I wondered if we should give the money to the church."

Adam hesitated, scratched his head then said, "Well, I guess the money is ours to keep. It's almost like we earned it. We should pay a tithe to Acts of Faith, though."

Lillie agreed with Adam, but still felt a twinge of guilt for keeping the cash. Tonight, she got a taste of both real ministry and the power that came along with being the lady in Adam's life. She'd be sure to meet with Lady Abigail and get that ring on her finger before the prophetic word spoken over her came to pass.

TWENTY

L ILLIE STAMPED her foot at CoCo when she met her at the door with a mangled pump hanging from her mouth. *Dang! This is the sixth pair. Ruined!*

When CoCo started behaving in this manner, Lillie took her to the vet, who donned a stupid separation anxiety diagnosis and even tried to write a prescription for the condition. Lillie refused to label her pet and give her meds, so instead, she choose an excellent dog sitting service that worked like a charm. Since Adam's preaching engagement surprised Lillie, she forgot to make plans for CoCo and of course, her shoes paid the consequence.

While Lillie pried the shoe from the canine's mouth she reflected on the evening. Accompanying Adam to this event proved to be a fruitful experience, with the exception of the altar work. Lillie enjoyed being with Adam, but she'd have to get used to ministering to folks. She made a mental note to stop by Moments with Majesty to pick up a few books on the subject. Despite her state of elation, Lillie was disturbed by the fact that

Bianca was her only friend to attend the service. She decided to stop by Grace's place to find out what was going on. She walked outside then into Grace's condo, not bothering to knock.

"Hey, Lillie." Grace and Masseri sat on the silky throw cushions on the living room floor playing Scrabble. They both rose to hug Lillie, while CoCo barked incessantly until Masseri picked her up. Lillie noticed that they both wore silky hip scarves laced with beautiful gold circles that looked like coins. They jingled like bells on Christmas every time they moved.

"Wow! You two are awful jingly today," Lillie teased.

"Oh yeah. Masseri added a belly dancing routine to the Global Fusion class. We ordered these and plan to sell them to the ladies in the class," Grace explained with a chuckle.

"I know they'll be a hit. They used them in the classes I taught in California." Masseri gyrated her hips as she turned in a circle to show off her new workout gear. Like a sleek panther on the prowl, Masseri's sleek moves exuded an exotic heat.

"Um, that's a little much for me," Lillie admitted.

"Humph," Masseri grunted.

"I missed you two at the second service. You know Adam brought the house down." Lillie held her head up high and smiled brightly.

"Humph." Masseri rolled her eyes. "I bet that's not all he brought down." Grace and Masseri shared a laugh.

Lillie decided not to take the bait and ignore the derogatory comment. Instead, she got straight to the point. "Why didn't you come?"

Grace and Masseri exchanged a knowing glance then sat in silence. Finally, Masseri, always the bolder of the two, spoke up. "I'm actually glad you asked so we can get this on the table. We heard you and Adam making love the other day and we were sort of . . . shocked." Masseri paused and inhaled deeply. "I mean, he's trying to be Super Pastor and all. The way he had you screaming and moaning just wasn't right." Grace nodded her head in agreement, donning a smug grin.

Lillie's mouth dropped so wide open you could run a Mack truck through it. Obviously, the paper-thin walls leaked the story Lillie tried to hide. Only Adam made it quite impossible with the amazing things he did to her body. She couldn't help but express her appreciation with screams of delightful passion. Of course, the response excited Adam and he added his own vocal praise to the chorus. Reflecting back on that evening, she could only imagine what they heard.

Grace must have sensed Lillie's discomfort as she tried to make light of the situation. "I mean, I'm not hating on you for getting your groove on, but it's going to take me awhile before I can listen to Adam bring the word again. And you . . . coming in here judging our hip scarves. You're a trip.."

"Grace, you're not perfect. Neither are you, Masseri," Lillie shot back.

"As true as that may be, you need to be more discreet. You're dating a minister, in case you forgot. You know Ms. Blakey's granddaughter told the whole choir she saw you and Adam getting down on the swing in his backyard last week. What's up with that?" Masseri challenged.

"All we're saying is that . . . you're foul. You're chasing after the desires of your Mars sign instead of your Sun sign. Mar equals boyfriend. Sun equals husband." Grace crossed her arms across her chest and exchanged a knowing glance with Masseri.

"What? You confuse me with all that astrological mess. Sounds like hogwash to me."

"You wouldn't get it because you'll open your mind up to sex with someone who's not your twin flame, but you'll close your mind to the planets and signs connected to the universe." Masseri rolled her eyes.

"Okay, let me put it in terms you can understand. The two of you aren't even trying to hide the fact you're sleeping together. In his backyard, Lillie. For Pete's sake! What were you thinking? Everyone knows it, and on top of that, no pun intended, he's all up Pastor Andrews butt." Grace defended her point like an expert attorney.

"I thank you two for being honest with me; however, neither Adam nor I have to answer to you or anyone else about our sex life or lack thereof," Lillie declared.

Grace looked at Masseri and they both shook their heads in disapproval.

"I've about had it with you two. Call me when you have something else to talk about rather than my love life," Lillie growled as she grabbed CoCo and stormed out the door. When she arrived in her condo, she slammed the door for effect, knowing that Grace and Masseri could hear it.

Stressed out by the events of the day, Lillie relaxed with a cup of lavender chamomile tea. She grabbed her leopard print snuggly blanket and hopped in the hammock on the patio. To take her mind off her friends and their jealous ranting, Lillie recalled Adam's command of the pulpit this evening. The people were so receptive to his message and his leadership. With Adam by her side, they could be a serious power couple. She'd just have to step up her game in the ministry space. Surely, it couldn't be that hard. Sipping on her tea, Lillie envisioned them traveling the world and ministering together. Maybe they could co-author a few books to add to their ministry. Cuddling up to her pillow, she fell asleep with a smile on her face.

TWENTY-ONE

O VER THE next few months, Lillie and Adam continued to pursue the next level of their relationship. He and his children won Lillie's heart and she enjoyed their presence in her life. Her family and friends didn't approve and she chose not to concern herself with their judgmental thoughts. Adam confirmed her decision when he preached about haters putting negativity into the atmosphere to mess up what you've got going on. He said that you needed to speak just the opposite into your life, in the name of Jesus. As much as she loved them, she decided to take on her honey's perspective and cancel out all the bad thoughts they shared.

"I bind your spirit of negativity and loose favor over my life, in the name of Jesus" became Lillie's canned response to their rants.

As promised, the men of COMA continued to work with Adam, while the ladies worked with Lillie. They learned about the nuances of church life, how to be great preachers, and the aspects of influential congregation leaders. Even though Adam hadn't officially proposed, they'd started their pre-marital counseling with Pastor Andrews and Lady Abigail. Here, they learned about the serious commitment and compromise involved in marriage.

When Lillie shared these details with her parents, they offered a different perspective. As she drove home from their house, she couldn't help but think back on the conversation.

"That man is full of . . . and he's leading you astray," Sophia fussed.

Lillie couldn't believe her mother almost cursed. She'd never heard that type of language from her before.

"Baby girl, I have to agree with your mother. What kind of pastor counsels a couple with no ring or formal engagement? That makes no sense to me," Sam said.

"Daddy. Are you mad because there's no ring or because he didn't ask you for my hand in marriage?" Lillie challenged her father's old-fashioned beliefs.

"That's just it. You used to believe the same things as us. Since you've been with this Adam character, you are changing and not for the better."

The truth of Sam's words stung Lillie like a honeybee at a church picnic.

"You're right. I have changed. Enough to know that as much as I love both of you, I don't have to sit here and listen to this. Unless it's Theo, you won't be happy anyway."

"We've talked about this time and time again. You and Theo were meant to be together and I'm not sure why you're fighting it," Sophia pleaded.

"You know where I stand." Sam pursed his lips and crossed his arms in front of his chest.

"Well, I see this isn't getting us anywhere, so I'll see you guys for Sunday dinner." Her parents sat in silence while Lillie grabbed her Coach purse and matching trench coat. She left without sharing a departure hug and kiss.

Lillie jumped in the shower to take her mind off the fight with her parents. Then she kicked back to relax on the sofa and watch her favorite sitcom. The busy day got the best of her because she fell fast asleep. To her surprise, the ringing of her cell phone jerked her awake.

The clock read 11:15 p.m. Who's calling me at this time of night?

She answered the phone in her groggy voice and pepped up when she heard Adam's voice.

"Umm . . . I really need to talk to you. I'm in the parking lot. Can you meet me down here?"

That's strange. Unlike Theo, Adam typically didn't stop by without calling first. She grabbed a pair of sassy pink flip-flops and checked the mirror to make sure her hair was in place. When she opened the door and peeped his Range Rover in her driveway, she noticed Adam's children asleep in the back seat.

"Hey, honey." Lillie planted a kiss on his lips and he squeezed her firm behind, arousing her senses right away. He didn't hesitate to reciprocate when she wrapped her arms around him. When they parted from the embrace, his eyes looked weighed down.

Lillie and Adam woke the children and led them into Lillie's condo. She sent them to her guest room so they could get back to sleep. They had spent many nights there since Adam typically worked late. CoCo Chanel followed them and jumped on the doggie chair at the bottom of the king sized bed.

Always the protector.

The catatonic stare on Adam's face worried Lillie, so she grabbed the anointing oil she'd purchased online from Heggai Ministries and anointed her hands. Then she began to pray for him in the spirit. Lady Abigail told her that every first lady needed to be filled with the Holy Spirit. So she came over late one night and tarried with Lillie until she flowed in tongues. Then she told Lillie about the spiritual attacks most pastors experienced and taught her how to pray for Adam. A pastor's wife served as her husband's personal intercessor and prayer warrior, covering him from all angles. Even though they weren't married yet, he was her husband-to-be, so Lillie felt it was her job to block negativity in the spirit realm.

As Lillie prayed, tears fell from Adam's eyes. His silent sobbing caused her to pray with more fervor. He lay face down in front of her fireplace and began crying out to the Lord. Lillie continued to pray as she walked around the room. She determined to tarry with her man until she sensed a breakthrough. Adam must have been in the same vein because he remained prostrate on the floor for about thirty minutes.

When he finally rose, she grabbed his hand and led him outside. They walked to the trail by the wooded ravine. Usually, this trail was their romantic get-a-way, but Adam's needs were different tonight.

"What's going on?" she asked with compassion in her tone.

Adam sighed softly and took a deep breath. "Lillie, I don't want to lose you."

"Lose me? Why would you lose me?" Puzzled by Adam's statement, Lillie probed for more. She also remembered Lady Abigail's teaching about unconditional love in a marriage. "Honey, we're in this together. You know you can tell me anything. I promise, no matter what it is, we can work through it." Then she recalled they weren't married just yet.

"You see, some things have changed in my life." Adam sighed again. "My family is expanding, effective tomorrow."

"Huh? Expanding tomorrow? What are you talking about?" Lillie demanded an answer. She was starting to have second thoughts about this whole unconditional love thing. Lady Abigail didn't mention sticking in there though problems like this.

"Here's the deal. I'm not just the father of Ajay and Aliyah. I have more children. Two more, to be exact."

"Two! What do you mean you have two more children? The whole time we've been together, you mean to tell me, you haven't been honest with me?" Lillie couldn't believe her ears. Nothing Lady Abigail had taught Lillie thus far could have prepared her for this.

"Yeah, their names are Andrew and Adrianne. Adrianne is my baby girl. They're coming tomorrow, and I want you to meet them." Adam's sullen demeanor changed to one of strong pride and love when he mentioned the names of his children. Even still, Lillie wasn't moved by this display.

"Meet them? What? You've got to be kidding me," Lillie yelled.

Adam squared his shoulders and spoke boldly. "I've told you what I expect from the woman I plan to marry when it comes to my kids."

"First of all, that was when there were only two in the picture. Second, you can't just drop something like this on me and expect me to adjust so quickly." Lillie defended her position like a champion fighter about to lose his belt.

"Well, if you can't accept my kids, you can't accept me," Adam declared.

"Get real. This is not about accepting your kids. This is about you lying to me over and over again." When Lillie mentioned the root of the issue, Adam winced.

"Okay, I'm telling you now," he said with acrimony in his voice.

Lillie's anger elevated to such a high level, she saw white light. "Thanks for being so real and transparent," Lillie sniped. "By the way, where's their mother?"

Adam's face turned bright red. It was even noticeable in the dark. "Um . . . her name is Jonna. She lives in Chillicothe. Nowhere near Shannon, though."

Lillie was already getting frustrated trying to keep track of his babies' mamas.

"What's her deal? What kind of mother just packs her kids up and sends them to live with their dad at the drop of a dime?"

"Well, she has kept the children from me for years. I guess Jonna and Cassie met for a play date when Ajay and Aliyah were visiting. Then the next thing I know, Jonna called me and said that if I had Ajay and Aliyah, I should have all my children."

"That doesn't sound right. No woman who's not in a relationship with a man flips out on that level, unless . . . Adam, please tell me you weren't . . . "

"Why would you even think I'd do something like that to you? You have to trust me."

"Trust you? Trust you? Oh my God, you're such a liar. And not only are you a liar, you're an egotistical jerk. That's probably why all of your kid's names start with an A." With tears pouring, Lillie shot Adam a sneer.

"Look, this is no time for crying," Adam chastised.

"You just don't get it. You're ruining our life. We're supposed to get married and be this awesome ministry team. How can we do that now with all these lies between us?" Lillie questioned Adam.

"Lillie, my kids come first; so you can step anytime. I don't need a woman in my life who won't support me. How can you say you're a woman of God and act like this?" Adam's hypocritical and manipulative statement sent Lillie over the edge.

"What? How can you say you're a man of God even though you lie and fornicate? Preaching and singing like you're somebody special." Lillie's accusation must have hit home because Adam's face was beet red.

"You ungrateful wench," Adam yelled furiously.

Oh, no he didn't!

Lillie reached back and smacked him with all her might. To her surprise, he grabbed her and started to shake her violently. He returned Lillie's slap with brute force. She grabbed her face to soothe the sting, leaving herself defenseless. Adam took advantage of the opportunity and began to drag her by the hair. Lillie couldn't believe this was happening. Somehow, she broke free from Adam's abusive hold and ran towards her condo. Just as she rounded the curb, Theo and Grace pulled up. Without hesitation, Theo exited the car and stood next to Lillie.

"Lady Bug, are you okay? What's going on? Did that cat hurt you?"

"Hey, Adam, I mean, Theo … umm …I hit him first." Lillie stumbled over her words.

"Grace, get Lillie to your place. I see him walking across the street, and I'm going to handle this." Grace didn't say one word. Instead, she gave Lillie a signal to follow her lead. Lillie ran inside her condo, grabbed CoCo Chanel, and made sure her door was unlocked so that Adam could retrieve his children and leave.

Then, she went to Grace's place.

"Have you had enough of your singing pastor yet?" Grace asked. "He only wants your money and will tell you whatever he needs to get it."

"It's not like that at all, Grace," Lillie defended Adam between tears. "Adam doesn't need my money. His job and preaching will sustain him just fine. He loves me, but he's struggling through some challenging times."

"If he loved you so much, then tell me this: Why is he taking your loving without so much as a ring on your finger? Why did he just manhandle you? Why, Lillie, why?" Grace screamed.

"Stop it! I've had enough," Lillie snapped.

"Yeah, you've had enough. The problem is you think you can't get enough of his—"

Appalled at Grace's blatant vulgarity, Lillie cut her off mid-sentence. "Don't go there, Grace. I mean it." Lillie's anger permeated through her tear-stained face.

Theo waltzed through Grace's front door with an alpha male swagger. "You better thank God that Grace needed a ride home tonight. Otherwise, I wouldn't have been here to save you from getting beat down by the love of your life."

Frustrated, yet simultaneously grateful, Lillie responded, "Thank you, but please stop it. I can't take your teasing tonight." Lillie worked hard to hold back the tears.

Sensing his friends' humiliation, Theo changed his tune. "Okay, I'll stop, for now. I just wanted you to know that it's safe for you to go home, now. I threw that zero and his kids out. So, grab CoCo and let's go," Theo directed.

As Lillie gathered her belongings, Theo turned to Grace and said, "Thanks for being there for Lillie."

"Anytime. Even though she's making some dumb decision, I'd never leave her hanging." Grace smiled smugly and Lillie rolled her eyes. She was glad the ordeal with Adam was over and they were leaving Grace's place.

Theo and Lillie exited Grace's condo and entered Lillie's. When they stepped inside, Theo hugged her tightly. He kissed her on the forehead and sat on the couch.

"Are you going home?" Lillie didn't want to be alone, yet she also didn't want to ask Theo to stay.

"Naw. I'm not leaving you here with the potential of your Mr. Caramel Latte Nightmare trying to come back once he thinks I'm gone," Theo responded sarcastically.

"Thank you." Lillie's words sincerely expressed her gratitude to her best friend.

"You're welcome," Theo responded. "Girl, throw me that snuggly blanket so I can get some sleep. All of your relationship drama has made me tired." Lillie retorted by hitting Theo on the head with the pillow. He grabbed it from her along with the blanket.

Lillie chuckled as she realized only Theo could wrap up in a snuggly blanket and still exude manliness. He smiled and licked his lips, then laid his head on the pillow. He was so handsome, and his heroic efforts made Lillie love him even more. She bent down to kiss Theo on the cheek, and to her surprise, he pulled her close to him and held her tightly. Lillie felt so comfortable in his arms, and she began to sob. Theo stroked her hair gently and began praying for her peace of mind.

After the prayer was over, Lillie lay on the couch with Theo until they both fell asleep. About an hour later, she awoke and headed to her bedroom, leaving Theo to continue resting on the couch. As she lay in her bed, she thought about her next steps. For some strange reason, she was confused. In love with Theo for years, yet afraid to cause a problem in their friendship, she'd avoided dealing with the obvious. She wasn't ready to let go of Mr. Caramel Latte Dream, even though the voice in her head told her to run for the hills. Lillie pondered on her encounter with Grace that evening.

Maybe Grace is right, Lillie thought. Even if she wasn't, Lillie needed to know how to handle this situation, so she decided to call Lady Abigail first thing in the morning. She always knew just the right thing to help Lillie with Adam.

TWENTY-TWO

LILLIE THANKED God as she walked into Urban Bistro, one of the many restaurants the Andrews owned in the city. The sweet, tangy, and spicy aromas blended so well that Lillie's stomach growled like a little lion. When Lady Abigail walked in, heads turned from every direction. Known for beauty, class, and style, she was arrayed in an elegant, custom fit cream pants suit and salmon sling back heels. She sported designer glasses with rhinestones on each side that complimented her other accessories. First Lady definitely was a divine picture of class and grace.

"Lillie, it's so good to see you. Girl, you look great,"

Knowing she'd be dining with the first lady, Lillie selected her wardrobe with care. Her tailored ivory halter dress fit each and every curve on her body. Lillie's chic apparel couldn't be denied. She chose a necklace of sable polished brownstones and matching earrings from the Premier Design Jewelry collection. Stiletto heels and a soft, buttery leather Prada bag topped off the ensemble.

"Why thank you, First Lady. You look great, yourself. I have to get a pair of those shoes," Lillie responded.

"Amen. The catalog is in my office at the church. I'll give it to you tonight at Bible Study. Enough about my shoes. What's going on with you, little sister?"

"I really don't know where to start, so I'll just get to the point. Adam and I are having problems," Lillie admitted, even though she was quite embarrassed.

"Honey chile, all couples have problems." First Lady tilted her head back and let out a gentle laugh. "Shoot, there's not a week that goes by I don't get mad at your pastor, girl. One time—"

"No, you don't understand. Last night . . . he . . . umm . . . he got physical with me."

"Physical? What do you mean by that?" Lady Abigail drilled Lillie.

"He . . . umm . . . he hit me," Lillie admitted as she shrank down in her seat.

"What? He hit you? Are you okay?" Her concern was genuine and comforting.

"Yes and no. I hit him first but I never imagined it would go this far. Thank God Theo and Grace were there to help me."

"Okay. Don't worry. He won't hit you again. I'll have pastor talk to him." Lady Abigail grabbed her phone out of her Coach bag and typed a text message. Lillie assumed that this was her way of informing Pastor Andrews. Once she returned the phone to its original location, she leaned in close to Lillie and spoke in a hushed tone. "Sometimes, being married to a man of power can be challenging. You have to learn to use your yoni power."

Confused by Lady Abigail's statements, Lillie sought clarification. "Yoni? What's that?" Lillie took a sip of her coconut water.

The elder woman sighed then spoke slowly and deliberatively. "Your yoni. You know? Well, maybe you don't. Your vagina, your sugar walls."

Lillie choked on her beverage and coughed incessantly.

"Baby, if you think Pastor and I are unaware of your level of intimacy with Adam then you're sadly mistaken. Since you are, you need to know that you have the power to stand up to Adam, put him in his place, and make him respect you. Pastor can threaten to take away his position to make him stop hitting you, but you need to establish some authority of your own. If you do it right, he'll understand who's the boss."

Lillie stared in the eyes of her pastor's wife trying to find a hint of a joke. Instead, she saw a stone cold glare that let her know this woman had been through some things. As they sat in silence, she made a mental comparison of the first lady's advice with what she'd learned from her mother over the years. A true Corven woman, Sophia would have told Lillie to leave Adam and don't worry about playing games because relationships weren't about manipulation. With such wisdom, she wondered if meeting with the first lady was a waste of time.

"You're an intelligent business woman, so you know exactly what I mean. As your first lady, my job is to pray for your soul. Woman to woman, though, I'd be remiss if I stopped at prayer or sat here and quoted a bunch of scriptures, don't you think? What you need right now is some practical advice."

"Practical advice is good, but there's more I should share with you." Lillie stirred her water with a straw.

"Adam and I—" Lillie tried to explain.

"Stop right there. I don't need to know all of your business. That's another thing, one day, you'll learn that less is more. What I do know is this—your sex life with Adam is between you, him, and God. But since you've started playing married, you're going to have to be woman enough to deal with married people issues." First Lady's tone had transitioned from sweet to firm.

"I—" Lillie started to speak and the first lady interrupted.

"Sweetie. It's not a fairy tale, but it's your story, so live it out. Since you've already opened the door and wouldn't close it even if I told you, use it to your advantage."

"That's sexual manipulation. Okay, this is totally different advice than I expected from you. I have to admit I'm challenged because I also heard your husband give Adam some . . . let's say . . . interesting advice."

"Think what you want, but know this—men who pretend to live by the Word don't deserve the benefits of a submissive wife. In public, you show the people what they want to see. At home, it's a different story. You can play the submissive role all you want, but it won't get you anywhere with a man of the cloth who hasn't been delivered, if you know what I mean."

Lady Abigail's gritty advice was just a little too "real" for Lillie's taste. Instead of challenging it, she simply shook her head in agreement.

"I've been a first lady longer than most people have even been saved. I've seen it all, and yes, I admit, I've done it all. Do you want to be with Adam or not?" Lady Abigail challenged Lillie on the spot.

"I do, but I don't want this to turn into a serious abusive situation," Lillie stated.

"Here's how you make sure Adam doesn't hit you ever again. Make him feel the pain. Ignore his calls for five days because five is the number of grace."

"So I'm going to grace him with my presence?"

"No. You're giving him grace by even answering his call."

Dang! First Lady is cut-throat!

"The sixth day is the day of man, so you know he'll be all in his flesh and you don't want him to seek out another woman. So when he calls, accept his invitation to come over. Play the coquettish role when he tries to kiss or touch you. Reluctantly, let him get you into bed then flip the script."

"Flip the script?"

"Well, yeah! Pull out your bag of tricks and give him a night he'll never forget. Whatever you do, don't stay the night. Leave like you're perplexed about what just happened and don't answer any of his calls or allow him in your home until you feel a breaking in your spirit."

"What if I never feel it?" Lillie asked.

"Que sara, sara. Whatever will be, will be." She laughed heartily. "In other words, he's not the guy for you."

Lillie left the restaurant with her head down. She appreciated First Lady taking the time to meet and share her brand of wisdom but she wanted to hear it from a man's perspective. Not in the mood for Theo's jealous antics or her father's weed induced philosophies, she decided to call her god brother instead.

"Hey, Lady Bug. It's good to hear from you, sis. What's going on in Coldhio?" Now that Alvin resided in Hawaii, he'd coined a new phrase to describe the unpredictable cold weather in Ohio. They casually chatted awhile then she jumped to her point.

"Let's say a girl hit her man and he hit her back. Should she leave him?"

"Now, you know I'm not a fan of domestic violence. Especially after watching that stupid man smack my mother around." Alvin's icy tone made Lillie shiver.

"Her husband?" Lillie screeched. She never knew him to be a violent man.

"No. The one she used to sneak around with. I tried to kill that bas—"

"Whoa, partner! Relax. Let's not relive the moment and mess up our energy."

"Our energy? You sound like Grace talking about energy frequencies and vortexes. Do you know she sent me some white ceremonial sage and frankincense? What's that for?"

Lillie chuckled because Grace had given them all the same "gift" when she learned about clearing your home of negative presences and increasing the positive energy vibrations.

"So, what should your imaginary friend do? She should keep her hands to herself, ditch his trifling behind then call her big brother. He'll hop on a plane and be there in less than a day to wreck a brother's world."

Lillie changed the subject and ended the call with Alvin reminding her he was just a plane ticket away. Despite Lady Abigail's advice, Lillie chose to go with Alvin's perspective. Over the next month she ignored Adam's communication attempts. She even attended the early service to avoid seeing him. To make matters worse, she decided to bar access to her place of employment, so each time he attempted to visit, the security officer kindly blocked his entrance. Unfortunately, Adam's tenacity circumvented her continued avoidance efforts. To Lillie's surprise, he attended the early service and cornered her in the hallway afterwards.

"Hey, babe. I've been missing you."

Adam reached to stroke Lillie's cheek, and she grabbed his arm with a force that even shocked her.

"I don't take kindly to a man putting his hands on me; especially you."

"You do know that you hit me first, right? What was I supposed to do? Just stand there and let you clown me?"

Lillie glared at Adam like he stole her Christmas presents. "That's no excuse, Adam and you know it."

"Okay, I see where this is going. I love you and I believe we can work this out. I've been talking to Pastor Andrews and he's helping me get to the root of my issues. I'm sorry for taking them out on you."

"Save it. Excuse me, please?" Lillie pushed her way through Adam's corner barricade.

Before he could respond, Lillie followed a crowd of people walking out the door. Knowing he wouldn't make a scene played out to her advantage. She did heed one part of First Lady's advice. Since Lillie didn't feel a break in her spirit Adam wouldn't be getting back in her good graces anytime soon.

TWENTY-THREE

T HEO HAD a knack for attracting wealthy clients of color to the firm. This time, he landed the opportunity to represent a family who owned several natural markets throughout the state. The larger farms were trying to put them out of business, and they knew Theo's desire to rid the world of genetically modified, pesticide filled food would drive him to secure a verdict in their favor. Winning this case would mean establishing himself as a formidable opponent in the Central Ohio legal landscape. To keep her mind off Adam, Lillie volunteered to provide thought leadership on the business end to assist him with his strategic approach.

Adam called five times as Lillie made her way to Theo's restored miniature mansion turned office in Olde Towne, a historic district near downtown Columbus. In its day, only the crème de le crème could afford a home like this. The neighborhood changed over the years and became a drug infested haven until up and coming buppies decided to gentrify the area. Theo and his partners were totally against this idea so they brought out all the property on the street and restored the homes to their original glory. They decided to focus on selling the property to successful people of color who wanted to live in communities with people who looked like them. The homes sold in no time and they reaped the benefits by keeping the money in the community. They petitioned to keep out trendy coffee shops and malls that the residents around the corner couldn't afford anyway.

Lillie barely missed running into Sharon, the young lady from the table group at Adam's singles gathering. Despite the near accident, she managed to balance a few boxes of Adriatico's pizza.

Why is she heading to Theo's office with our favorite pizza?

The delicious smell of homemade tomato sauce, fresh veggies, and unpasteurized cheese took Lillie's mind to another place where nostalgic memories of study nights flooded her psyche. She, Theo, Grace, and Masseri would gather on the top floor of the OSU student union with Adriatico's pizza and Masseri's fresh squeezed lemonade.

Lillie greeted Sharon and followed her to Theo's office where he typed frantically on his sleek silver laptop. Lillie couldn't help but notice the immaculate cherry wood desk as she took pride in Theo's prestigious accomplishments. With the exception of Masseri, they all came from the same middle class neighborhood, surrounded by successful people of color. This atmosphere opened the door for Lillie, Theo, and Grace to be successful entrepreneurs. Their client groups consisted of friends from high school and college, as well as some of their parent's friends.

Theo walked around his desk to greet his friends. Lillie almost peed her pants when Theo hugged Sharon first. For all the years they'd known one another, he never hugged another woman first in her presence. Green with an envy she didn't understand, Lillie jerked away when Theo finally decided to give her a hug.

Why am I tripping? He's not my man.

"Lillie, you remember Sharon from—"

"Yes. I remember her quite well. So what brings you here today, Sharon?" Lillie poured a cup of tea from the set on Theo's desk and took a sip. Chai, how nice.

"Girl, you know how it is. Gotta make sure my man gets his dinner."

Lillie choked on her tea as she stared at the couple in disbelief. Theo ran to her side and patted her on the back.

When Lillie recovered, she asked, "How long has this been going on?" She twisted her hair vigorously.

"Going on? What do you mean going on?" Sharon flipped her kinky hair and cocked her hips. The defensive stance caught Lillie off guard.

"Um . . . Lady Bug, stop twisting your hair like that. Don't make me call Lisa."

"You're deflecting." Lillie tapped her foot like she was channeling Gregory Hines.

Theo walked over to Sharon and put his arms around her shoulder. Then he slid down to sit next to her. "What Sharon meant to say is that we've decided to go out on a few dates and see where it goes." Theo stood up and planted his feet.

"Well dang! I know we're just dating, but don't make it sound like it's nothing."

Now that she has Theo, I guess she can stop taking bubble baths and lighting candles for Jesus like he's her man.

Lillie grunted and stuffed her mouth full of the thin crust pizza, pulling the cheese with her fingers. While Sharon fixed his plate, Lillie took off the Tiffany's bracelet Theo gave her for her last birthday and placed it on his desk. He shook his head as if he understood and put the bracelet in a box in his drawer. When his new love returned with his dinner, he shared the details of the case. Lillie reluctantly shared her thoughts from the business end. Once the conversation ended, Lillie decided to leave. She refused to watch Theo cuddle up with another woman. *A kooky Jesus is my boyfriend type at that.*

Lillie sulked the whole way home, realizing she'd lost a good man in Theo. Her godmother once told her the danger of the love game.

"Baby. Love is such a game. You don't know how much you want a man until you see him with someone else. Not just any old person, but a person who's comparable to or even better than you. We're fickle that way."

Aunt Diana's practical advice rang true for Lillie that night. She'd even dialed Theo's number a few times and hung up before the call connected. She wanted him badly, but didn't have enough nerve to say it. Plus, the whole Adam situation complicated the matter even more. Lillie knew that she hadn't closed that chapter in her life yet. No need to put Theo in the middle of all of her drama.

I guess I'll just have to get used to it.

Lillie arrived home to find the night air still warm. She lit some candles and lay out on her patio for a while to take her mind off Theo's new found love. Her mother helped decorate the patio with a "peace" theme so Lillie could have a serene place to escape from the rest of the world. They'd planted trees and beautiful plants for the sake of both beauty and privacy. The patio served as Lillie's home away from home, and tonight, serenity was in order. She put on some Zen music and lay on the reclining chair, while sipping on hot raspberry mint tea.

When Lillie heard footsteps outside of the gate she jumped out of her seat. She calmed down when a whiff of familiar cologne landed in her nostrils. Without even looking, she knew it was Adam. Lillie debated whether or not she should go in the house to avoid him. Before she could make a decision, Adam blessed her ears with the audible pleasure of his silky, smooth voice, serenading Lillie with one of her favorite songs. His passion united with the melody to lure her into his seductive spell. Perfect pitch flowed out of each note from Adam's throat, beckoning the inward parts of Lillie's soul to reconnect. As Adam's melody made love to her psyche, she longed for his touch. He opened the gate and made strides toward Lillie dropping deep pink rose petals with each step. Lillie's resolve broke down slowly, surely as he poured honey on her bare legs and licked it off with gentle flicks of his tongue. The familiar smell revealed that it was the same honey in her dreams. Then he bellowed out the chorus as a lone tear fell from his mesmerizing eyes.

"Never felt this way about your lovin' . . ." he crooned.

Adam bent down, swooped Lillie into his arms, and kissed her gently as he stroked her hair. The honey dripped from her legs and Adam rubbed it with his fingers, putting them in his mouth one by one. The sweet sticky substance dripped all over the bed of roses. She gasped with desire while he sang softly, making up his own sweet words to the song. Against her better judgment, Lillie returned Adam's affection, causing their love volcano to erupt with passion. She was his puppet and Adam knew just how to pull her strings. They made love on the bed of honey-laden roses as he sang sweetly in her ear.

To Lillie's surprise, she still didn't feel the "breaking" in her spirit that Lady Abigail mentioned during their lunch date. She knew she was treading on dangerous ground, but she couldn't deny the heat generating between her thighs. Was Adam a wolf in sheep's clothing or the love she'd waited for her entire life? As always, Lillie knew that time would reveal the true meaning of it all. So, she exhaled and continued to surrender love to her mate over and over and over again.

TWENTY-FOUR

IT'S FUNNY how time flies when a woman's life is full of chaos. After the sensual honey rose encounter, Lillie forgave Adam. She held on to the notion that their love would prevail, but lately, she began to wonder how she'd tangled herself in this sticky web of drama. Lillie jumped out of her seat when the shrill, ear-piercing ring of the phone interrupted her thoughts. Rosa typically answered the calls but Lillie's intuition took over so she grabbed the phone and greeted the caller.

Her world crumbled right before her eyes when she heard the operator say, "Collect call from the Franklin County Correctional Institute. To accept the charges, press one, otherwise, press two."

Who in the heck is calling me from the county jail on my office phone? Even though she asked herself that question, she knew the caller's identity in her heart of hearts. Reluctantly, she pressed one. Just as she thought, she heard Adam's voice.

"Adam, why are you calling me from jail?" she demanded.

After a pregnant pause, Adam directed, "We only have about fifteen minutes on this call, so listen carefully."

"What happened? Tell me everything and don't hold back one bit of information," Lillie commanded.

"It's a long story. Let's just say that my past has caught up with me."

"Your past?" Adam seemed to be full of surprises lately. This one, however, topped the cake.

"Okay, Lillie. I haven't been totally honest with you. This is embarrassing, but I'm not going to lose you over my pride."

Lillie rapped her manicured nails across the desk, as she waited to hear Adam's explanation.

"When I lived in Chillicothe, I had some domestic violence issues."

"Really, Adam . . . noooo!" Lillie jeered. "Remember, we broke up not too long ago because you thought you could put your hands on me."

Adam continued to tell his story. "So, Jonna and I . . ."

"Jonna? Why in the hell were you with Jonna?"

Adam didn't answer right away. When he finally spoke, he said, "She wanted to see the kids and you know, she'd been drinking and —"

"Drinking?" Lillie yelled, forgetting her location for a brief moment.

"Yeah. She's a full-fledged alcoholic now. I tried to talk to her about it and she wasn't hearing me so I told her she couldn't see the kids until she got it together and she flipped out."

"So you just had to restrain her, right? I'm sure you were the perfect role model in this situation." Lillie blasted Adam with a few more choice words then regained her composure when she remembered Rosa.

"Come on now. Let's not fight. I'm going to be here for quite some time, anywhere from thirty to ninety days; so please get the kids from school, and let them stay with you."

"Adam, I live in a two-bedroom condo, and you're asking me to bring four children to live there? You've got to be kidding me."

"You know I wouldn't ask if I really didn't need it. I'm in a bind," Adam cried. "Elaina isn't going to hold my job, either. That b—"

Without hesitation, Lillie shut down Adam's attempt to curse Elaina before he could finish.

"Now, you wait one minute. I won't have you cursing her on the collect call that I'm paying for. Elaina has a business to run. You going off to jail wasn't in her forecast, I'm sure."

Adam sighed then spoke with a new strategy.

"Remember that honey love? Don't you want more of that, baby?" This man had a way with words that could make a nun disavow her celibacy. Lillie moved back and forth in her seat as her libido rose to meet the occasion.

How can this stupid imbecile arouse me from a jail cell? Ugggghhhh!

"Let's do this; my visiting hours are every Tuesday and Thursday, ten A.M. to two P.M. I know you missed today's, so can you come on Thursday? I need to see you, baby. You give me hope."

Lillie got nervous just driving past a jail, let alone going inside one. Even though she boiled with anger, her heart broke at the thought of her man in that small cell. She wondered about the stories she'd heard. Were men really having sex with other men in jail?

I can't see Adam bending over for any man. She tried to shut out that thought. Jesus, please keep him.

"Lillie, when you come to visit, can you bring my magazines? They let us have those in here."

"Uh . . . yeah, sure, Adam. I'll come on the next visiting day."

"What about the kids? I wouldn't really trust them with anyone else." Adam's plea for his children broke Lillie's heart. Then, her godmother's words rang in her head.

"Love shouldn't be this complicated."

She played scenarios over and over in her mind while Adam talked about his dilemma. Caught up between love and reality, Lillie's ignored the well-traveled cautious route and instead took the more risky road.

"You have one more minute before your call ends," warned the recorded voice.

The recording overpowered Adam's words of love then the system ended the call. Lillie laid her head down on her desk and a river full of tears poured from her eye. She and Adam made love on this very same desk just last night.

This can't be happening.

Once she regained her composure, Lillie decided to search the online offender and municipal court databases to see just what kind of man she'd gotten involved with. She shivered as she keyed in his name and social security number in the criminal offenders site. Lillie held on to the sleek keyboard with an intense vise grip that would have choked the life out of any human. She watched the progress meter build on her screen while she waited for the result. The screen popped up and showed a number of cases against him from both of the mothers of his children and a name she didn't recognize, Tia Reyes.

Chills of fear collided with shards of anger and Lillie ran to the bathroom to vomit. As she hugged the toilet, the infamous night in the park flashed before her eyes and she wondered just how far Adam would have gone if Theo hadn't interfered. With a record like this, who knew what he was capable of doing.

But he did say she attacked him. And I hit him first, too.

⅜ ⅝

What a stinky place!

The line of people wrapped around the interior of the building three times as people waited to visit their loved ones in the county jail. The large entry room was full of women carrying crying babies, thugged out men with braids and sagging pants, shiesty attorneys, buff corrections officers, and an array of other interesting characters. Lillie couldn't believe she'd agreed to visit Adam in this seedy place. This was on top of the overabundance of collect calls she continued to accept from him.

Trying to keep his incarceration a secret was pointless. Somehow, all of her friends and family found out, so she'd been avoiding their calls. When Pastor Andrews found out about the situation, he suggested that Lillie take Bianca with her.

"No woman should be in a man's jail. You definitely can't go alone. As a minister, I can visit him anytime so I won't infringe upon your time. Bianca will gladly accompany you."

"I don't know how I always end up in these strange situations. I mean, prison ministry is not my thing." Bianca turned her nose up at the dirty baby sitting in the chair next to her. Lillie wondered when the mother had last changed the child. The ripe smell coming from his diaper told her it had been a long while.

"First of all, Bee, this is not a prison, it's a county jail. More like a workhouse."

"Oh, so now you've got the lingo down." Bianca raised her eyebrow to show her skepticism. "On another note, are you paying for his commissary too?" Rolling her eyes, Bianca's mocking remarks were beginning to make Lillie angry.

"I—" Lillie started to answer.

"Don't even answer the question. You need to maintain at least a shred of dignity." Bianca's judgmental sarcasm made Lillie regret bringing her.

Despite the sweet phone calls and letters, this county jail escapade taxed their relationship and Lillie's intense passion for Adam faded. Absence didn't make her heart grow fonder. Ironically, Theo called to check on Lillie more than usual. His dedication touched Lillie deep down in her soul. Bianca interrupted Lillie's thoughts with a smart comment.

"How does it feel to be an instant mommy to four little rug rats?"

A mother herself, Bianca found Lillie's dilemma entertaining. Lillie didn't dare return the sarcasm because Bianca had been a life-saver over the past few weeks. Since she couldn't tell any of her friends about Adam's drama, she'd depended on Bianca and Elaina to help her with the children. Thank goodness they both loved children because they were at Lillie's disposal when something happened to the children she didn't know how to handle.

"To be honest with you, Bee, I'm overwhelmed. That's why I'm praying they let him out early," Lillie admitted.

Bianca stopped her teasing and hugged Lillie. The tender moment provided an opportunity for Lillie to be vulnerable. Tears streamed down her face, and Bianca stroked her hair to help her relax.

"I talked to his mother about his situation," Lillie shared. "She's surprised his past is coming back to haunt him since he turned his life around."

Bianca sighed. "I'm just not sure why she didn't feel it was important to tell you about his past."

"She said that Adam is an adult, and she wanted to give him the opportunity to tell me everything." Lillie was just as confused as Bianca, but at the same time she respected Ms. Johnson's stance. "Now, she seems to be sharing more. For instance, she said that Adam's problem started when he witnessed his father's cold-blooded murder."

"What?" Bianca shouted in shock.

Lillie shared the gruesome details of Pastor Johnson's murder with Bianca. Her mouth dropped wide open and she shook her head in disbelief.

"Despite his issues, he was able to graduate from college and preach down at Pastor Green's church in Chillicothe. You know, New Bethel."

"Yeah, I've seen Adam preach when he was down there. I can't imagine watching my father be killed by his mistress. Adam was probably confused out of his mind."

"Yeah. After his father died, he started to change. During his teen and college years, he drank alcohol to cope. So of course, that led to other issues. He spent some time in jail, which led him to make some changes. Pastor Green and his mother stood by him all the way."

Bianca grabbed Lillie's hands and said, "Now that you know the truth, what are your plans?"

Lillie paused, took a deep breath, and responded. "I don't know, Bee. This time away is helping me sort through my feelings for him."

"Sis, I know this is hard on you. I still don't like you in this situation; however, I'm here for you, no matter what. Missing your man is a painful experience that no one should have to go through alone, especially under these circumstances."

Missing Adam was only half of the issue. His children, as much as she loved them, were driving her crazy. They were sweet enough, yet juggling their schedules, paying for daycare, lunches, and all the food they consumed was getting to be a bit much. That didn't include the extra household supplies, toys, and games she'd purchased to keep them occupied. Adam's mother helped as much as they could. Even still, four children in her home was an overwhelming experience. CoCo was also not taking kindly to the situation. She used to love Adam's children, but things changed when they moved in. The boys terrorized her whenever they had a chance. Of course, the space invasion caused CoCo to bark more than ever. She even bit one of the children when he tried to chase her around the house.

Elaina had not only fired Adam, she didn't hold back her feelings. During her last visit, she had a heart-to-heart conversation with Lillie. As Lillie waited for her turn in line with the rest of the visitors, she reflected on what Elaina had shared, while nervously twisting her hair.

"So, how are things going with you and Adam?"

"Things couldn't be better," Lillie exclaimed. "He's such a wonderful man and we're so in love."

"Love?" Elaina's voice increased a few octaves as she challenged Lillie. "You mean magnified lust, right? Love's not the same thing as lust. If you've never been in love for real, you don't know the difference."

Lillie gasped in disbelief. With a grunt of irritation, Elaina pressed an extra firm crease in Aliyah's pants.

"I can't believe you said that. We do love each other and, for your information, we're not having sex."

"Umph! I'll just let you figure that out for yourself." Elaina flashed Lillie a motherly smile.

"And about this sex thing, I was born at night, but I wasn't born last night. Girl, I can tell you the day it happened."

Lillie cheeks were beet red and she stared at the ground refusing to make eye contact with Elaina.

"Don't feel bad; he had me fooled, too. I hired him because he was clean cut and seemingly holy. Especially since he was Pastor Alvin Johnson's son."

"He didn't fool you. He's the man you thought he was. You'll see. In fact, we're talking about marriage."

"I want to point out that there's still no ring on your finger. All these promises and he still hasn't come through."

Lillie's wait was finally over. A county jail staff member escorted her to a cubicle with a glass partition. She sat on one side and Adam on the other. He smile beamed from ear to ear when he saw her.

"Adam," Lillie exclaimed, excited to see him.

Normally, Adam's very presence aroused Lillie. Seeing him in this state did just the opposite. Typically clean-shaven with a fresh haircut, she hardly recognized this wooly mammoth.

"You're a site for sore eyes, and I miss you like crazy," Adam said as he locked his eyes on her with a mixture of seduction and longing.

Unfortunately, she couldn't say the same to him. Lillie wondered if this was the "jail talk" Theo had warned her about. He said men in jail say anything to tickle the ears of the ones who pay for their commissaries. Lillie wondered if that was true. Guarded, she decided to keep the conversation focused on good reports and the well-being of the children. Naturally, he was sad he couldn't see them because Lillie had made an executive decision about their visitation. She concluded they shouldn't see their father in a place like this.

Instead of wasting their time fighting about the children not coming, Adam shared a few updates with Lillie. He'd started a Bible study group in jail. So far, there were fifty faithful attendees, and ten inmates had given their lives to Christ. The converted inmates were already witnessing, so Adam expected to see additional new believers as a result. The pastoral call on his life made Adam operate in this manner, no matter what the circumstances were. Despite the complex situation, Adam seemed excited about the opportunity to minister. To Lillie's dismay, the visit was over just as quickly as it began. The couple said their goodbyes, and she walked into the lobby. As soon as she entered, she heard a woman screaming at the intake officer.

"What do you mean I can't see him? He already had a visitor?"

"Ma'am, our inmates are only allowed to have one visitor per day. Unless you're his lawyer or clergy, you can't see him. Remember, you can come back on Thursday, the next time visitations are allowed," the intake officer retorted.

Lillie walked over to the vending machine to get a bottled water. While she inserted her cash, she continued to listen to the juicy confrontation at the intake desk.

"I'm his wife! I can't believe this . . ." Storming away from the intake desk in a frenzy, the woman bumped into Lillie.

"Get out of my way!"

Oh, no she didn't. She's lucky I know Jesus, Lillie thought.

She was ready to "touch and agree" with this woman in a bout of "heated fellowship" until she noticed the deep-seated pain in the woman's eyes. Lillie's heart went out to her, despite what had just occurred. Without hesitation, Lillie decided to minister to her.

"Excuse me, can I help you?" Lillie asked with concern.

"No! Obviously, no one in this place can help me. At least you got to see your man or whoever you came to visit," the woman said with envy in her tone.

Compelled to help this woman, Lillie continued to speak with her. Bianca joined her, and as they walked outside, Lillie invited the woman to walk with them. "My name is Lillie Corven, and this is my friend, Bianca. And you are?"

"Tia Reyes-Johnson," she said proudly.

Johnson? Why does her name sound so familiar?

"Really? My boyfriend's last name is Johnson," Lillie responded, wanting to know more now.

"Yeah, it's my married name. My husband and I have been apart for quite some time; so when I found out he was here, I thought it was for the best to at least try to visit him." Bianca arched her one eyebrow, then rolled her eyes.

"I hear you. My boyfriend is here, so I'm in a similar situation. The Lord is helping me get through it, though. By the way, what church do you attend?"

"Right now, I'm attending Bedside Baptist with Deacon Drapes and Pastor Pillow."

The three women laughed loudly as they walked to the parking lot.

"Hey, that sounds like a great church. I know you're getting fed the Word there, right?" Lillie joked. "My mentor tells me that in times of pandemonium, sometimes the Lord is trying to get our attention."

"Yeah. I bet he is. I haven't paid him any attention at all since my marriage failed. I put everything into it, but my husband was a preacher with drama, and nothing has changed. He played the part with such precision no one believes how he contributed to the failure of our marriage. They think it's all me." Tia breathed deeply and scrunched her face to hold back tears. "To make matters worse, I'm hearing that he's moved on with some other woman from his church."

"Oh, wow! I'm sorry to hear that."

"It's probably for the best. That man took me through so much. You know how that can be, girl." She smiled.

"Um . . . unfortunately, yes, I do. That's why I'm here right now. I believe God can change them if we just keep praying." Lillie tried to offer a word of encouragement to Tia and herself at the same time. She took a drink of the ice-cold water she'd been holding.

"Girl, I can tell you love Jesus. Because if you knew Adam Johnson, I'm not sure you'd be saying those words."

Lillie convulsed as she spit water all of Tia. Then everything went black.

TWENTY-FIVE

Y ou can't leave me at a time like this. I need you," Adam begged and Lillie let out an exasperated sigh.

"Yeah, right. You should have thought of that before you began this stream of lies."

"I told you, we're getting a divorce, so there was no reason to mention that to you. What else does it take for you to understand my heart belongs to you?"

Lillie was appalled at the fact that Adam was making excuses for not revealing his true marital status. Now it made sense that he delayed putting a ring on her finger. Didn't he understand this type of behavior was unacceptable, no matter what the circumstances may be?

"Whatever! Go beg your wife for help and leave me the hell alone."

"I can't believe you're cussing at me." Adam screeched in shock. "What's gotten into you?"

Even Lillie couldn't believe the words that flowed so freely from her mouth. Cursing wasn't typically part of her vocabulary, but today, she couldn't hold back.

"Better yet, what's gotten out of me? YOU! I'm getting you out of my system as we speak. In fact, don't bother calling me ever again," Lillie yelled with a fury Adam had never heard from her before.

"You have to have faith in me, babe. You can't abandon me now."

Lillie thanked God when the recording came on telling them they only had a few minutes left on the call and the system ended the call. She couldn't believe the level of manipulation he tried just to get his way.

What a jerk!

Lillie took a few deep breaths and plopped on her bed. She burst into tears while she punched the pillow and kicked at the air. Distraught over Adam's deception, she cried and cried until there were no more tears. Suddenly, a feeling of extreme exhaustion snuck up on Lillie, causing her to go into a state of drowsiness. Before she knew it, she fell fast asleep.

Hours later, Lillie woke up feeling just as bad as she did prior to the nap. She looked at her caller ID and noticed that Adam tried to call collect several times. Impulsively, she called the phone company and added a collect call block to her phone. Now, there was one more thing to do. She called Adam's mother to discuss the children because in reality, they should be with legal family, not Lillie.

"Hi, Ms. Johnson. I want to get right to the point."

"Lillie, you don't have to say a word. I already knew in my spirit that you wouldn't be staying with Adam. You can bring my grandchildren anytime." Ms. Johnson was definitely a woman of God with strong discernment. Lillie was actually glad she didn't have to figure out the words to share the news.

"Thank you, Ms. Johnson. They're with Elaina and her grandchildren right now. Can I bring them tomorrow morning?" Lillie asked.

"Sure, baby. Come on. I'll have breakfast ready when you get here." Ms. Johnson and Lillie both paused for a moment and silence did the heavy lifting. "Do me one big favor. Don't tell the children what's going on. Let them think they are coming to visit me, and I'll break the news to them. This isn't your battle, and I won't make you fight it."

This woman never ceased to amaze Lillie. No matter how awkward their initial interactions had been, she'd changed so much and opened up to Lillie over the past few months. She and Ms. Johnson said their goodbyes, and Lillie called Grace.

"Hey, sis. What's up?" Grace greeted Lillie.

"Grace, I really could use your help . . . if you have the time. I need to pack up Adam's children and take them to his mother tomorrow morning. Your SUV will come in handy. Can I borrow it?"

"I knew it! This morning, I did your natal chart and I heard the creator speak clearly to me about the end of your situation."

"How in the heck can you do my natal chart without my permission? And how did you find out what time I was born? You know what... Forget it! What about the SUV?"

"Not only can you borrow it, but Masseri, Theo, and I will be right over to help you with the packing. You won't have enough room for everyone if we go, so we'll bring Theo's truck, too. I'm assuming you finally came to your senses and dumped Adam," Grace teased.

"Yes, I dumped Adam and I never lost my sense. I just want to get these little people out of my house, and I don't want to talk about it anymore, okay?" Lillie snapped. Grace burst out laughing and said, "Aye, aye, Captain. We're on our way."

Thirty minutes later, the trio walked in with boxes and tape. Lillie called Elaina to explain what was going on. She volunteered to keep the children overnight, then pack them in her minivan to bring over in the morning. Like the others, she was happy to help Lillie end the flaky relationship. Theo didn't say one word to Lillie as he helped with the packing. Once they filled and sealed all of the boxes, he placed them in Grace's SUV.

The next morning, when Elaina arrived with the children, the crew caravanned to Chillicothe. When they arrived at Ms.

Johnson's house, she met them at the door and invited them in for breakfast. Lillie's three friends were reluctant because of their strict eating habits. Knowing how awkward the situation was, Ms. Johnson cajoled then with buckwheat pancakes and real maple syrup. They practically knocked Lillie down to get in the door.

After breakfast, Ms. Johnson asked to talk with Lillie in the sunroom. Lillie couldn't help but notice how the lush green plants and the beautiful fountains brought a calming peace to the place. She was pleased to feel the warmth of the plush white cushion when they sat down on a wicker sofa. Ms. Johnson reached for the photo album on the matching coffee table and handed it to Lillie. When she opened the album, Lillie was amazed to see a man who looked just like Adam, but older. He was handsome and dressed to the nine standing behind the pulpit of an old country church.

"Before you and your friends get on the road, I want to commend you for your attempt to maintain a relationship with Adam, despite the circumstances."

"Thank you, Ms. Johnson. You don't know how much that means to me."

"Adam's a lot like his father, you know. After he was murdered, I found out that he had several mistresses. In fact, one of them was my armor bearer. Can you believe that?"

"Not at all. It was hard to believe that a man of the cloth could be so promiscuous. Then passed it on to his son through a generational curse."

Lillie sobbed vehemently, and Ms. Johnson rocked her in her arms as if she was her own child.

"Baby, it hurts me that my son caused you so much pain." Ms. Johnson's words soothed Lillie's soul.

"It's not all Adam's fault. I'm owning up to my responsibility in this situation," Lillie admitted.

"That's what I like about you. My son will be sorry he ruined this relationship, for sure." Ms. Johnson spoke with firm surety as she wiped the tears from Lillie's eyes.

"Let's get back to your friends. I know they have other things to do and I don't want to hold them up."

Lillie went to the bathroom to wash her face and then met her friends in the kitchen where they were finishing the dishes.

"Oh! Thanks so much for cleaning the kitchen," Ms. Johnson exclaimed.

"You're welcome, Ms. Johnson," Theo responded.

"We appreciate your hospitality. It's the least we could do to repay you," Grace said.

"The food was delicious, Ms. Johnson." Masseri's expression matched her words.

Ms. Johnson hugged each of them and they said their goodbyes to the children. The quartet made an exit and headed back to Columbus. The trip home seemed much longer than usual. Lillie held back tears for most of the ride. Even though the pain in her heart felt like it would never go away, she refused to let this situation bring her down. She'd gained an appreciation of prayer from this relationship so instead of sulking, she prayed for herself. She asked the Lord to heal her heart and take the pain away. The comfort of the prayer lulled her to a peaceful sleep.

⁚ ⁝

Once they got off the road, Lillie's three friends stayed for a while to comfort her. Bianca and Lisa drove over to join the crew. Grace walked through the place with her white ceremonial sage. She swore the house needed to be smudged and cleared of negative energies. She diffused some frankincense essential oil after she completed her ritual. Elaina's Christian principals wouldn't allow this to happen so she followed closely behind Grace with prayers and anointing oil. Lillie hated to admit it, but she felt positive vibrations and a spirit of peace permeate her household. To get it back to normal, she'd have to repaint and clean her carpets. Lillie spent the next few months doing just that.

From time to time, she wondered how Adam and his wife were doing. Had they decided to reconcile or were they moving on to greener pastures? Out of respect, Lillie didn't reveal her identity to Tia at the county jail. Adam wrote letter after letter, apologizing to Lillie and making lame excuses for his neglect of the truth—: his father's death, pressures of the ministry, and seeking all the wrong solutions. For some unexplainable reason, despite her anger, Lillie still had feelings for Adam and she really missed him.

Grace, Masseri, Elaina, Bianca, and Lisa came over almost every day to check on Lillie. When Lillie cried about the break up, Masseri said, "Don't let that man get you down. Come on to my Brazilian funk class so you can work it out." Grace gave Masseri a high five.

"Or you could try kickboxing and pretend that you're kicking Adam in his—" Grace started.

"Stop it, Grace! You can be so insensitive at times. That isn't what I need to be doing or even thinking about," Lillie scolded. She also didn't want to reveal how much she missed him.

"Say what you want, but it does release stress and tension. I can't help it if imagining someone's face helps in the process." Grace shook her head as if she'd done this before.

"Lillie, I know this has been a crazy time for you. You've done nothing but go to work and the salon. You need to get out," Masseri said firmly.

"We're going to Flow tonight for Ladies Only Flow. Elaina let me and Grace plan the event so we're celebrating all aspects of womanhood to include health, wellness, relationships, the beauty of our moon cycles, resolved infertility, unassisted births, breast-feeding, and just being a woman."

"Oh wow. That's quite amazing. Will men be there?"

"Yes. Originally, we didn't want to include them but Grace decided that men are an integral part of the female experience so we'll do this event with men and the next one will be for women only."

"You know you want to come," Grace encouraged and teased at the same time. "With all this Adam drama, I bet you've written some great stuff. Maybe sharing it will help you feel better."

Lillie thought about Grace and Masseri's proposition. Lisa had mentioned the event to her earlier that week, since she and her husband, James, planned to be there. He was bringing some brothers from his motorcycle club that he ran for saved bikers. The club was so successful, even unsaved bikers who didn't want to deal with the other clubs frequented his spot. Lisa enjoyed playing matchmaker and felt that one of the guys would be a great distraction for Lillie.

"Theo is coming to pick me up at seven. Do you want a ride?" Grace asked. To Lillie's surprise, she felt a twinge of jealousy. Even though she'd made her decision about a romantic relationship with Theo, it still bothered her that he was dating Sharon. She wished them the best, yet deep in her heart, she was hoping that the relationship would fail.

"I still can't believe he's dating the 'Jesus is my boyfriend' chick," Lillie pouted.

"Really? Why should she let a perfectly good man go to waste." Grace tried to give Masseri a high five, but Masseri rolled her eyes.

"Yeah, some women need a man to validate their femininity. Not my style," Masseri said as she stared daggers at Grace. The tension suddenly became unbearably thick.

"I'll drive myself to Flow," Lillie said as her friends made their exit.

Something wasn't right with those two. She'd been so busy dealing with Adam and his issues Lillie had overlooked just how strange their relationship had become. She'd have to make a point to keep her eyes open. Her ultimate goal in this situation was to protect Theo and she would do whatever it took to make that happen.

Lillie plunked down on the plush Victorian single end show frame sofa in middle of her bathroom. The mere size of the condo attracted her from day one and she never regretted making the purchase. Having enough space for furniture in this room was a rare find these days. She kicked back to relax before getting dressed for Flow and began drifting off to sleep. Reality beckoned her back with a heinous growl out of nowhere.

GRRRRRRRR!

What is that?

Of course that deep-seated growl couldn't have possibly come from CoCo Chanel. Lillie jerked her head from one direction to another seeking out the source of the eerie disturbance.

GRRRRRRRR!

Lillie closed her eyes and began to pray.

"Lord, if you're real, let me see what's growling at me. Pleeeeaaaasssse?"

She peaked slowly through one eye and then the other. The hideous site before her unfolded into a nightmarish ghoul surrounded by ethereal clouds. She jolted in the air as a high-pitched squeal escaped from the bottom of her throat. Lillie lifted her legs and tried to run for cover but a magnetic force literally glued her to the sofa. The clouds disintegrated and a giant dark bird-like creature appeared before her in all its demonic glory. It had to be at least eight feet tall. Even Lillie's high ceilings were no match for its evil presence. Prickly little goose bumps invaded Lillie's arms. She wanted to scream but for some strange reason, her voice abandoned its abode. The horrendous beast flailed his gigantic black webbed wings infusing a spirit of terror throughout the room. It reached out to grab her with the arm extensions that protruded from its weaved appendages. She kicked at the monstrosity only to find that her feet went straight through its body.

Once she found her voice, Lillie wailed, "Somebody help me please!" over and over again at the top of her lungs. She closed her eyes to avoid seeing the gargantuan's taunts. Just when she couldn't take it anymore, she heard Grace's voice.

"Lillie, are you okay? Why are you in here causing all this ruckus?"

"I don't know what's going on, Grace."

Grace tried to turn the doorknob to no avail. She continued to rattle it and Lillie hoped she could get in to rescue her from this nightmare.

"I'm armed, " she screamed out.

Lillie wondered why she screamed that statement, then she remembered when Grace obtained her concealed carry license, she'd learned the requirement of informing the intruder. Red eyes pierced Lillie's inner being as the beast tried to lock in control of her mind. Lillie fought in the spirit realm by praying in tongues.

"Why are you in there speaking in tongues? Jesus, the angels, and the ancestors would have intervened by now if he wanted to. They must have better things to do. I guess that's why I'm here."

Grace kicked the door four times in an effort to tear it down. No luck. Lillie peeled herself from the imaginary glue on the seat and slid between the creature's legs to escape. She opened the door to Grace's gun pointing right at her face. Thank goodness Grace hesitated before pulling the trigger. It gave Lillie just enough time to duck and watch her decorative vase smash to pieces and the bullet permeate the back wall. Lillie's scream alerted Grace to her presence. The growling stopped and when Lillie turned back around, the room looked normal.

"Did you hear that? The growling stopped."

"What growling?"

Seconds later, the shrill ringing of the phone woke Lillie out of a sleep she didn't even remember falling into. She ignored the phone and immediately dropped to her knees to pray.

TWENTY-SIX

A S USUAL, Flow was packed to the hilt. Lillie made her way through the crowd to Bianca's table. Still a little shaken from the crazy nightmare, the familiar presence calmed Lillie's spirit.

"What's up, Bee? It's so good to see you." Bianca was fiery and spunky with her spiked hair and long sundress. She had on makeup tonight, which was rare.

"Now that you're not all booed up with Adam, we get to see you." Bianca smiled as she gently punched Lillie in the arm.

"Girl, slang does not become you. 'Booed up.' You're hilarious." Lillie sat down next to Bianca.

"Lillie, I've been meaning to talk to you. I need your help," Bianca said.

"Okay, what's going on?" Lillie wasn't sure how to handle this situation because Bianca rarely asked for help. This had to be something major. Glad to stop talking about her soap opera life, she welcomed listening to Bianca's problem.

"Oh heck, Here's the deal. My marriage is failing." Bianca held her head high in an attempt to appear to be confident. Unfortunately, Lillie knew her all too well, and it wasn't working.

"Failing? You and Todd make the perfect couple. I know he was laid off for a while, but now he's back in action, right?" Lillie asked.

"That's just it. This layoff took a toll on his mental state. He's gained weight and he's perpetually negative. I can't take it anymore."

"That can be overwhelming, Bee. You still love him, right?"

"He's my high school sweetheart. I'll always love him. I took things too far, though." Bianca paused, holding back tears. "I need you not to judge me for what I'm about to share with you," Bianca said with caution. Even though Bianca was judgmental at the county jail, Lillie decided not to return the attitude.

"Okay. Do we need to pinky swear?" Lillie asked, trying to lighten the mood.

Bianca burst out laughing and said, "No pinky swear necessary. Here's what I'm dealing with, though. I've been sleeping with an old friend from college, and I feel like crap."

Stunned by Bianca's revelation, she blurted out, "Whew! I thought you were having an affair with Pastor Andrews."

"Huh? Who does that?"

"Well, apparently not you."

"Yeah, he's so not my type."

Embarrassed by the information she'd just shared, she decided to change the subject.

"So does Todd know?"

"Todd? You see that's part of the problem. He knows I'm having an affair, he just doesn't know with who and I don't plan to tell him, either," Bianca said assuredly.

"Bee, this isn't a judgment, it's what I know, and I wouldn't be a true friend if I didn't say it. You have to break off this affair. I'm sure this guy is a big boy, and trust me when I say this. He'll be fine," Lillie tossed her hair to the side.

"I'm embarrassed to say this, but, Lillie, I can't. Every time I try, he does this one things to me, and—"

"Hey, hey, hey! That's TMI! Too much information." Lillie was appalled at Bianca's revelation. "Bee, I hope you know what you're doing."

Their conversation was interrupted, as Lisa and James, approached the table with the guy they wanted Lillie to meet.

"Hey, Lillie and Bianca." The group exchanged hugs and sat down.

"Lillie Corven, I'd like you to meet Garrett Carter," James said. "He's one of the brothers from the motorcycle club." Garrett stepped forward to shake Lillie's hand. His smooth chocolate skin complimented his shiny white teeth. He must have ridden his bike because he had on leather chaps. His trimmed goatee added pizzazz to his stocky stature and wavy hair. Garrett was someone worth checking out. A yummy man riding a motorcycle was just the distraction Lillie needed to take her mind off her problems. Lisa shared that he owned a profitable motorcycle repair shop on the east side, so he was a man of his own means who could provide for a family when the time came.

Bianca stood up and said, "Hi, Garrett. I'm Bianca." He shook her hand politely.

"Why don't you all have a seat," Lillie suggested. Lisa made sure that Garrett sat right next to Lillie. Right at that moment, Elaina announced Lillie as the next artist. She excused herself and walked to the stage.

Lillie adjusted the mic, took a deep breath, and began to read her poem.

The Brink of Insanity

The brink of insanity closes in quickly
Negative spirits try to control my thoughts
Driving me crazy trying to steal my joy
Joy they don't even own or know how to get

As I try to find peace in the midst of this chaos
They try to infuse my mind with negativity
Minions try to grasp hold of my soul and break me
I fight, I scream, I holler, I cry out
I climb to the top to escape their pinching claws
Backbiting crabs keep trying to pull me back down
Misery loves company and they don't want me to go
I rebuke them, resist them, shun them, smack them
They spit at me, hit at me, yell at me, curse at me
Saying, "You don't have what it takes to make it,
Serving a weak God who let us terrorize you.
You're a meaningless statistic with no power
We bought you. We own you. Resistance is futile."
I kick and scratch at their words and accusations
Making my way out of the slimy barrel of haters
They try to zap my energy and steal my dreams
Pushing me towards the Devil's flaming fire
Trying to consume me, rule me, take over my soul
I refuse to burn in the enemy's lair
So, I take it all back and own my destiny
The enemy can't impede my progress at all
No matter how he tries to run his conspiracy game
I'm liberated. I'm free. All I do is win
This is how I know that . . .
The brink of insanity will never do me in

The audience roared and rendered thunderous applause and Lillie's spirit overflowed with good vibrations. She hadn't read in a long time, and it felt good to be back in the game. Garrett waited patiently at the edge of the stage and escorted her as she descended. The walked hand in hand back to their seats.

What a gentleman!

"I'm impressed with your poetic expression. Girl, you can flow. Your words. They are quite . . . soulful." Garrett complimented Lillie on her performance.

"Thanks. You seem to know a little something-something about poetry."

"Yeah, I know a little something. Don't let the motorcycle fool you." Garrett winked his eye and Lillie giggled as she brushed her hand across her rosy cheeks.

"So tell me about Lillie Corven. Who are you in the big scheme of the cosmos?" Garrett requested as he smiled, showing off his dimples. Lillie couldn't help but wonder if he'd be a better match for Grace. His free spirit and love of the universal soul aligned with her friend's perspective on life. He might not be her soul mate, but he could truly pass for her twin flame.

They talked for a while, until the next artist came to the stage. He even ordered her favorite tea, which let her know that Lisa had been filling him in. Grace and Masseri gave her high fives and thumbs up signs from their table on the other side of the room. Theo on the other hand, avoided eye contact. His dedication encouraged Lillie and gave her hope that not all men were jerks. As much as she wanted to grab Theo and kiss him, he was Sharon's man now and she had to respect that. Garrett definitely made a good substitute for her sorrow.

No Theo. No Adam. Welcome Garrett!

Garrett, Lisa, and James rose to leave, as they had to get back to James's club for a party.

"Lillie, you should go with us," Lisa urged. "You know you need to have some fun tonight."

"I'm already having fun, Lisa," Lillie responded.

"No doubt, but you'll have even more fun watching a bunch of bikers do line dances and drink Kombucha," James teased. "Nobody parties like us, Lillie and you know it. Come on, girl. You can keep Garrett here company." James playfully punched her in the arm.

"I'd love to be in your company, Melancholy Poet." Garrett asked, still showing off those handsome dimples. Lillie swooned at his nickname.

"I'd like that." They followed Lisa and James locked arm in arm.

The Queen's Blues

My love left me last week and I am drowning in my lack of sleep
Why would he leave a godly queen like me?
His heart, I treasured, so much that nothing could measure up . . . to him
Putting him first caused me to put myself last
With God somewhere in between, slowly, losing my identity
Making a sista want to holla and scream and throw up my hands in frustration
Face dripping with perspiration
Because I slipped up and went outside with no deodorant
Got himself another queen, tall, thin, and lean
Just the opposite of me, so let me see
Was I not good enough for him?
Not small enough?
Not tall enough?
Not smart enough?
Not pretty enough?
Treated him like a king so why did he leave this queen?
Was it because I didn't put out?
Shoot! I was waiting for this brother to marry me
Guess he missed having beautiful brown babies with me
No more collard greens
No more fried chicken dinners cooked with lots of love
Glad I kept my eye on the prize,
Focused on the God above
I thank him in advance for bringing me a real king
A man who gets that he should write me love letters
And send flowers and candy
And simply love on me, a godly queen!

The audience roared as they snapped their fingers when the young lady closed her piece. Her passion was undeniable, and her pain quite evident. In spite of all her heartache, she used her poetic ability as a form of expression. Elaina hugged the young woman and they shed a few tears as she began to pray. Almost every person in the building circled around her and joined in. Lillie could feel the charge in the atmosphere. A train of glory manifested itself like a thick cloud all over Flow. Those who weren't praying stood in awe.

Lillie wished Garrett had been able to make it out tonight. It had been two months since they had met. They spent countless hours together and he even accompanied her to the HR Talent Showcase banquet where she was presented with the Human Resources Innovator of the Year award. She'd started hanging out with him at James' biker club. No matter how hard she tried, she just couldn't shake thoughts of Theo nor Adam. Garrett was a wonderful man but he couldn't hold a candle to the two loves of her life. Since neither of the two were an option, Garrett would suffice.

Once the prayer ended, Elaina pulled Lillie onto the stage with the young lady, and she sang a prophetic song to both women. Then she spoke edifying words of encouragement.

"God has not forgotten you. He's removing each and every distraction from your life. As you continue to release your heart and pain unto him, revelation will open up to you. As you cry each tear, your drink offering is received by the Lord. Each one of your tears is stored in a vial in Heaven. Even now, the Lord is pouring your tears on the pages of his book. As the tears are poured out, words appear on the pages. The Lord not only hears your cries, he records them in his book and sends angels to answer on his behalf. Even as you stand before me, angels are all around you, ready to watch out for you. So rise, warrior woman of God. Rise up, mount up, and fly like an eagle. You're about to soar to altitudes where everyone can't go. So spread your wings and fly."

This charismatic ministry catapulted Lillie into a phase of forgiveness and healing. She fell to her knees and worshipped the Lord like never before. But Elaina wasn't through with her. She bent down next to Lillie and whispered, "Beloved, you've sought the Lord and he's heard your cry. He says, 'Guilt and shame are not your friends. I am that I am!' Soon, the Lord is going to test you with a major decision. Don't be led astray. Seek the Lord, and he'll direct your path."

With all she'd been through, Lillie couldn't imagine facing yet another decision. Not able to stop crying, Lillie went to the rest-room to recover. As she made her way, she could've sworn that she'd seen Adam sitting with the sound crew, but he hadn't been release from jail yet. Lillie washed her face, refreshed her make-up, and returned to her seat.

Just as she waved the waiter down to order a cup of Oolong tea, Adam set a steaming cup on her table.

Oh, my goodness. What is he doing here?

Without saying a word, he caressed Lillie's cheek and smiled. For a few seconds, Lillie melted, then she remembered she hated him. She rolled her eyes and snatched away from his touch. Adam chuckled as he turned to walk on the stage, pulling out a piece of paper from his pocket. This was odd since he'd always flowed straight from the heart in the past.

"As many of you know, I was recently incarcerated." The crowd started mumbling and whispering. "Don't worry. The Lord dealt with me during that time and showed me the purpose of my time away. While I was there, I started a Bible Study. Over two hundred inmates at the workhouse gave their lives to Christ. Some of them have been released and are attending Radical Faith right now." The audience clapped for Adam. "I also was able to work with the warden to negotiate some educational opportunities for the inmates." They clapped again. "During this time, a special person sent this poem to me." Many of the patrons turned to gaze at Lillie. "So tonight, I want to dedicate this to her. She knows who she is, and obviously, so do most of you."

Manifestation of My Dreams

The state of my dreams became the state of my reality
The moment you waltzed into my life with a cup of Oolong tea
A spoonful of honey was all the sweetness I needed

The manifestation of my dreams
Your natural flavor completes me
No need to fantasize about your twin flame
I'm your helpmeet, the right one
Even though you're not present in my space
I feel your spirit is here with me each day
You're my second thought when I awake
No offense, Jesus is my first
And my second to the last thought after my prayers each night
The unique quality of our love will transcend the test of time
Eventual wedded bliss is the splendor of our plan
Now that you're here, I can see you, feel you, touch you, and love you
I see beauty when I look into your eyes
Thank you, Lord, for bringing her to me
Because she's the manifestation of my dreams

The crowd applauded and Adam bowed. Overwhelmed with erotic intensity, all the feelings Lillie had for him flooded her psyche. He joined Lillie at her table where she sipped her tea. She played the coquettish role and said, "So Adam, I know you didn't think you could bring me some raggedy tea and read my poem to get back in my life."

Adam beamed his pearly whites and Lillie fought the effects of his mesmerizing smile.

"Lillie, you stopped answering my calls, yet you never officially broke up with me; so I thought we were still a couple."

Oh, no he didn't! What would make him think I'd want to be with a married man?

Lillie gritted her teeth, ready to give Adam the verbal beat down he deserved until she remembered they were in public.

"You're not exactly free to be my man; so I didn't have to call it off. I don't date married men. I can't marry someone who's already taken, right?" Lillie smirked.

"You'll be happy to know that Tia brought divorce papers to me to sign before I ever met you." Lillie rolled her eyes and rose from her seat to leave. Adam buried his head in his hands. His apparent state of despair attracted attention because many of the patrons watched and whispered.

"Dang, Lillie. Give me a chance to explain. She had me sign the papers over a year ago. Can you believe she never filed them?" Lillie stared at Adam in amazement. "She promised to file them this time around. If things go my way, you should see the divorce announcement in the newspaper soon."

"I still don't understand why you didn't tell me you were married, previously married, married because papers weren't filed, or whatever the case may be." Lillie's voice screeched above the music and more patrons turned in her direction.

"Lillie, can we go somewhere private?"

"No. I don't want to go anywhere with you. Plus, I came here to have a good time and that's what I plan to do."

Adam continued to sit at the table with Lillie as they enjoyed the readings. For some reason, between sets, he decided to bare his heart. He shared that his landlord evicted him from the rental home during his incarceration, so he was staying with one of the deacon's from the church. Lillie kindly let him knew that she wasn't the least bit interested in his supposed plight. Frustrated with the conversation, he excused himself. Unfortunately, Lillie knew his departure was only temporary. She knew it would only be a matter of time before he sought out her company again.

TWENTY-SEVEN

WHEN LILLie arrived home, she felt a surge of fear shoot through her mind. No matter how many positive affirmations she spoke, she couldn't shake the feeling that someone lurked in the shadows. The nightmares of the growling beast and the California tike in the dingy gingham dress haunted her nights. Now, these eerie feelings were starting to invade her peace at home. As she walked through the living room to the kitchen, she heard noises coming from her bedroom.

Where's CoCo? Then she remembered kenneling her after she tore up yet another pair of designer pumps. She pulled out her cell phone just in case she had to call the police. Suddenly, Lillie heard glass break then large feet pounded the pavement outside of her condo. She fell to the ground and gasped for breath. Her heart beat so fast it felt like it would jump out of her chest. Something in her spirit told her the intruder hadn't left. In her mind, she saw him lurking in the bushes.

Once she recovered, Lillie called the police to report the intruder then grabbed a baseball bat from the pantry and ran to her bedroom to find a broken window with glass on the outside.

"Ahhhhhhhh," the intruder screamed loudly as a man jumped from the shadows and wrestled him to the ground. Lillie grabbed her flashlight from the nightstand drawer and shined it on the two men. She was shocked to see Adam putting the man in a headlock.

"Adam," Lillie screamed.

He continued to restrain the perpetrator who yelled a few choice obscenities.

Before she could say anything else, the sound of police sirens permeated the air. The officers exited their vehicles and surrounded Adam and the intruder. Lillie ran outside to help sort out the issue.

"Officer . . . "

"Guinness. Officer Guinness. Ma'am, do you know either of these men?" Adam held on to the criminal with all his might.

"He's the robber." Lillie pointed at the grimy man in black pants and a T-shirt. In turn, he scowled at her. Adam went to Lillie's side and placed his arm around her shoulder. The other officer cuffed the intruder and read him his Miranda rights. Officer Guinness collected information from Lillie for the report and they were on their merry way.

"Adam, what were you doing out here?"

"I came over to talk to you in private since you've been avoiding me."

"Oh really?"

"Yes, really. In fact, I will be here at your house every day until you take me back, so get used to seeing me," Adam spoke with a new confidence.

Lillie blushed and smiled. "We'll just have to see about that, won't we?"

෮ ෭

Adam traced the pattern of the henna tattoo on her belly like a piece of his favorite candy.

"Being with you has me all excited." He laughed nervously. Lillie understood his anticipation since they hadn't been together in a while. He'd kept his promise to visit her every day until she took him back. He filled her home with candy, flowers, herbal teas, and a plethora of other gifts to get back in her good graces.

Since he'd left Nirvana on such good terms, they eagerly welcomed him. Not only did they rehire him, the new job came with a pay increase and a luxurious office. This was unheard of for a former inmate. He loved the job with the exception of a nosy co-worker named Brandi who told everyone's business. Lillie viewed this opportunity as a fresh start for Adam, which meant a fresh start for the two of them as a couple.

"Let's not beat around the bush. I can forgive you for your past, but what I can't do is live with lies and secrets." Lillie paused and took a deep breath. "What else should I know about you?"

Adam looked up at the ceiling and took a minute to respond. He paused and scratched the back of his neck. "I don't have anything to hide from you, babe."

"Okay. If that's true, spill the beans, now."

"There is one thing I'd like to share. Even though I have custody of all of the children now, I still owe their mothers back child support."

"What?" Lillie exclaimed. "You've got to be kidding me." All she could see was dollar signs flying out the door.

Adam's revelation jarred Lillie's memory of Elaina's disapproval of their relationship. "Lillie, marrying a man with a bunch of kids is like paying a credit card bill you didn't create. Why would you pay someone else's bill when you don't have to?"

Now, Lillie felt the impact of those words more than ever. Her thoughts were interrupted when Adam hung his head low as tears flowed from his eyes. Lillie had never seen him this vulnerable. Strangely, she even appreciated his decision to pursue honesty.

"What else, Adam?" Lillie anticipated the next blow.

"Nothing. That's it, Lillie. I know you're worried about the money I owe but I'm working at Nirvana again. With my salary increase, the back child support issue will be taken care of sooner than later."

She didn't allow her surprise to show. There was one more question on her mind.

"What about the domestic violence issues that helped land you in jail?"

Adam grinned. "You know, I was waiting for you to ask me that question. For your information, Jonna and I have reconciled our differences. I've been meeting with her sponsor and she assured me that Jonna's on the straight and narrow. We've known Gabrielle for a long time. In fact, she went to college with us."

She caressed Adam's arm and said, "I want to thank you for being honest with me. So when do I get to meet this miracle working sponsor?"

Adam flashed Lillie a coy grin.

"Why are you worried about meeting her at a time like this? That's Jonna's issue, not ours."

He kissed her gently, picked her up, and carried her to the bedroom. Thoughts of Jonna and her sponsor dissipated and the passion between the two lovers increased. They made love for the entire night and Lillie fell asleep in Adam's arms. She dreamt about riding on a rainbow slope. When she reached the end of the arc she was delighted to see a pot of shiny gold coins. Without warning, a green leprechaun appeared and waved Lillie towards the treasure. She reached out to grab it and the leprechaun transformed into the California tike with the dirty gingham dress.

"Hickory Dickory Dock . . . " She sang the fairytale song in that familiar eerie voice, like fingernails scraping a chalkboard. Lillie put her hands over her ears and cried out. Then, the little girl transformed to the blob beast she heard growling in her bathroom nightmare. The beast planted its feet on the ground and growled as it continued to block Lillie's access to the treasure. She turned to run but the beast grabbed her and began to squeeze the very life out of Lillie. She choked to catch her breath then the beast shouted, "You chose to play with fire, and you got burned. Your skin is numb to it now, yet soon, you'll feel the excruciating pain. If you touch this gold, it will melt, so I must keep if from you. Know this, a seed has been planted in your fertile ground, and your life is about to change forever."

Lillie gulped and let out a shriek that pierced a hole in the rainbow wall. Unable to stand the sound, the beast dropped her to cover his ears. Then, just as quickly as he appeared, he melted into a puddle of green liquid goo. Lillie touched the remains and the acid ate away at her hands. Her piercing scream jolted her out of her sleep. Surprised by her outburst, Adam tried to comfort her with hugs and kisses. When Lillie opened her eyes, an aura of red, hot flames were consuming him, yet he didn't even seem to notice. Just as quickly as she saw the disturbing scene, it disappeared. Adam reached to grab her hands.

"Babe. Are you okay? Why are your hands so hot?"

TWENTY-EIGHT

LILLIE'S LONG nights of love-making and nightmares continued for the next two months, leaving her a mess each morning. She found herself unprepared for client meetings and even forgot to complete menial tasks. Yesterday, she'd fallen asleep at her desk and missed an important appointment with a potential investor. This wasn't the first time either, so Lillie knew she had to get back on track quickly to continue operating her business. Being an entrepreneur meant she always had to be on top of her game, despite whatever was going on in her personal life.

The phone rang and she saw it was Garrett. Since Adam's reentry in her life, she'd been dodging him and the guilt was killing her so she decided to tell him the truth.

"Lillie, I get the sense that you're not really interested in me," Garrett said.

"I enjoyed your company and riding motorcycles with you brought a sense of freedom into my life that I've never felt before. It's just that when we met . . ."

"You were just getting over a relationship, right?"

Impressed with Garrett's insightfulness, Lillie responded, "Was it that obvious?"

"Yes, Lillie. I'm afraid it was, but I totally understand. Maybe another place, another time?" he proposed.

"Yes, that sounds appropriate. Goodbye, my friend."

Naturally, Lillie wondered if she'd made the right decision. As she pondered on the situation, Rosa entered her office, confused. "Lillie, there's a Mrs. Tia Reyes-Johnson here to see you."

"I can't believe she came to my job. Does anyone have respect for the workplace these days?" Lillie ranted as she stomped to the front of her desk.

"Who is she?" Rosa inquired with suspicion in her voice.

Instead of answering Rosa, Lillie ignored her question. "Thanks, Rosa. Please send her in."

"I just don't understand why you let that piece of man back into your life." Rosa shook her head back and forth in disapproval. "Lillie, if you don't mind me saying…get out of this relationship while you can… before something happens that…you'll regret."

"Rosa, I do mind. Let's stick to work at work, okay?"

"Humph! I'll send Mrs. Johnson right in. Enjoy your catfight. I'm sure it's not the first and it won't be the last as long as that jerk is in your life." Rosa stumped out of the office, agitated by the whole situation.

Moments later, Tia walked through the door. Her white Donna Karen suit showed off her petite, curvaceous figure. In five-inch stilettos, her presence towered over Lillie's. The polished appearance caught Lillie by surprise because she looked much different when Lillie saw her at the county jail.

"Hello, Lillie. I'm sure you remember me," Tia sassed. Hearing the belligerence in her voice jarred Lillie's memory.

"Hello," Lillie cordially greeted her. "Yes, I do remember you. Please have a seat." Lillie led her unwanted guest to the sofa. "Would you like something to drink?"

"No, thank you," she snapped.

"So, to what do I owe this honor?" Lillie's inquisitive tone seemed to frustrate her more.

"I have one question for you." She cocked her hip and plopped her hand on it. "Why did you neglect to tell me the truth about your relationship with Adam?" Tia banged her fist on the end table in anger.

"That's an excellent question, but you won't get far by attacking my furniture. In case you've forgotten, sister, this is my place of business, so act like it."

"Whatever! Don't try to change the subject. You need to answer my question," she demanded with authority.

"You're funny, but let's not waste anymore of my precious time, so here's my answer." Lillie leaned closer. "When you said Adam's name that day, I was shocked out of my mind. Here I am trying to minister to you in your time of need and you say the most unexpected thing."

"Minister to me? You're screwing a married man and you were trying to minister to me? Ha! That's why I can't stand Christians!"

"But you married a pastor?" For the sake of her business, Lillie decided to back down. "Look, I'm not making excuses or lying to you. I didn't want to hurt you or make rash decisions," Lillie rationalized.

"I want to believe you, but you continued to be involved with Adam after that. There's no excuse. You were seeing a married man, and you knew it," Tia accused.

As much as Lillie wanted to smack the woman and send her on her merry way, she couldn't help but feel some of her pain. "Like I said before, that day in the parking lot, I got excited about ministering to someone who was in a similar predicament. Unfortunately, I didn't have enough courage to tell you the truth," Lillie admitted.

"What part of married don't you understand? Married means off limits to single hussies like you." She spat the nasty words then jumped up from her seat and slapped Lillie in the face. Taken aback, Lillie grabbed the crazy woman by the hair and dragged her to the other side of the desk. Not willing to lose this battle, Tia clawed at Lillie until she drew blood.

"Ahh!" Lillie screamed in agony. Struck by the sudden pain, Lillie's anger amplified and she smacked Tia across the face repeatedly.

"You husband stealing tramp," she screamed as she flipped Lillie over and tried to put her in a headlock. Lillie wasn't having it, so she pulled Tia's weaved hair until chunks came out.

"Lillie Corven! You're nothing but a home wrecker," she screamed as a beautiful vase of flowers fell and hit her in the head. A stream of blood trickled down her face. Fortunately, the site of Tia's blood jolted Lillie back to reality.

"This is foolish. We're grown women fighting over a man. One who you're divorcing, right?" Lillie's tone dripped with sarcasm. The two women stood eye to eye with less than an inch of space between them.

"Hell, no. I'm not divorcing him, you stupid—"

"Woo, woo, woo! Wait one minute. You will not call me out of my name in my own office. In fact, get out!"

"Not until you apologize to me."

Lillie fumed as she called out, "Rosa, please call security." Rosa was two-steps ahead of her as she walked in with the security officer.

"What in the heck is wrong with you two?" Rosa shrieked as she stepped in between the two women. She flashed a stern look, clearly warning both of them to stay on their sides of the imaginary boxing ring.

"I can't even deal with you, right now, you home wrecker." Tia stormed out of the office in a whirlwind fury.

"You're not exactly worth my time either," Lillie yelled after her.

"Are you alright, Miss Lillie?" the security officer asked.

"Yes. Thanks for asking," Lillie responded.

"Good. I'm going to make sure she actually left the building. If you have any more problems, call me."

"Thanks so much, Bill." Lillie watched as he left her suite and entered the elevator.

"Are you sure you're okay, Lillie," Rosa asked.

"Yes," Lillie responded reluctantly. "I'm going to clean myself up and get back to work." Lillie's tone let Rosa know that this wasn't the time to talk any longer.

Once refreshed, Lillie called Adam to let him know about his wife's visit.

Without greeting Adam, Lillie said, "Guess who just left my office, Adam?"

"Oh, hello, to you too, Lillie. Who just left your office? Let me guess. That dude Theo is sending you flowers again? Or maybe it's that biker you told me about," Adam teased.

"No. I wish it were that simple." Lillie sighed. "Your wife stopped by and the tramp had the nerve to start a fight with me. She also mentioned not divorcing you. Explain that, Adam!"

Adam didn't respond and Lillie seethed with anger, cursing him out with a fury. She didn't make a habit of using those kinds of words, but at that moment, her anger was off the charts.

"Lillie, I can't believe how you're talking to me. A lady wouldn't act like this." Adam's accusation was just what Lillie needed to hear to take it up a notch.

"Practice what you preach, Adam. I'm sure if God forgives us for all of the fornication we've been commitment, he'll forgive me for this, so, I guess I'll cuss now and repent later." She was not about to let Adam get away with this.

"I know one thing, Adam Johnson. I'm giving you three days to fix this. If at the end of that period, you haven't taken care of this little situation, you can forget about a future with me. Do I make myself clear?"

"Crystal," Adam said. "But, I'm going to need you to relax that tone, Lillie."

"I'm not relaxing anything, Adam Johnson. Like I said, handle it, and do it now.."

"Relax! I'll take care of it," Adam yelled.

"You better!" Lillie hung up the phone and threw it across the room. She dived onto the couch in her office and cried until the tears would no longer flow. Lillie vowed to herself, If Adam doesn't come through this time, I'm out.

∞ ∟

"I have a surprise for you, babe." Adam poured organic soil into the gigantic aerated stone pot while Lillie and CoCo Chanel chilled out on their special patio seat. The patio garden was just one of Adam's many birthday gifts to Lillie. She'd made some fresh lemonade early that morning and it came in handy to quench their thirst on such a hot day.

"Is it someone who can maintain this garden for free?" Lillie asked sarcastically.

Adam handed Lillie a manila envelope. She ripped it open and was pleased to see a divorce decree.

"Um . . . is this real? You know, I heard that people fake this type of documentation every day," Lillie accused.

"What would make you say that, Lillie?" Adam's irritation was obvious. "Pastor Andrews hooked me up with a lawyer who took care of everything."

"So, are you saying this is real?" Lillie's excitement escalated. She'd have to make a point to meet his sponsor and thank him for the assistance, soon.

"Yes. In fact, you will see it in the paper soon, just in case you need to verify it." Adam's confident demeanor assured Lillie that he was telling the truth.

"Praise God," she exclaimed. "You came through."

Adam chuckled and pulled Lillie close to him. "I've been thinking, you are the perfect woman for me, and I don't want to lose you." He kissed her gently. "I love you, Lillie."

Aroused, Lillie returned his affection. Since the patio was private and secluded, Adam removed Lillie's clothing one item at a time. She obliged and removed a few of his. He grabbed the cushions from the lawn furniture and spread them across the patio. Taking Lillie by the hand, he escorted her to their love pallet and romanced her. While they made love, Adam placed an engagement ring on her finger and began to sing a Brian McKnight tune sweetly in her ear. The same tune he sang the last time they'd made love on the patio.

After all they'd been through Lillie was one step closer to being Adam's bride. Her overwhelming emotions added to the affection they traded while making love. Adam's intensity took her to higher heights on the mountain of love with ease. Wrapping her legs around him tightly, she cried out over and over again. Lillie buried her face in Adam's chest to muffle her screams of passion.

As she lay in his arms enjoying the beauty of the love they'd just made, Lillie said, "Life can't get any better than this, can it?"

Adam chuckled as he stroked her cheek gently and said, "Why, yes it can, the moment you become Mrs. Adam Johnson." Tears of joy streamed down Lillie's face and Adam kissed each one. They spent the rest of the evening gazing at the stars as they loved one another over and over again.

TWENTY-NINE

PREGNANT!" LILLIE cried as she stared the nurse in the face. "You've got to be kidding me." It made sense, yet Lillie didn't want to hear it. For the past few months, her breasts had been sore. The slightest smell sent Lillie to the bathroom, hurling up her goods. Furthermore, she'd been irritable, tired, and sleepy. Rosa had stepped up and handled some of Lillie's caseload on the days she couldn't get into the office. Just last night, Lillie didn't make it to the bathroom in time so her white carpet got a taste of the bile in her stomach. It took her forever to clean it all up.

Frustrated, Lillie took three deep breaths.

Why did I listen to Adam's stupid pulling out idea?

She wanted to kick herself and smack Adam as she remembered his stupid pleas.

"You're my rib and our flesh desires to be one. We don't need a latex barrier complicating our union."

If Lillie had been on her toes, she would've told him the marriage covenant is what seals the deal, not whether or not they used a condom. Adam's faulty logic cost Lillie more than she was willing to pay.

"The ability to create life and give birth is the most beautiful experience in the world. It's what makes being feminine divine. Divine and sacred." The sweet nurse meant well. She went on to share her philosophy about the baby being a part of Lillie's life path and a woman's ability to give life being characteristic of a goddess. If she closed her eyes, she could picture Grace's face. These are words she would speak.

I'm pregnant by a man with a record, no home, an underpaying job, and four other children. Being a goddess is the last thing on my mind right now.

"You've just made it out of your first trimester, Lillie." As she spoke, the nurse's bubbly nature permeated the atmosphere. "We'd like to see you back in two weeks for the ultrasound and a consultation with me," the nurse said with a bright smile on her face. Then she slipped Lillie a brochure and walked out of the room. Lillie opened the tri-fold paper to find information about the danger of ultrasounds on the unborn fetus.

Why did she tell me to schedule an appointment, then give me this brochure?

Lillie sat dumbfounded when the nurse popped back into the room. She took the brochure out of her hand and placed it in Lillie's purse while she shared stories about her four children. At that moment, Lillie realized that this nurse didn't agree with everything prescribed by the practice. She made a mental note to look up this information on the internet. By the time Lillie's visit ended, the nurse had shown Lillie pictures and invited her to her youngest son's birthday party. She and her husband were planning a party with food catered by one of the popular vegan restaurants in the city.

Lillie knew she should be excited about her pregnancy, despite the circumstances, but all she could do was cry. As she walked to her car, Gloom and Doom followed her like a shadow. When she opened the car door, the hairs on her arms rose when she saw a black cat sitting on her seat.

Aaaaaaahhhhhhhhhhh!

As she swung her purse to beat the feline out of her car, she screamed over and over again, only to realize that the cat's presence was just a figment of her imagination.

Now I'm seeing things again! Uuuuugggghhh! My mind's playing tricks on me.

The negative spirits that followed her to the car beckoned her into a melancholy funk. She sat on the smooth leather seat and slid down until her head faced the steering wheel.

What the hell am I going to do with a baby?

Out of nowhere, she heard a sweet, gentle voice say, "Kill it. Why bring a baby into this world in this situation?"

Clear as day, she heard another more authoritative voice shout, "No! Thou shall not kill! It's not your life to take."

An urge to see Adam interrupted the voices in her head. She needed to see her man right now, so she decided to stop by Nirvana. He needed to know about their bundle of joy who would change the course of the rest of their lives.

THIRTY

AN OMINOUS energy cloud followed Lillie from Dr. Samuelson's parking lot. Thick fog saturated the atmosphere making it hard for her to see. To make matters worse, rain poured buckets out of the sky. The flow of her tears synchronized with the cacophony of drops pounding the windshield. The sudden storm defied the weather forecast just as Lillie's broken heart contradicted her life plan.

Usually, when she visited Nirvana during the day, she found Adam in his office trying to book the latest and greatest jazz artists and musicians. Today, she was surprised to find his office empty. Lillie recognized the young woman at the front desk and decided to probe for information, even though she couldn't remember her name. Sandy and Candy came to mind, but she knew that wasn't correct. Just then, she recalled a conversation with Adam when he referred to her as Brandi, the club gossiper. Despite Adam's warning, Lillie continued to be friendly to the receptionist. When Lillie approached the front desk, Brandi immediately greeted her with a smile.

"Hey, Lillie. It's so good to see you. Are you coming to pick up Adam's things?" she asked, pointing to the boxes stacked in the corner.

"Adam's things? What do you mean?" Lillie asked.

Brandi flashed Lillie a blank stare, then she raised her eyebrows as if she'd uncovered a great mystery.

"Girl! Look at that ring. When did you and Adam get engaged?" Brandi asked.

Lillie responded and allowed her to gawk at the ring a little more.

"So back to Adam's job."

"Um . . . well . . . He no longer works here." Brandi dropped the news like an atomic bomb that smacked Lillie right in the forehead.

"Are you sure, Brandi? That seems strange to me. Bill rehired him not too long ago."

"I'm sure. Bill refired him two days ago." Brandi's matter-of-fact expression let Lillie know that her information was on point.

Confused by her statement, Lillie questioned Brandi. "Refired? Refired isn't even a word, Brandi."

"Yeah. You know Bill's wife Deena, right?" Brandi's inquiry reminded Lillie of her first night at Nirvana when Mallory serenaded Adam and gave him a shout out. She'd met the owners that evening. Bill reminded Lillie of a rock singer with his long hair that he wore in a ponytail, while Deena reminded her of a Latina Pamela Anderson. Her silicon breasts were huge and her bleached-blonde hair was as bright as the sun.

"Bill fired him just last month because he thought Adam and Deena were fooling around. For some reason, she rehired him the next day."

"Are you serious?"

"You know Bill ain't no fool. She's not the only one, either."

"Woooooooo. More?"

Brandi vigorously nodded her head in an affirmative manner.

Just as Lillie asked the question, Mallory, the voluptuous singer, walked in. She'd performed there on Adam and Lillie's first date. Also, Theo saw Adam embracing her in an intimate manner at Easton Town Centre when she and Adam initially started dating. Mallory didn't stop to talk. Instead, she rolled her eyes and continued walking.

Brandi whispered, "There's his queen bee right there."

"What?" Lillie screamed as she twisted her hair with fury. All she could do was shake her head. The great Adam Johnson had played her for a fool, yet again. Brandi might be the club gossiper but the girl supplied accurate information. Adam was a cheating, lying, unemployed jerk.

"Oh yeah. I almost forgot this part. I overheard Adam talking to Mallory about living with one of the deacons from his church. You know that's not true, right?"

"Oh really?"

"No, it's not. When he's not sleeping at Mallory's place, he's sleeping at your place and he's telling both of y'all the lie about living with the good deacon. He lived there for about two weeks when he initially came back, though. He's been at Mallory's when he claims to be at work. In fact, he's there now. Here's the address. Thought you'd want to stop by and pay him a visit."

"Thank you for sharing this with me." A lone tear escaped Lillie's eyelid and Brandi handed her a tissue.

"There's one more thing. I've watched Adam over the years and he typically operates in threes. So don't be surprised if another woman pops into the picture."

"Another one?" Lillie's head throbbed from the pain of thinking about Adam's indiscretions.

"I can't say for sure but I do know Adam's pattern. I promised myself that I'd tell you everything I knew if I ever had the opportunity to talk to you alone. Women need to stick together, right?"

Lillie shook her head then glanced at the address on the paper. She almost peed her pants when she saw the New Albany zip code. She reflected back to the day Adam left dinner at her parent's home early. Later that evening, she'd seen him at the

New Albany carryout with Aliyah and another little girl. Lillie couldn't remember her name, yet she remembered Adam's strange behavior.

"You're about to find out who the real Adam Johnson is. By the way, be careful. Mallory might be beautiful, rich, and classy, but she doesn't play about her man. She's packing!"

ℴ ℻

Magnificent scenery astounded Lillie as she drove the back roads to New Albany. She couldn't deny God's majestic creation of trees, foliage, and flora. Opulent million dollar homes greeted her when she turned into Mallory's upscale neighborhood. The new contract must have been more than generous because only the wealthy residents of central Ohio could afford to reside in this prestigious community.

Lillie whipped around the cul de sac and settled on a parking space across the street from her destination. She cracked her window only to encounter the eerie sound of the whistling wind in concert with the rain. Dark fog hovered like the scene out of a Stephen King movie. With no game plan in mind, she wasn't sure what to expect of this visit, so she just sat in her car. After about ten minutes, a yellow school bus pulled up and a little girl jumped off. Lillie couldn't shake the feeling that she'd seen this child before. She couldn't think about it anymore because her cell phone rang. The caller ID revealed the call was from her parent's home. She wasn't in the mood to talk to either one of them, but she answered the phone anyway. Putting on her best happy voice, Lillie greeted the caller with a hearty, "Hello."

"Hey, Lady Bug." It was her mother's cheery voice.

"Hi, Mama. How are you?"

"I can't complain, baby. It wouldn't do any good, would it?"

"Mama, you've been saying that since I was little." Lillie laughed.

"And I'm going to keep on saying it, because it's the truth."

"So, to what do I owe this great honor?" Lillie asked as she watched a few neighboring children join the little girl in the front yard.

"I had a dream about you last night, and I need to see you face to face." Sophia's prophetic gift irritated Lillie when it came to her personal business.

"Really, Mama?" Lillie teased, as she twisted strands of her hair.

"Umm hmm. I bet you're messing in your hair right now."

Lillie chuckled. "Mama, you don't know everything."

"Don't get sassy, young lady. I do know one thing. Lisa Keyes is not going to take kindly to it either. She'll set you straight at your next hair appointment."

Sophia's intuition had always been an issue for Lillie. In third grade, the cutest boy in the class wrote a letter asking Lillie to be his girlfriend. His instructions directed her to circle 'yes,' 'no,' or 'maybe' and then return the note to him. She circled 'yes' and followed the return directions, then they exchanged a kiss. Little did he know, Lillie's parents forbid her to have a boyfriend. As soon as she hit the door, Sophia confronted her.

"You've been kissing a boy, haven't you?" Sophia accused.

Before Lillie could respond, she said, "Don't lie to me either because I saw it in a vision."

No matter what Lillie said, she knew her mother would know the truth. The sound of her mother's sweet voice interrupted the nostalgic moment.

"So when do I get to see your smiling face, Lady Bug?"

"Mama, I'd love to see you, but I don't have much time this week," Lillie lied.

"Humph! I already know you're back with that trifling preacher. I need to come see you."

Dang! How does she always know so much? Lillie wondered.

"Plus, if you came over here, your daddy will play his kitchen commentator role."

Lillie knew her mom had a point. Maybe it was best for her to come to Lillie's place.

"Okay, Mama. My place it is. Maybe we can order take out from that place at Easton that does the Hibachi meal thing to go. You know the place that serves brown rice?"

"Take out? Your mama's coming to visit and all you have to offer is take out? That's not like you."

"I haven't been feeling well lately so I'm not up to cooking."

"I see."

Sophia's pregnant pause made Lillie uncomfortable. Not wanting to take this conversation any further, Lillie decided to give her mother a politically correct dismissal.

"Mama. I'll call you when I get home so you can stop by." Lillie rushed her mother off the phone.

"Uh huh," she said in a suspicious tone. "You do that, baby. I love you."

"Love you, too."

As Lillie ended the call, Mallory's three-car garage opened and the little girl walked to the middle car with her mother, giving Lillie a clear view of her face. Then it dawned on her why she looked so familiar. Deidra. The little girl with Adam and Aliyah in the New Albany carryout parking lot. Lillie remembered how Adam cut the child off when she mentioned her mother. Now, it all made sense. Deidra belonged to Mallory and Adam wanted to hide it.

As Lillie forced her mind to transition from the memory to the present, she placed her attention on the contents of the garage. The three-car garage housed a Hummer, an Escalade, and a Lexus sedan. Right before Lillie's eyes, another one of Adam's lies unfolded. He told Lillie the good deacon allowed him to borrow one of his Lexus sedan since the finance company reposed his Range Rover.

He's such a liar! Driving me around in some other woman's car. Who does that?

Not able to take anymore, Lillie decided to head back to work. She had clients waiting who weren't concerned about her personal life. As she turned onto the next street, a crazy driver cut her off without warning. Lillie jerked the steering wheel in an attempt to steady the car. Instead, she spun in several circles, barely missing the cars in the oncoming traffic. She screamed at the top of her lungs, as she saw her life flash before her eyes while she skidded into the grass median. Aware of her location, Lillie managed to pry herself out of the car when she noticed a surly woman walking toward her. Is that...

"What's wrong with you, you crazy, witch," Lillie screamed as she exited the car. "I can't believe you ran me off the road!"

"Can't handle a little reckless driving?" Mallory teased in a sadistic tone.

"I could've been killed. What were you thinking?"

"I was thinking that you have some nerve sitting out in front of my house, like some freakin' private investigator," Mallory accused.

"This isn't the day to mess with me, especially since you're messing with my fiancé. You know we're engaged, right?" Lillie flashed the ring in Mallory's face with a fury.

"So, I finally get to talk to the great Lillie Corven. I hate that it had to happen this way." Mallory's voice dripped with sarcasm, making Lillie want to smack her. Instead, Lillie rolled her eyes at the crazy woman and proceeded to step up to her face. Despite the pain from the accident, Lillie's adrenaline rose to unnatural levels.

Mallory glared daggers into Lillie's eyes and then she raised her hand to smack her in the face. Lillie caught it in mid-air, preventing contact. She'd already had a bout with one of Adam's women, and would've fought this one too, until she remembered her delicate condition.

"No you didn't try to slap me. I can't believe this."

"Well, believe it! Just think, he wanted to marry you because he didn't think I'd make a good pastor's wife." Mallory laughed so hard, she sounded like the Joker on the Batman movie. "I don't know why I'm wasting my time with you anyway. He always comes running back to me," Mallory gloated as she walked back to her car.

Unable to retort, Lillie did the same. Amazingly, there was not one scratch on the vehicle.

Funny how God was there for me even when I was one hundred percent wrong.

As she pondered on this miracle, Lillie gathered her senses and drove away from the pitiful scene. To calm her spirit, she prayed for peace of mind and clarity. Soon and very soon, Adam would no longer be a factor in her life.

THIRTY-ONE

L ILLIE PAID dearly for the unexpected time she'd taken off that morning. Her workload seemed to have quadrupled, which made her think about sharing more of her caseload with the consultant Rosa hired. Her prestigious clients rang the phone off the hook when their deliverables were late. Having this baby would mean she'd definitely need the extra help. Running a company certainly had its benefits and presented challenges all at the same time.

Hours later, Lillie looked up and the clock read 8 p.m. The lights were out in the front office, which meant Rosa must have stepped out during her last teleconference. Lillie packed up her belongings and headed to the parking garage. On her way home, she decided to change up the treadmill regimen she'd followed religiously for years. She had to keep her figure tight during the pregnancy. After much contemplation, she decided to go for a light run in the park next to her condominiums. After her run, Lillie stopped at the stretching bars to release the tension in her limbs.

As she bent into a downward dog pose, she overheard two women talking. Strangely, their voices sounded familiar. She turned to see who was walking her way and caught a glimpse of the two women kissing.

No! There's no way in the world! It can't be!

To Lillie's surprise, it was Grace and Masseri. Not only were their lips locked, they had the nerve to caress each other's face and gaze intently into one another's eyes. Lillie hid behind a tree to avoid being discovered. She thought back to how they'd teased her about having sex with Adam on his backyard swing and instantly, she became disgusted by their hypocritical behaviors.

She wondered what Alvin would think of this scenario, so she pulled out her cell phone, snapped several shots, and typed a message. As the couple walked to the park entryway, they froze dead in their tracks when they spotted Lillie. With a resolve like crazy glue, Lillie planted her feet to make sure Grace and Masseri knew she'd seen their romantic interaction. Without another thought, she clicked SEND.

"Um . . . Hi." Grace's voice shook when she greeted Lillie.

"Hi yourself. What brings you two out today? Shouldn't you be at the studio?"

"Oh, we decided to take the day off and practice some new routines," Masseri responded with candor. Somehow, Lillie knew she wouldn't be embarrassed one bit.

"So that's what we're calling it now. A new routine. Wow! You two are really . . . um . . . dedicated."

"Lillie, we saw you hiding behind that tree?" Grace's voice no longer shook.

"What?" Lillie looked Grace dead square in the eyes and spoke her peace. "I guess Ms. Blakey was right about you all along, Grace. She's been saying you loved the girls since we were children."

"Oh, really? Then she must be right about you, too."

Ouch. That hurt.

Masseri's words stabbed Lillie in the heart like a sharp, silver dagger and to make matters worse, she knew she deserved it. Ms. Blakey did have a way of making someone's sin into an instant church scandal. Right now, Lillie and Adam's love affair was at the top of the list. Grace and Masseri's lesbian love affair definitely took second place.

Before either of them could respond, Lillie continued speaking with an authority they'd never seen from her before. "I always knew there was something different about you two. Now that I've had the displeasure of seeing it with my own two eyes, I'm amazed at your audacity. You know, I expected this from Masseri, but you, Grace. We've slept in the same bed, dressed in front of one another, and have been way too personal for me to be comfortable with this."

As she stood glaring at her friends, her cell phone played a Brian McKnight song, and she knew it was Alvin.

"Lady Bug?" His tone was surprisingly calm. "Tell me that this text pic is fabricated. I know you have some serious photo editing skills, so why would you do this?" Alvin accused.

"I guess this is the day for everyone to come out the closet." Lillie laughed like a mad hyena. Grace and Masseri on the other hand didn't crack a smile.

"What? You've got to be kidding me. Grace is like my little sister and I've got serious love for Masseri, too. For God's sake, this is devastating."

Lillie responded, "Yeah. I'm looking at both of them right now trying to find the love in my heart to continue our friendship. They treated me like yesterday's garbage after my ordeal with Adam."

Masseri stormed off and Grace followed her.

"Well, that's a whole different story." Alvin paused. "I need to hear Masseri's side. I'll call you later."

When Alvin hung up, Lillie dialed Theo's number to tell him the news.

"And you're shocked because?"

Lillie couldn't believe Theo's response. She expected him of all people to see things her way.

"She's playing my brother and they've both lied to us. Don't you even care?"

"I care, but not enough to get all upset. Alvin will get over it and so will you. They're just experimenting. Trust me when I say that."

I bet he wouldn't feel the same way if they were two guys!

"I can't believe you're a man of God condoning what they're doing."

"Woe! Woe! Woe! I'm not condoning it. I'm just not surprised by it. Oh hold on, that's Sharon. I gotta go."

Theo disconnected the call before Lillie could respond. Lillie gasped and stared at the phone in disbelief. In the history of their relationship, he'd never put another woman before her. She walked back to her condo in a state of mass confusion, unable to control her emotions. Tears dripped down her cheekbones as she realized that Theo had moved on. Even though she'd been with Adam, Theo meant a great deal to her. She never imagined that he wouldn't wait it out.

Just as Lillie unlocked her condo door, her stomach lurched, threatening to evict its contents. She ran to the bathroom and blessed the porcelain bowl with thick, chunky vomit. Lillie gagged when the horrid stench hit her delicate nose and upchucked some more. She grabbed a towel from the rack to wipe the residue from her mouth then felt sharp, tingly, itchy bursts in her watery. A sudden dizziness took over and Lillie hit the floor. The all too familiar image of Adam in flames invaded her psyche. She closed her eyes to try to escape the visual; however, it just became more apparent.

A sinister laugh penetrated the atmosphere so she put her hands over her ears to escape the sound. Unfortunately, her efforts were in vain because it didn't go away. Lillie screamed and cried until she couldn't even see straight. Finally, the vision subsided and she stopped the piercing screams. An eerie silence took its place, leaving Lillie to wallow on the floor in a pool of self-pity. She mustered enough energy to grab the sink and fell flat on her face. Too weak to fight, she surrendered to the pain, while tears poured from her eyes like the rain showers on the way to Nirvana. When she couldn't take it any longer, she fell into a comatose sleep.

ॐ ☺

The abrupt, piercing sound of the ringing doorbell interrupted Lillie from a deep sleep. She reluctantly pulled herself up and made the painful-stricken trek to the front door. When she looked through the peephole, she saw an older version of herself staring right back. She'd forgotten to call her mother. As much as Lillie loved Sophia Corven, she wasn't in the mood for her prophecies.

"Lillie Michelle Corven. I know you're standing there. Girl, let me in."

When Lillie heard her government name, she knew her mother meant business. When she opened the door, Sophia quickly bolted inside. Lillie's stomach growled like a bear at a beehive when the scrumptious smell from her mother's bags met her olfactory glands. Sophia made her way to the dining room and unloaded the contents on the table. Once she finished, CoCo challenged her to a playful boxing match, their ritual greeting. Lillie sat back on the sofa and chuckled while she observed their faux battle.

"Mama, I'm so glad to see you." Lillie's feigned excitement like an Oscar-winning actress. She took a sip of her mother's fizzy probiotic beverage.

"I bet you are. I've been dreaming of fish." Lillie choked on her drink and coughed incessantly.

"So, Mama, what exactly does dreaming about fish mean?" It took the entire wherewithal she could muster not to laugh, since she knew exactly what the dream meant.

"Now, you're my child, so I know you know what it means. Don't try to pretend you don't." Lillie smirked to herself.

"Here, let's wash our hands and fix our plates. I'm hungry, and I know you are, based upon my dream." Lillie avoided her mother's soul-penetrating stare. Over the years, she learned her mother focused on the eyes, since they were the doorway to the soul. Through this visual portal, she discerned intentions and levels of honesty.

"Did I ever tell you the story about your Aunt Diana?"

"Yes, Mama." Lillie wondered how all of this related to her. Little did she know, she was about to find out. "Dying in that mental institution about killed Alvin."

"Medically, they say she had a heart attack. Spiritually, she died of heartbreak. And by the way, she didn't die in a mental institution. She was incarcerated. We just never wanted to tell you."

Lillie furrowed her brows, scrunched her eyes, and hunched her shoulders.

Sophia responded to her daughter's perplexed demeanor by continuing to tell her story.

"When your godmother and I were younger, we met two handsome men who happened to be brothers who wined and dined us for an entire summer. Even though they were fun companions, we knew they would make horrible husbands." Lillie saw the writing on the wall and it made her want to leave the room. She'd be a fool to walk out on her own mother, though. Sophia Corven didn't tolerate such behavior.

"Diana loved her some Alvin, though."

Alvin? Oh, this must be Alvin's dad.

"When he went to the army, she cried every night. You know they drafted him." Sophia rolled her eyes. Lillie knew her mother's stance on the military. She could just see her now with an Afro and a dashiki, with picket signs in hand. Her mother had always been the eccentric type.

"He promised to send for her once he could, and she promised to wait for him. Now you know the man lied to her. She went to visit him a few times and he came back home to see her as well. Kind of like Masseri and Alvin have been doing for years. But they're serious, though."

Years? What did she mean years? How long have Masseri and Alvin been seeing one another behind my back?

"So God gave her a gift wrapped in sore breasts and morning sickness. She tried to tell Alvin, but found out he'd been deployed to fight in the war. You know that your godmother loves Jesus like nobody's business so she saw abortion as a sin and adoption as abandonment."

"Did Mr. Alvin die in the war?" Lillie asked.

"That sucker didn't die. He got married to his high school sweetheart. Remember when I told Adam he looked familiar to me?"

Lillie shook her head in disbelief as the story unfolded in her mind. Sophia reached out to hold her and she jerked away as she realized her Aunt Diana killed Adam's father! Lillie folded over to succumb to the sick feeling in the pit of her stomach.

"Yes. So, Adam has a brother. His mother's death wasn't the only thing that drove him to the army."

Lillie always wondered why the Johnsons hadn't named Adam Alvin Jr. Now she had her answer. That excuse about him having his own identity was a bunch of crap! The color drained from Lillie's face as she realized the magnitude of this issue.

"Yeah. I figured it out yesterday. I couldn't understand what drove you away from Theo into the arms of Adam. Now, we know. He reminded you of Alvin. We always choose the familiar for some reason. Whether the man is like our daddy, our brothers, our uncles. Baby, you don't have to say a word. I already know you've gotten yourself in a bad situation. Just know your options are different than Diana's. Theo will marry you and take care of your baby. He's a good man."

"Mom! He has a girlfriend. He's moved on."

"We'll see how long that lasts."

"Maybe I'd have a chance if . . ."

"If what? Don't you go do nothing crazy, now. That's life. You don't have the right."

The idea of trying to make things work out with Theo sounded quite appealing, based on Adam's behavior as of late. But it might be easier with the baby out of the way. She couldn't help but think back to the prophetic warning in the dream she had on the night he read her poem at Flow. "Lillie, you'll be tried by the fire, but you're coming out gold." She was definitely being tried by the fire, and each bad decision she made resulted in her getting burned. With this horrible track record, she definitely wasn't coming out gold.

Lillie and her mother continued their dinner in silence. When they finished, Sophia rose to do the dishes and kissed her daughter on the forehead. To Lillie's surprise, she whispered, "Go rest. I know I shared a great deal of information with you this evening. And don't worry about Grace and Masseri. It's just an experiment."

"Huh? How did you . . ." Then she remembered her mother's gift. Sophia winked at Lillie and went to the kitchen.

An hour later, Lillie heard the door open and close. She tried to relax but all she could think about was getting rid of this baby. She decided to read up on the subject so that she could make an informed decision. Her search resulted in a variety of different perspectives. The debate over whether or not a fetus is a living being at conception or birth stood out to her. Most right wing sites believed the life started at conception while many left wing sites disagreed. An herbalist who claimed to be a follower of the occult offered a different perspective. He shared that the soul hovers around the mother waiting for the child to be born to incarnate. Once the baby is born it took about seventeen minutes for the soul to connect to the physical body. That's why it was important to not cut the umbilical cord until it stopped pulsing. He also supported abortion when the mother knew the father wouldn't be in the picture.

Perplexed by the decision, Lillie didn't know which way to go. She didn't believe in abortion, yet she didn't want to have this baby either. Adoption wasn't an option because she couldn't bear to part with a child after carrying it for nine months. Plus, she remembered all of the nights she comforted Grace who would give up all her organs just to get a glimpse at her birth parents. If she kept the baby, Adam's instability would be her burden for the rest of her life, unless she totally wrote him off. Maybe the herbal guy had a valid point. Just her luck, it would be a boy and he would turn out to be just like him.

THIRTY-TWO

It was a dreary Saturday morning and Lillie lay on her bed, engulfed by a sea of white throws. The décor that once brought peace and clarity now lacked spirit. She twisted her hair with a fury then stopped when she heard Lisa's voice in her head. Split ends ran rampant in place of the once shiny smooth mane. Frustrated, Lillie switched to punching the crap out of her pillow as she cried a river of tears. The piercing ring of the phone interrupted her personal fight fest. Bianca's name popped up on the caller ID.

"Hey, Bee. What's going on?"

"Not much. Girl, are you okay? You sound horrible."

Why do people tell hurting people they sound horrible?

"Yeah . . . um . . . I'm okay."

"If you say so," Bianca sassed.

"What's going on with you?"

"Girl! The better question is what's not going on with me." Bianca went on to share how she hated Todd and didn't know what she was thinking when she married him. She even broke down in tears when she revealed her thoughts on a potential divorce.

"I'm so disgusted with him, I don't even want to talk about it anymore. What's going on with you? I'm not stupid. I know pain when I hear it."

"I have some good news and some bad news."

"Don't leave me in suspense. Tell a sister what's going on."

"Well…" Lillie hesitated. "The good news is I might be having a baby."

"Might be having a what?" Bianca exclaimed.

"A baby, Bee. A baby."

"I have five of those and might is not an option. Either you are having the baby or not," Bianca stated.

"Do you want to hear the bad news now?"

"Um . . . yeah . . . I'm not sure I can handle it. It definitely can't top what you just shared."

"The bad news is . . . I'm having Adam's baby and all I can think is why, Lord? Why me?"

"Pardon me for what I'm about to say, Lillie. But come on. You're a grown woman who hasn't gotten pregnant in all these years. Why now?" The truth of Bianca's words stung Lillie like a swarm of killer bees.

An avalanche of silence overtook the conversation and Lillie fought hard to maintain her composure.

"So I guess you're protecting yourself when you're tipping out on Todd, right?" Bianca blessed Lillie's ear with the slamming of the phone. No longer able to take her frustration out on her friend, she fought the temptation to call Adam and give him a piece of her mind. She no longer referred to him as Mr. Caramel Latte Dream. With everything she'd found out, he was more like Mr. Caramel Latte Nightmare.

"Footsteps in the Dark" sounded out from her cell phone. She clicked on the line item and a picture appeared. Lillie's stomach tightened as the picture downloaded to reveal a newspaper article featuring Adam and some strange woman kissing. They were on a Ferris wheel and the byline read, "Couple finds love at The Ohio State Fair."

Who is this woman, and what is Adam doing kissing her?

Then Lillie recalled Brandi's warning—he always operated in threes. This woman completed the trio. Tears rolled down Lillie's face as she read the article. Her name was Gabrielle Warren and she owned Sheer Bliss, a prominent wedding consultant firm. The name of the firm sounded familiar to Lillie, then it hit her. Lisa used their services when she and James married. The article went on to say they'd met in college and kept in contact over the years on a friendship level. Lillie's stomach lurched when she read Adam's comment, "She helped a friend of mine through some really hard times recently and it brought us closer together."

Despite her better judgment, she continued to read the article. The reporter met his wife at the fair ten years ago and profiles couples who either meet at the fair or have a monumental event in their relationship while on a ride. He quoted Adam and Gabrielle saying this kiss solidified their official decision to become a couple. First Mallory, then Tia, now Gabrielle. Lillie sobbed vehemently until there were no more tears to cry.

Within the next hour, she made an appointment with her gynecologist for a pregnancy termination consultation. She loved how they tried to make it sound like a simple medical procedure. Whatever they wanted to call it, she wanted to get rid of it as soon as possible. Lillie refused to deal with Adam's shenanigans for the rest of her life. He'd proven himself unworthy of fatherhood. A strange feeling of remorse set in as Lillie thought about Theo. They'd loved one another since elementary school. She knew her mother was right. He would've never placed her in this position.

Like clockwork, Lillie's phone played "Footsteps in the Dark" again.

Theo: *Lillie. Are u okay?*
Lillie: *What do u think?*

Theo: *Want me to come over?*
Lillie: *No, thx. 2 emotional rt now.*
Theo: *Call me if u need me. Still love u.*

She stared at the phone in disbelief and texted back.

Lillie: *What about Sharon?*
Theo: *She's history.*

Lillie almost dropped the phone when she saw those words.

There's still a chance. Thank God it's not too late!

She wanted to tell him the truth about the baby and her intentions. Unfortunately, she couldn't swallow the heavy load of pride she carried on her back. So instead, she called him and lashed out.

"Why would you do this to me? What were you thinking?" Lillie screamed.

Theo chuckled, yet he remained cool, calm, and collected. "What was I thinking? I guess the same thing you were thinking when you sent Alvin the text pic of Grace and Masseri kissing."

"Oh, so you've been talking to my brother. Did he put you up to this or is it your revenge? I pray that it's sweet."

"No, Lillie, it's not my revenge. I'd never hurt you. You know this text just saved you from a lifetime of misery."

More than you'll ever know.

"Now that you've shown me this, I should be eternally grateful, right?"

Theo paused and responded in a low, sexy tone. "Lady Bug, you're my lady in waiting. Adam's loss can be our gain."

Immediately, Lillie thought back to the night at Flow when she'd met Adam. Theo's poem was for her, yet at the time, she denied it. With all she'd been through, he was one of the only people she trusted. No longer able to hold back, she decided to tell him everything.

"Theo, I'm pregnant," Lillie blurted out. A thick silence fell over the atmosphere like a blanket of Alaskan snow.

After what seemed like an eternity, Theo responded. "I guess that means I'm going to be a daddy a little sooner than I anticipated."

Dang! Mom was right once again.

"Umm, no. I'm taking care of that situation soon." More silence.

"You don't have to do that. I'll support you, no matter what, and I'll take care of this baby as if it's my own. I'm coming over now to hold you."

"You'd do that for me? Take care of another man's baby?" Lillie asked skeptically.

"Yes, Lady Bug. I love you. I know you've made up your mind, but please pray. An abortion is not the will of God. I'm with you, so you won't be alone. We can get married as soon as you're ready."

"Okay, but I can't make any promises."

Lillie hung up the phone and cried. When Theo arrived, they didn't exchange words. She cried. He held her. They were in perfect peace.

THIRTY-THREE

GETTING READY for church seemed like a chore. Thank goodness Theo offered to pick Lillie up for the morning service. Typically, Lillie cooked breakfast and dined on her patio, but the pregnancy drained her to the extent that she decided to forgo the Sunday ritual. Her growling stomach challenged the decision. Theo arrived just in time, walking in the door with three bouquets of calla lilies and a spread of breakfast goodies from the church's restaurant.

"Oh, Theo! How'd you know I hadn't eaten?"

Theo smiled and kissed her on the forehead.

"I've known you since we were ten, Lady Bug. I feel your ebb and flow in my spirit." Amazed at his intensity, she planted a passionate kiss on his lips.

"And the calla lilies. You know they're my favorite. Why three bouquets, though?"

"One for each phase of our relationship. Getting to know one another as children. Strengthening our bond as adults. And now, finally opening the door to our love."

He'd amazed her once again. She'd watched him grow from a bossy, overprotective fifth grader into the man before her today. Their closeness created a connection she tried to ignore for years. Now, she was following her heart.

Theo and Lillie enjoyed their pastries and light conversation on the patio. Happy to see her human comrade, CoCo jumped on Theo's lap. A far cry from her interactions with Adam, whom Lillie hadn't talked to in three days. Since she hadn't officially broken up with him, technically they were still a couple. When Lillie mentioned this to Theo, he said, "I'm not concerned about that little technicality. I still need to 'officially' break up with Sharon, too. In fact, if you're in need of my services, I'm offering a two for one special. I can break up with Sharon for me and Adam for you."

Lillie giggled like a schoolgirl.

"Thanks, but I've got this. You just make sure you handle your business with Sharon." Lillie pushed Theo and they wrestled like two teenagers in love.

As they were leaving to go to church, Grace walked out of her condo. Seeing Theo and Lillie, she dropped her head to avoid making eye contact with them. When Masseri walked out of the door behind her, the reason for her avoidance became obvious. Lillie waved at the couple, just to be malicious. Both women stood staring at them, yet neither one of them waved back or offered a verbal greeting.

ॐ ♋

When Theo and Lillie pulled into the church parking lot, they noticed a swarm of women surrounding the front steps. Before they could get to the crowd, Bianca grabbed Lillie's hand and whisked her away to the other door. Theo followed suit.

"Hey, Bee. Why'd you move us away? I want to see what's going on." Lillie pouted.

Bianca was shaking a little bit. "Girl, that was nothing. Typical church gossip. You know how these women can be."

Theo smiled and chimed in. "Yes, we definitely know how they can be."

They walked to their normal seats and greeted their friends. Lillie noticed that Grace and Masseri sat together in the balcony.

"That's odd," Theo commented once he caught sight of their friends. "Why do you think Grace and Masseri are sitting in the balcony, Lady Bug?"

"Maybe they're afraid that we'll call attention to their relationship. I bet Ms. Blakey can smell that one a mile away." Lillie and Theo chuckled. Sure enough, Ms. Blakey was staring in Grace and Masseri's direction from her seat with a disapproving scowl on her face.

Just as Lillie turned around, Gabrielle Warren walked in, followed by an entourage of women. She went directly to Lady Abigail and gave her a hug, then she showed her the diamond ring on her finger and giggled coyly.

Dang! I'd hoped to avoid this. How do they know each other?

"Hey, Soror. So the article in the paper was true. You and Adam are serious about one another and getting married, too?" The first lady asked.

"Yes, we are. I'm so excited."

"Well, congratulations." Lady Abigail flashed a concerned look to Lillie, who in return shrugged her shoulders. "Make sure you call Bianca to make an appointment for counseling." First Lady's fake smile didn't cover up her confusion but Gabrielle's state of bliss must have caused her to not see it.

"Oh, we did that yesterday. No need to waste time. My consultants are already busy planning."

Wow! I bet she doesn't know Adam is technically still engaged to me.

Gabrielle flashed a radiant smile showing her perfect, pearly white teeth. Lillie couldn't help but admire her beauty. Her super model looks would easily align with Adam's celebrity pastoral persona. She'd heard that he'd taken on a full-time position as the assistant pastor. Even though Lillie was extremely jealous, she felt sorry for Gabrielle. Unfortunately, she must be oblivious to Adam's shenanigans.

Bianca smiled and said, "Girl, that's why I pulled you away. I wanted you to hear it from me instead of being a part of all this drama. I'm sorry, Lillie." Bianca hugged Lillie, and then Theo picked up where she left off.

"I found out yesterday at the service pastor hosted to welcome Adam to his staff. Don't you know he proposed to her right in front of everyone? Knowing they were all wondering about you. No explanation, no nothing."

Theo tightly embraced Lillie as tears welled up in her eyes. When she broke the embrace, she was face to face with Ms. Blakey. Theo walked to the balcony to talk to Grace and Masseri.

"I was never a fan of your relationship with that scoundrel piece of trash. It's the only thing me and that triflin' daddy of yours have ever agreed on. You know that, right?"

"Yes, ma'am. I am quite aware of how you feel about my daddy and other people's business."

"Hey! Don't be sassin' me. You see, good preaching and a handsome face don't fool me. I discern things in the spirit. Things nobody wants to talk about or they pretend like they don't see." The sternness of Ms. Blakey's face revealed a deep-seated annoyance. "If you'd have kept your fast behind in fellowship with the Lord, you wouldn't be in this predicament. Anybody with eyes can tell that you're expecting, child."

Lillie responded in surprise. "Me, pregnant? No way." She turned up her nose.

"Walking 'round her with your nose up that boys butt with that fake promise you're still wearing on your finger, I might add."

"Ms. Blakey!" Lillie responded as she pulled the ring off her finger. She'd forgotten all about it and was surprised that Theo didn't mention it either.

"Hush, girl, and listen. Now that Smith boy, I know his people. That's Deacon Smith's grandson, right?"

"Yes, ma'am," Lillie affirmed.

"He comes from good stock. If you marry him, he'll take care of you and that baby like it's his own. Don't be a fool like I was. I've been in your shoes."

Maybe that's why you're so bitter, Lillie thought.

"I've also done what you're thinking about doing."

Lillie almost choked on her spit when she heard those words.

"Keep your baby. It's not your life to take away."

Lillie started to cry because Ms. Blakey's rude transparency touched her heart. This was definitely a Titus moment where the seasoned women shared their knowledge with the younger women.

"Now, you keep Sam Corven in line. You know I pray for you momma every day."

Lillie burst out laughing as she hugged Ms. Blakey tight. Surprisingly, the older woman returned the affection then went back to her seat. Theo popped up with Grace and Masseri tagging behind.

"Let's go to church with my parents today," Theo suggested.

This was the best idea she'd heard thus far. She turned around and followed him back to his car. Right before Lillie climbed in the car, Adam strolled past her whistling like he didn't have a care in the world. She stared daggers at him and he flashed her a sinister grin.

GRRRRRRRR!

Lillie jumped when she heard the familiar sound. A shiver ran down her spine as she was reminded of the night she was stuck in the bathroom with the demon.

GRRRRRRRR!

She didn't even bother to ask Theo if he heard it. What was the point when she knew he didn't?

THIRTY-FOUR

THEO'S IDEA to visit his parent's church turned out to be just what Lillie needed. The service blessed Lillie's heart. It was refreshing to see a humble pastoral husband and wife team. They ministered in the pulpit together as one. After service, Deacon and Mrs. Smith had a chat with Lillie and their son.

"How did you enjoy the service?" Mrs. Smith asked as she gave Lillie another one of her famous bear hugs, squeezing her so tight, she could barely breathe.

"Amazing!" Lillie answered once she caught her breath.

"Baby girl, you need a change of pace from all the drama over there." Deacon Smith wasn't one to hold his tongue or put up with mess.

Theo chimed in changing the subject. "I don't know about you all, but I'm starving. Let's go to the Polaris Grill."

"Yeah, their brunch buffet is just what I need right now." Lillie smiled as Theo pulled her into his arms, planting a juicy kiss on her lips.

Theo's parents stopped in their tracks.

"Does this mean…"

"Yes, Mom. We…" Before he could finish the statement, Deacon and Mrs. Smith embraced Lillie and Theo. Tears flowed down Mrs. Smith's face.

"We've always wanted the two of you to get together. Let's invite your parents to brunch too." Lillie called her parents who willingly joined them.

While the families dined, Lillie's cell phone vibrated, notifying her of an e-mail from Adam. Reluctantly, she read the contents.

Lillie,

By now, I'm sure you heard I'm getting married. Not to you and not to Mallory. Why? Because I was never with Mallory and I regret being involved with you. My mother told me that you weren't cut out to be a pastor's wife. Theo called me to tell me about his intentions with you and the baby. He had the nerve to tell me not contacting you would be in my best interest. I'm still pissed you told him about our baby and not me. Your actions let me know you don't love me as much as you say. I bet that baby isn't even mine. You're just like all the rest of the tricks. And you better check your crazy, weed-smoking dad. He came into my church office threatening to shoot me with his archaic shotgun. I'm a grown man, and I don't have time to deal with a weak woman who can't stand on her own. You need Theo and your dad to fight your battles. Gabby is the kind of woman who intuitively understands my needs. Unlike you, she was there for me when Jonna was going through her alcohol addiction. Bet you didn't know she was her sponsor. She's a recovering alcoholic and she has her stuff together more than you. I need a woman who has what it takes to be a first lady and we all know that you don't. You're lucky I stooped low enough to date you with all your worldly ways and occult-practicing friends. As assistant pastor of Radical Faith, I suggest that you, Mr. Smith, and the lesbian lovers (bet you thought I didn't know) find a new church home.

Adam

Lillie dropped her phone on the ground, sickened by Adam's crass letter and her level of naivety. She never questioned the fact that he was hanging out with Jonna's sponsor. Especially when he said they all went to college together. This wasn't the Adam she'd met that night at Flow, or was it? She continued to steam while Theo picked up her phone from the ground.

"Is everything okay?"

"No. Not at all. Read this crazy note. I can't believe that stupid jerk."

No longer able to hold back tears, Lillie ran to the bathroom. She slammed the stall door and locked it so no one could disturb her. The pain in her heart continued to increase, so she cried until her eye ducts could no longer make tears. Desperate to get rid of any traces of Adam Johnson from her life, she decided to keep the appointment with her OB/GYN Theo had asked her to cancel. Lillie was determined to end this pregnancy.

When she came out of the bathroom, both her mother and Theo's mother were waiting. Without saying a word, they embraced Lillie, giving her the comfort she needed.

"Lillie, baby. I know you're hurting right now. Theo ordered a little something for you to take home so you can recoup from this devastation in private." Her mother kissed her on the forehead and led her back to the table. Lillie was thankful for the gesture.

"Oh don't worry, Mom. I'll take good care of her. That cat has to answer to me for what he did." Theo hugged all of the parents and said his goodbyes. Then, he and Lillie walked to the car and drove to her place in silence.

The moment Theo dropped Lillie off at home, she called Bianca to share the events of the day and ask her to take her to the appointment. She also wanted to talk about Bianca breaking off her relationship with her college friend.

"Bee, what's up, sister?" Lillian greeted her friend.

"Hey, Lil. I'm glad you called."

"I have a favor to ask."

"Shoot."

"Okay. I need a ride to the—"

"Don't say the word. I'll take you but I don't want to talk about it. When?"

Relieved, Lillie shared information about the appointment with Bianca.

"Now that I'm getting rid of my problem, I wanted to talk to you about getting rid of yours," Lillie shared.

"First of all, your baby isn't a problem. I wish you'd see how much of a blessing he or she could be to your life."

"So, your affair is a blessing to yours?" Lillie razzed. "How are you keeping up with your man and Todd anyway?"

"Let's just say orgasms drain you at first but give you energy in the long run. You should know that." Since she made such a nasty comment about the affair, Lillie ignored Bianca's crass statement. Hell would freeze over before she stepped foot in Radical Faith Church again. She'd lost all respect for Pastor Andrews. Plus, her wounds were too raw to bear seeing Adam and Gabrielle in their state of pre-marital bliss.

Now that Lillie had secured a ride, she felt relieved. She wondered what would be worse—having an abortion or giving birth to Adam Johnson's fifth child. Full-fledged baby mama's status.

I'll take the abortion for $1,000, Alex.

THIRTY-FIVE

L ILLIE ARRIVED at the consultation appointment not knowing exactly what to expect. Dr. Samuelson wasn't her normal OB/GYN, so this experience was totally new. Once she completed the Targeted History Form, the doctor conducted a physical exam. Next, he sent her to another room with the ultrasound technician so they could confirm how far along she was in her pregnancy. Once these procedures were complete, the nurse ushered her to Dr. Samuelson's office to discuss the options for the procedure.

"Are you serious?" Lillie exclaimed. "This is a list of abortion options."

"We like to refer to them as pregnancy termination choices," Dr. Samuelson corrected Lillie as he plastered on a fake smile.

I guess that's supposed to make it sound better, Lillie thought.

"Okay, I get it. Can you help me go through these options?"

"Yes, that's why we're here today. First of all, you're sixteen weeks along. For this reason, I suggest that you be sedated during the procedure."

"Sedated?" Lillie shrieked in surprise. "I don't claim to be an abortion expert, but is sedation really a necessary option?"

Dr. Samuelson put on that fake smile again and responded. "We coach our clients according to their stage of gestation. Most people terminate their pregnancy earlier, so we typically don't even discuss sedation with them. That may be the reason you've never heard about it."

Lillie only knew of one person who had an abortion and she did it at nine weeks, so the doctor probably had a valid point.

The doctor paused and made a note on the chart. "The procedure is longer and much more uncomfortable at this stage. Also, since you are so far along, we'll have to dilate your cervix."

"Dilate my cervix? Why do we need to do that?" Lillie raised her eyebrow.

"Good question. Once again, most people only know about the abortion process in the early stages, so I get why you're confused."

"I'm glad you understand."

"Of course. I don't mind explaining. We have to dilate your cervix so that the contents of your uterus can easily pass through. Here's the process. First, we'll swab your cervix with Betadine, which is a cleaning solution. Then, we'll insert a small, sterilized stick in your cervix."

"Will this hurt?" Lillie asked. "I want to be prepared just in case."

Dr. Samuelson chuckled and responded. "Since I don't have a cervix I wouldn't know."

Lillie knew he was trying to put her at ease with his jokes, however, she didn't appreciate his familiar bedside manner. Her mother always said that a man had no place in women's business. Especially when it comes to our bodies. Now, that statement made so much sense. Once Dr. Samuelson realized her displeasure, he cleared his throat and continued.

"Some women say they can barely feel it while others say it's quite painful."

"Makes sense. When do you do this?"

"We'll schedule an appointment for you on the day before your actual procedure. The goal is to ensure that your cervix has ample time to dilate. Well, that's all I have to share for now. What questions do you have for me?"

"I don't have any more questions, yet. Thank you for explaining all of this to me."

"You're welcome, Lillie. I want you to know that we conduct these procedures many times each day. You're in good hands and there's no reason for you to feel bad."

Lillie was surprised by the doctor's candid statement.

"When I reviewed your chart, I noticed that you selected Christian as your religious belief. Most Christians I know aren't advocates for abortion, so I can see why this is a challenging decision for you."

"Well, I love the Lord, but just like everyone else, I make mistakes. I shouldn't have to live with that for the rest of my life."

"That's why we give you twenty-four hours to change your mind. In your case, it will be twenty-four hours prior to the cervical dilation procedure. The receptionist will give you some literature when you sign out and make your next two appointments."

"Thank you, Doctor. For some reason, I feel better. Not better about the decision, but better in general."

"Don't worry about explaining. I've seen enough patients in your shoes to understand," Dr. Samuelson reassured her.

Lillie closed out the consultation at the front desk and headed to her car. To her surprise, Theo was standing there waiting. He ran to Lillie and passionately embraced her.

"I can't believe you are really going to go through with this," Theo said as he stroked Lillie's hair.

"How did you know I was here?"

"I know this sounds crazy but last night I had a dream about this place. Then, on my way to work, I noticed that you had dropped a brochure on the floor in my car. The appointment time and date was written on the back."

What are the odds of that?

"Unfortunately, I was too late to get her when the appointment started, but I'm here now."

"Why did you come, Theo?"

"To tell you that you don't have to do this. I told you I'd take care of you and the baby."

Touched by Theo's sincerity, tears flowed down her face. He embraced her tightly and began to pray for her right there in the parking lot. She cried and cried until she couldn't cry anymore. Lillie knew this was one of the most crucial decisions she ever had to make. As much as she loved Theo, there was no way she could see him taking care of Adam's child. That was a burden she just wasn't willing to put on him. She knew she'd live to regret that decision but it was a chance she was willing to take.

THIRTY-SIX

L ILLIE RECALLED a sermon she'd heard a few months ago. "If you play with fire you'll get burned. The funny thing is most victims don't sense the heat until they're in the midst of the blaze. The temperature creeps up a few degrees at a time, while the flame beckons its unsuspecting prey to come closer. The enemy hides the deliberate intention of harm, ensuring the ultimate transition to the third degree zone. Without warning, the fire consumes the naïve prisoner's entire being. The result is an aftermath of ashy residue and gruesome scars."

Fallen victim to a cauldron full of pain, Lillie refused to allow her agony to be soothed. Instead, she sat in the clinic lobby, swallowing an excruciating heartache, giving in to a lethargic spirit. The purple walls closed her in to a circle of misery, accented by track lighting that drove her to the brink of insanity. Catching a glimpse of Bianca's tear-stained face, Lillie's agony only increased. Torn between the desire to console her friend and the need to find a sense of peace, her heart beat at a furious pace.

"Please stop crying, Bee." Lillie gently squeezed her shoulder. "You're making this harder."

Bianca turned from Lillie's gaze and dropped her chin. "I'm only here in this backwoods clinic on the hottest day of the year because I promised to support you during this horrid ordeal," she retorted with sharp abruptness. "I never said I agreed with your decision."

"I'm not asking you to agree with it. Just make sure this stays between you and I. There's only one other person who knows and I'd like to keep it that way."

"What? There's no way I'd admit to coming here to this seedy place with you. You ought to be ashamed of yourself. I know I am."

Not wanting to make a scene, Lillie straightened her long, flowing sundress as she reached to grab Bianca's arm. "Bee, what am I supposed to do? I can't have this baby. You know what I'm up against."

"Lillie Corven," the nurse barked in a sterile, unsympathetic tone.

Bianca's uncontrollable sobbing magnified the brokenness of Lillie's spirit. Without further hesitation, she made her walk of shame to the reception area, only a few steps closer to sealing the deal. Thanks to the preparatory procedure the night before, she couldn't turn back even if she wanted to. Lillie tried to reach into the depths of her soul to turn off any emotional connection she had to the unborn child. Like a dead woman walking, she gasped for breath as she held back the tears.

For the first time, she noticed the others in the room. The young lady sat next to Bianca who appeared to be about sixteen years old, yet her boyfriend seemed to be pushing forty.

He could be her father, but does it even matter? I guess not. Wait a minute, only crazy people talk to themselves and actually answer.

"Second call for Lillie Corven." The nurse's irritating screech sent Lillie over the edge.

"Shut up, you old hag! I'm coming!" Lillie's buried anger surfaced like a geyser. She regretted the outburst when a vision of the psychic reading those tarot cards flashed before her eyes. Overwhelmed by the memory coming to life, she stumbled on the ground and instinctively covered her stomach. She pulled herself off the ground and caught a glimpse of herself in the mirror behind the desk. Then she screamed like a banshee when she saw the Grim Reaper's walking closely behind her. Bianca ran to her side and rubbed her back gently. The cloaked villain didn't disappear, though. Instead, he hovered, carrying a sharp scythe in his right hand. Lillie shrieked in horror when she envisioned the old spirit using this instrument to pick away the ice from her heart.

Why did it have to end this way? He was supposed to love me. Not get me pregnant and leave me hanging.

"First time, huh?" The nurse stopped writing and glanced up from the chart. "I can always tell."

The realization of the grave situation stifled Lillie's speech. The stench of the baby-killing factory attacked her nostrils like a cougar preying on a gazelle, causing her stomach to lurch.

"Don't worry about a thing. We'll take great care of you. Plus, the receptionist said you have great health insurance to be self-employed." She instructed Bianca to return to her seat.

Lillie sneered as she recalled acquiring group health insurance coverage from a representative at the church who specialized in working with entrepreneurs. Who knew the plan she purchased to preserve her life would offer enough coverage to kill another.

A staff member escorted Lillie into a room where a nurse proceeded to take her blood pressure and check her vitals. She then conducted the required silent ultrasound without saying a word.

If I were keeping this baby, there's no way I'd get near an ultrasound machine.

Relief filled Lillie's mind since she didn't hear the baby's heartbeat. Those quick palpitations tortured her during the initial consultation. Without warning, the familiar smell of sage assaulted her nostrils. She sniffed overtly, arousing the attention of the medical assistant.

"Is everything okay, Miss Corven? What are you doing?" The medical assistant scrunched her eyes and waited for an answer.

Out of nowhere, a young girl appeared. The same little tot from the psychic's home in California. Lillie just knew it was all a dream until she heard the familiar nursery rhyme.

"Hickory Dickory dock. The mouse ran up the clock. The clock struck one. The mouse ran down. Hickory ..."

"Get that little girl out of here," she screamed hysterically.

The medical assistant arched her eyebrow and responded, "What ... little ... girl?"

Despite the medical assistant's oblivion, the nursery rhyme continued to permeate the atmosphere.

"Hickory Dickory dock. The mouse ran up the clock. The clock struck one. The mouse ran down. Hickory ..."

"The one right there in the corner." Lillie continually pointed at the girl when she noticed the confused look on the medical assistant's face. "Can't you hear her singing?"

"Are you crazy or something?" The medical professional rose from her seat and began to back away from Lillie. Realizing her mind was playing tricks on her, she decided to be quiet. All of a sudden, Sage's sinister laugh took the place of the fading nursery rhyme.

"The spirit of death is all around you," Sage teased over and over again in between her evil laughter.

Lillie knew she was going crazy as the nurse continued to stare at her in disbelief. She broke out into an uncontrollable sweat, soaking through her Donna Karen linen jersey dress. Her skin was boiling so Lillie pulled a piece of paper out of her purse and began fanning herself. Then, the young girl vanished into thin air just as sudden as she'd appeared. The singing and the evil laughter faded with her.

"Are you ready to finish, now?" the assistant asked reluctantly.

Lillie hesitated for a moment. The pregnant pause enveloped the ambience of the room, causing this strange moment to be even more awkward.

"Yes. Let's finish," Lillie replied.

Still shaken from the strange vision, Lillie stared at the white ceiling while the nurse finished her business. The decontaminated smell of hospital antiseptic filled her nostrils. After she finished the diagnostic evaluation, the assistant handed Lillie a sterile cotton gown that felt like sandpaper. Her insensitive demeanor only confirmed Lillie's belief she was nothing more than a statistic, adding to the multiple layers of guilt and shame that piled on Lillie's heart.

"Change into this, remove your underwear, and take a seat," she ordered like a drill sergeant running boot camp. "Dr. Samuelson will be in soon with the intern."

Great. All I need is another person probing and prodding at my body, Lillie pouted as she stared at the tray of metallic silver utensils—instruments of death. Before she had the opportunity to fall deeper into self-pity, the doctor, intern, and an unknown third medical professional entered the room. Their presence crowded the space even more.

"Hello, Miss Corven." Lillie couldn't help but wince at Dr. Samuelson's greeting. His bedside manner was non-existent, which made it easy to distinguish him from his father. Moreover, abortions were never an option when the older man owned this practice.

I guess death and subsequent inheritance gives you the right to do what you please.

In addition to obstetrics gynecology, he and the other doctors who joined the practice offered an interesting array of services— liposuction, tummy tucks, Botox injections, cellulite presses, and vaginoplasties. Catering to the needs of vain women must be a profitable business since they'd opened two additional locations on opposite sides of town. Lillie shuttered just thinking about it.

"Hi, Dr. Samuelson." Lillie's feigned greeting was awkward.

"I need you to sign this release, stating you're aware Billy is an intern and you're okay with him assisting with this procedure."

Grabbing the pen from his hand, Lillie signed the form with extreme urgency. Once this catastrophic event was over, she could move on with her life.

"This is Shelly, the anesthesiologists. She'll sedate you so we can begin."

"Ms. Corven, please relax and count backwards from ten. I'll place a mask over your nose and mouth. I want you to find a spot on the wall or something in the room to focus on." Shelly's voice had a calming effect on Lillie. "There will be a brief moment of euphoria, and then, you won't know anything until you wake up when the procedure is complete."

"That easy, huh?" Lillie responded in a harsh, sarcastic tone that made Shelly flinch. At a loss for other options, Lillie followed Shelly's instructions. She concentrated on the rack of Good Housekeeping magazines while the hatred in her heart for Adam increased each moment. She prayed for forgiveness in her spirit then stopped abruptly.

God will never forgive me for what I'm about to do, so what's the point?

"Ten." *I'm sorry I ever met the jerk.*

"Nine." *Will I go to hell for this?*

"Eight." *I wonder if it hurts when they use those metallic silver instruments.*

"Seven." *Ooh, it tastes like grapes.*

"Six." *I wonder what my parents would think.*

"Five." *Wow. I'm in paradise. These meds are strong.*

"Four." *How did this happen to me?"*

"Three." *I'm so sleepy. Lillie yawned.*

"Two." *I can't believe…"*

"One"…

ö ℜ

Lillie awoke from the anesthetic sleep in a disoriented state of confusion. Once her vision stabilized, a row of beds filled with patients just like her assaulted her eyesight. Some slept, while others cried buckets of tears. A few of the women masked their pain, staring into space with no apparent expressions on their faces. Lillie touched her stomach, taken aback at the difference.

A sagging emptiness replaced the hardness of her abdomen. The hollowness seemed strange after experiencing life growing inside of her for sixteen weeks.

"Good, it's gone." Despite the ability to spit out those words with ease, a bittersweet cocktail of guilt and shame overwhelmed Lillie's psyche. Slamming her fist into the mattress repeatedly, she fought the urge to cry. The sound of feet scuffling quickly toward her bed interrupted the fit of rage.

"Miss Corven." It was the same nurse as before. "Are you okay?" Lillie stared at the ceiling, refusing to make eye contact, as she twisted her hair around her fingers.

"Yes, I'm fine as a woman can be after getting rid of her baby," Lillie responded, flat and void of emotion.

The nurse smiled and spoke gently, "Rest a little longer, and tell me when you're ready to check out." She walked out of the room, leaving Lillie to wallow in her miserable thoughts. To avoid drowning in pity, she listened to a young woman laying a few beds down from her. For some reason, she was talking on her cell phone, despite the restriction sign on the wall.

"I loved our baby enough to admit we're not fit for parenthood. We both work too much," she admitted. "Do I feel guilty? Hell no! Welfare recipients who pop out babies without restraint should be ashamed, not me." Her derogatory accusation seemed to deflect from the real issue, in Lillie's eyes. Disgusted, she decided to tune her out and eavesdrop on another conversation.

"I helped Mom raise our brother who had Down Syndrome, so when the amniocentesis revealed a positive result for the disease, we made the decision to do what was best for everyone involved." The woman's tone exuded an uncanny sense of confidence.

What a strange thing to be confident about at a time like this.

"I understand your perspective, Mrs. Candet. Mr. Candet, how do you feel about this?" Lillie recognized this voice as one belonging to the doctoral candidate from The Ohio State University who conducted an informational interview at the initial appointment.

"I support my wife wholeheartedly. We believe caring for a child with these issues will cause hardships for our family," the man added. "That's why we plan to pursue a sterilization procedure. You know, we're the proud parents of three beautiful children, and we're too old to have more without taking a big chance."

For Lillie, hearing a man's point of view on the issue was unsettling yet comforting all at the same time. *I wonder what Adam would say if he were being interviewed about this situation.*

"Plus, we can't stand the heartache again." The woman's voice trembled as she revealed her deep thoughts. Lillie heard the husband's footsteps as he went to his wife's side to give her comfort.

Tears rolled down Lillie's face as she listened in on these private conversations. Like her, they all believed they had a valid reason for ending a life. Lillie's spirit was unsettled by this sudden revelation and she decided it was time to break free from this baby-killing factory. She inhaled deeply, holding her breath in anticipation of her release since she couldn't take the atmosphere of death any longer. She exhaled, thanking the Lord for perfect timing as the nurse returned to the room.

"Miss Corven. We need to discuss aftercare responsibilities." She handed Lillie a packet and reviewed the contents. "Now, let's check your pulse and blood pressure. You'll be free to go if everything is normal. Of course, you must have someone drive you home."

The post examination results were favorable, so Lillie dressed with the speed of a cheetah. She checked out and picked up her prescriptions—an antibiotic to prevent infection and an anti-emetic in case of extreme nausea or vomiting. The drugs probably cost more than the procedure. Lillie still couldn't believe the abortion was covered but the insurance company wouldn't cover birth control pills. But then again, she didn't want to fill her body full of that hormonal nightmare waiting to happen.

As soon as Bianca laid eyes on Lillie, she ran to comfort her friend. She signed the release form, indicating she'd drive Lillie home. "Bianca, why are you still crying?" Lillie asked. "It's over now. If I'm not shedding any more tears, neither should you." Bianca's eyes pierced Lillie's soul as she grabbed her keys. "Let's go. I wonder how much we'll have to lay on the altar for this," Bianca yelled. Heads turned, trying to find out who was responsible for the crazy outburst. Lillie pondered on Bianca's thought, then, decided repenting wouldn't do any good. Despite what the Bible said, she didn't believe the Lord would forgive willful sin.

"How'd I allow myself to get into this situation?" Lillie asked as she twisted her hair around her fingers.

"I'm sorry for snapping at you. This situation is making me crazy." Bianca's tone changed from judgmental to empathetic. "Don't ponder on it, Lillie. Otherwise, your memories, guilt, and shame will overtake you. Trust me, I understand. I've got secrets of my own, you know." Bianca's facial expression showed sincere concern for Lillie's well-being. "Now that you've made this decision, you have to start over, allow yourself to be healed, and take steps to get back in the will of the Lord," Bianca advised. "And stop twisting your freakin' hair, for God's sake!

THIRTY-SEVEN

ILLIE, HE *loves you. Places no one above you. Let him back in. Back in your life again."*
Lillie and Rosa looked up from her desk when a group of singers walked into her office singing to the tune of a fifties song. Of course, they'd changed the words to match her situation. Three months had passed since the fatal day of Lillie's abortion, and she was trying everything within her power to keep it together. Frustration set in as she tried to ignore the guilt and shame that haunted her like the ghost of Christmas past. Unfortunately, no matter how hard she tried, she wasn't able to disconnect from her tortuous decision. So Lillie remained secluded from her friends the entire time. Especially Theo. Why would he want tarnished goods when he could have someone with less baggage?

The women continued to belt out the beautiful medley as Theo strolled in her office followed by deliverymen with what seemed like hundreds of calla lilies. After the ladies finished the song, they quietly exited the office. Theo didn't say a word. Instead, he pulled

Lillie close to him and kissed her with such intensity her cold heart melted. She returned his kiss with a fiery passion, not caring who witnessed the exchange. Theo escorted Lillie out of the building and she gasped when a stretch limo pulled up.

"For me?"

"No. For us."

Theo opened her door and helped her into the beautiful automobile. They rode around the city for the next few hours and talked out their differences. Then, the driver took them back to Easton where they dined at McCormick and Schmick's. When Theo dropped Lillie off at home, she was so giddy she couldn't sleep. The reunion made her want to reconnect with the rest of her friends. Since Bianca was the path of least resistance, she decided to give her a call first.

"Lillie," Bianca exclaimed with joy. "It's so good to hear from you. Oh yeah. I heard you won some kind of award for your business."

"Yes, I did. I'm the Human Resources innovator of the year. Anytime you win awards for your business, it opens you up to a new stream of clients. We've added another consultant, too."

"Wow! That's wonderful." Bianca's smile was evident even across the phone lines.

"So, how are things going with you and Todd?" Lillie was reluctant to ask Bianca about her marriage; however, she was determined to help her friend end this obsession with her friend from college.

"Hold on, Lillie." Bianca dropped the phone and scolded one of her children. "Lillie. I'm so sorry, but I have to handle this. I'll call you back."

Lillie and Bianca said their goodbyes and ended the call. Of course, Lillie knew the abrupt ending was Bianca's way to get out of discussing her affair. No matter what, Lillie was determined to help her friend break this pattern of negative behavior.

80 03

For the first weekend since they'd been a couple, Theo went on a business trip. Lillie decided to get some rest and relaxation, but thoughts of the great times she used to have with Grace and Masseri dominated her thoughts. Finally, on Sunday afternoon, she took a chance, walked over to Grace's condo, and rang the doorbell. This formality seemed strange yet with all that happened over the past few months, she didn't feel comfortable just walking in like she normally did. When Grace answered, Lillie wasn't surprised to see Masseri sitting at the island in the kitchen chomping on a hearty plate of food. Lillie's stomach growled audibly when the scrumptious smell hit her olfactory senses. Without speaking a word, Grace fixed Lillie a plate. Lillie washed her hands, sat down on one of the four island stools, and began to eat.

Masseri, the most spirited one in the group, broke the silence. "It's good to see you, Lillie. What took you so long to come to your senses?"

"Oh, this is about me coming to my senses? I think not. It's about the fact that both of you were living a lie and you involved my brother in your mess," Lillie challenged.

Masseri chuckled and turned up her nose at Lillie.

"Your attitude doesn't faze me one bit, Masseri. In fact, we'll see how long this little relationship lasts," Lillie shouted.

"Little? I can't believe you said that," Grace cried.

Masseri closed her eyes and screamed with passionate anger. "See, Grace. I don't know why you care what this hypocritical trick thinks."

"Look. Here's my issue. The two of you should have just been up front with your relationship instead of involving my brother and lying to us."

Grace stood next to her lover who kissed her on the forehead. Lillie couldn't help but be touched by their tender exchange. Masseri breathed deeply and exhaled slowly.

"I'm going to go for a walk in the park. You can keep talking to her if you want, but I'm done." Masseri marched out the door and slammed it behind her.

"Her temper has always been a problem and that's who you choose to love," Lillie spat.

"You've spoke your peace, now it's time for me to speak mine. I don't appreciate you telling Alvin what you saw before Masseri had the chance. People need to hear things from the source—"

Lillie interrupted Grace. "Uh uh. Stop deflecting from the true issue at hand. She should have told him a long time ago. In fact, their whole relationship was shaky. With her freaky behind."

"Now, she's my lover, and I won't stand here and allow you to talk about her, even if it's true." Grace gave Lillie a coy look, and they burst out laughing.

"Is that why you like her? Because she's freaky?"

"Lillie, you're always telling me that I need to take a diversity class. Look in the mirror, sister. I love Masseri for who she is, contrary to popular belief. Not because she's freaky or because she's a woman. You can't help who you fall in love with."

"So, let me get this straight. You don't like men anymore?"

"You're so closed minded. If you have to put a label on us, call it bisexual. Masseri and I are both attracted to men. We don't know if we'll continue to see one another, but for now, that's what we're doing. Alvin even gave Masseri some space to decide what she wants to do."

"Wow! My brother is an understanding man."

Grace rolled her eyes and said, "Hmm. People who live in glass houses shouldn't throw stones. Theo still wants you after your escapades with Adam and your little trip to the abortion clinic."

What? How did she know that? Lillie was perplexed, because even though some suspected, only Theo, Bianca, Adam, and the people at Dr. Samuelson's office knew for sure.

"I already know what you're thinking. Remember, these walls are thin, sister."

Just as Grace finished her statement, Theo walked in with Masseri, laughing and joking about a basketball game they'd both seen on television. "Lillie, I got back early just to see you and who do I run into? This crazy woman. How does Alvin feel about Grace stealing her away?" Masseri playfully punched Theo in the arm and he faked a karate stance, pretending to retaliate.

"If I could take her, she must not have been his in the first place," Grace sassed.

Theo scratched his head and said, "I can't believe I'm having this conversation with a woman. On a serious note. I may never understand this . . . uh . . . strange relationship, but there's no hard feelings between us. Cool?"

"Cool," Grace and Masseri said simultaneously.

"So let's eat and play some Apples to Apples. Adam's kids aren't here to win, so we might have a chance," Grace said.

Theo joked, "No more Be Be's Kids, so now it's heterosexuals versus homosexuals. The power of Jesus shall prevail."

Masseri shook her head and said, "I'm not even offended by that ignorant statement. Let's see if your theory is right, Theo."

Lillie flexed her muscles and shouted, "Let the games begin."

THIRTY-EIGHT

Silent Tears

Why do silent tears seem to hurt the most?
Tiny, bitter droplets encapsulating my pain
Purging the brokenness of my heart, oozing with hate
Beckoning me to wake up and smell the coffee
Hey you, over there! The face of my pain
Why do you have such a hold on me?
You won't let go, yet I don't want you
This is why I cry on the inside
Where you won't have the pleasure
Of seeing this treasure looted for a prize
Stop trying to take away my cry. It's mine.
You will never know that I am broken, wait . . .
Don't you get it? I'm only human. I hurt, too.
I'm not your verbal punching bag. Stop throwing blows.
Suck it up. Stop being a victim. Real women don't cry.

Get over it. Move on. Keep it moving.
Aaaaaaaaaaaaaaaawwwwwwwwwwwwwwww!
Can't you see my pain? It's written all over my face
If only you'd take the time to look
I'm dying on the inside, yet no one knows
I don't want to hear your stupid and insensitive advice
That's why I cry on the inside, in perfect silence
Yet, secretly praying that my tears are heard in the spirit
Even though it seems they aren't
Maybe that's why silent tears seem to hurt the most
Hmmmmm …

The audience at Flow gave a thunderous applause in honor of Bianca's dynamic performance. Her first reading was passionate, real, and exceptional. Bianca took a bow, and then shared her testimony.

"Prior to marrying Todd, I was involved in an abusive relationship. My esteem was low and I didn't trust anyone. Even though Todd is good to me, I never overcame the abuse I suffered. I decided to get some help and now, I'm experiencing healing for the first time in my life." The audience clapped and cheered for her victory.

"I'm a part of a group called Healing for Wounded Souls. The leader encouraged me to journal about my experiences. He's a strong believer in healing through artistic expression. I started writing poems in my journal and when I read them aloud to Todd, he encouraged me to share with you all here tonight. Your positive reception to my piece is a blessing." The crowd resumed their applause and Bianca took a bow. "Thank you for being a part of my healing." As she exited the stage, Todd and their children showered her with hugs and kisses.

"Great job, sister!" Lillie congratulated Bianca and gave her a bear hug. Lillie scanned her immediate surroundings to be sure that Todd and the kids were out of earshot. "So, I take it that you're…"

"Yes. It's over."

Lillie smiled and said, "You're definitely overcoming your demons."

"It became much easier when Todd went back to work. I definitely learned from this experience. I'll never put myself in the position to cheat on my husband ever again."

Tears streamed down Lillie's cheeks. "I'm so glad to hear that, Bee."

"It was an easy decision once I saw the relationship for what it really was. You'd be surprised at how many other women he's seeing."

"What! Are you serious?" Lillie had to admit, she was surprised. In innocence, she was under the impression that his indiscretion with Bianca was the extent of his sin.

"I'm glad you're taking accountability for your role in this and not pretending to be a victim."

"It takes two to tango, and I was a willing dance partner." Bianca and Lillie shared a laugh.

"Have you told Todd?"

"It's not that easy, Lillie. Todd's a new Christian. This might cause him to backslide. Plus, he wouldn't forgive me, and I can't risk losing him."

"I believe you shouldn't try to predict what he's going to do." They burst out laughing and Elaina joined them at the table.

"Well, enough about me. Let me tell you. If I didn't know for myself that Adam was a jerk, I'd swear he was the epitome of a man of God."

"How can you go to church where he's in leadership after what he did to me?"

Bianca turned to Elaina and asked, "Do you think people should leave a church when they find out the ministers are doing something against the word of God?"

Elaina paused for a moment and then responded. "Good question. I guess you do want the person leading you to practice holiness."

"Uh, yeah," Lillie chimed in. "I'm not big on telling people how to live but I do believe you should practice what you preach or get fired."

"But, what would happen if every time the pastor found out about one of our sins, he put us out of the church? Could you imagine this: 'Lillie, I'm kickking you out of church because you ate too much at that buffet last Sunday.'"

The ladies looked at one another and burst out laughing.

"For me, it's not about sin or no sin. As I grow, I don't believe God operates like that. At the same time, you have to be a role model for the way you're telling people they should live. I've failed miserably at that, so I should know." Lillie couldn't believe the words that came out of her own mouth, yet they felt right.

"I can't say I agree with you," Elaina paused for a moment then finished her thought. "I believe sin is sin so Adam not living what he's preaching about is no different than Ms. Blakey's nasty behavior. God sees all sin the same. Humans measure sin, not God."

"Makes sense but what if this life is about growing spiritually as and not about judgment? It's hard for me to not want Adam to rot in Hell, but with all I've been through, I'm not even sure Hell exists."

Bianca shook her head in disbelief. "Girl, what you're saying is so not in line with what's in the Bible so stop talking that foolishness."

Lillie chuckled. "Maybe pastor's do what they do because they know this is all a grand hoax. They've got us all caught up in this fear based crap to keep us in line and keep the tithes coming in."

Elaina and Bianca gasped in horror. "Lillie, you're going to bust Hell wide open talking like that. I know you're upset, but my goodness."

"What if I'm right?" Lillie's question left a thick cloud of heaviness in the room and they all sat in silence.

THIRTY-NINE

LILLIE RELAXED on her patio as she sipped on a cup of Ti Quan Yin. A magnetic force pulled her glance upward and she saw the most beautiful full moon ever. It was a beautiful sight, yet she couldn't help but remember her mother's old wives tale about strange things happening during this time of the month. For some strange reason, she had an eerie feeling, but she dismissed it, writing it off as superstition. A lone cloud slowly moved to cover the moon and CoCo barked with a fury, then ran to the edge of the patio. Not sure what the disturbance could be, Lillie shivered as she grabbed her cell phone, ready to call the police at any moment. To her surprise, a manly figure emerged from the woods. Lillie screamed hysterically, until she realized the identity of the shadow owner.

"What are you doing here, Adam?"

Like a lost puppy, Adam responded, "I had to see you. I needed some closure. I thought I didn't, but I do."

"Closure. That's interesting. How's Gabrielle?" Lillie asked with sincerity in her heart.

Adam rolled his eyes and answered, "She's fine."

"You two are newlyweds. So shouldn't you be home, tending to your new wife?"

"I didn't come here to talk about my wife. I want to talk about us."

"Us? Us, who?" Lillie retorted. Adam walked closer to Lillie and CoCo growled, protecting her owner.

"Can I come in? I have some things to share with you."

"Heck no! You can't come in. In fact, I want you to leave now."

"Come on, Lillie. Just hear me out and I promise to leave."

Lillie contemplated Adam's proposal, then responded. "You have fifteen minutes to state your case right here." As Lillie laid out the ground rules, memories of the times they'd spent on the patio flashed before her eyes. Almost as if he could read her mind, Adam moved closer and gently stroked her cheek. Ignoring CoCo's growl, he embraced Lillie and kissed her gently. Her resolve melted like ice cream on a hot, summer day.

"Stop! Don't you touch me."

Adam took advantage of her weakness and continued to lavish her with affection.

"I never meant to hurt you. Brandi lied about so many things, and I want to explain." Adam's deep, sexy voice beckoned Lillie to give in.

Lillie came back to her senses and responded, "You had your chance to explain, and chose to write that stupid letter instead. If it wasn't for Theo—"

At the mention of Theo's name, Adam stomped his foot and yelled, "Oh, Theo. If it wasn't for him, I'd probably be married to you today and not that controlling—"

"Oh, no! First, you were married to Tia during most of our relationship, so how could you have married me? Then as soon as you were free, you married Gabrielle instead of me, your fiancé. That's the wife you chose, and we'll not speak ill against her in my house."

"Oh, so now you want to front on me. What about the baby, Lillie? Were you even pregnant?"

"You've got to be kidding me. Did we ever use protection?"

"Whatever, Lillie. We didn't, and I was a fool for that, because you could have been sleeping with anyone. In fact, I believe Theo is the baby's father, not me."

Adam's accusation stung Lillie like a swarm of bumblebees at a church picnic. Holding back tears, she gritted through her teeth, "You've gone too far, and I'd appreciate it if you'd leave right now. In fact…" Lillie ran into her bedroom and grabbed the engagement ring that Adam had given her and ran back to the patio.

"You gave me this ring here, so I guess it makes sense that you get it back in the same location."

Adam took the ring from Lillie and put it in his pocket. "You don't look pregnant … Wait a minute. You didn't …"

"Didn't what, Adam? It's not like you cared, anyway."

"You had an abortion?" Adam yelled in disbelief. The bass in his voice could've rocked a late night party. Pointing his finger in Lillie's face, Adam barked, "You're a murderer and a sinner."

Lillie couldn't believe the words that were coming out of Adam's mouth.

He can't be serious. What makes him think he has the right to talk about me like this?

"Let's get something straight. I did choose to terminate the pregnancy, and I had my reasons. You'll never understand what I was going through. Especially since you were the cause of my pain."

"I have four children, and I didn't encourage any of their mothers to abort them. You had other options. Maybe if you'd have sat down to talk with me, we could have worked it out."

"You selfish … Oooh! You almost made me cuss. What was I supposed to do? We weren't even officially broken up and you were engaged to Gabrielle, and now she's your wifey."

"You know it should've been you." Like a piranha sensing blood in the water, he went in for the kill and kissed Lillie passionately. Instead of passion, her experience at the abortion clinic flashed before her eyes. Lillie pushed Adam away, grabbed CoCo, and ran into the house, locking the patio door behind her. After closing the blinds and locking the doors, she heard a loud thud. Lillie peeked only to find Adam banging on the glass patio door. Her first inclination was to grab her cell phone; then she remembered that she'd left it outside on the table. Adam's sinister grin sent cold chills up and down her spine as he picked up her phone, put it in his pocket, and continued banging on the glass door.

Suddenly, she remembered the violent snatching incident in the park the night he told her he had more than two children and the domestic violence charges on his rap sheet. Lillie ran to her bedroom and grabbed her house phone. Forgetting that she'd left the window open, she screamed like a banshee when Adam climbed inside. Then, she ran out of the room, and closed the door. Agitated by Adam's presence, CoCo barked and growled ferociously.

The thin walls that allowed Grace to invade her privacy finally came in handy. Grace and Masseri walked into the condo armed and ready to handle business. Adam rattled on the bedroom door.

"Look here, you jerk." Masseri dismantled her gun from the holster on her ankle. "I'm licensed to carry and I won't hesitate to shoot you're a—"

Before Masseri finished her sentence, Adam burst through Lillie's bedroom door only to meet the barrel of the gun. Theo walked in with a police officer, who immediately cuffed Adam as he read him his Miranda Rights.

"You have the right to remain silent. Anything you say can and will be held against you in a court of law."

While the officer continued his speech, Adam poked out his lip. He looked like a puppy who picked a fight with an alpha pit bull.

Theo ran to Lillie's side and kissed her. "Lady Bug, I came as soon as I received a strange text from your phone. I could tell you weren't the one who'd sent it. It was confirmed when Grace called and said she heard screaming and thumping at your place. They called the police."

"Hey, guys. Whatever you do, please don't tell my parents about this. They'll be worried sick." Lillie didn't want her dad standing guard at her door each night. She also wasn't fond of the idea of her mother having any reason to snoop around her place. "Don't tell Alvin, either."

"Too late. He already knows."

After the police left, the four of them went to the living room and sat on the couch. Grace made a pot of lavender chamomile tea to calm everyone's nerves. Lillie loved when Grace made this hot beverage, because she always put in just the right amount of honey and lemon. Not wanting to leave Lillie alone, Theo, Grace, and Masseri decided to camp out on her living room floor. Theo held Lillie in his arms all night. His calming presence soothed Lillie's fears and made her feel safe.

"Thank you so much, Theo. This means the world to me. You're always my hero, and I love you," Lillie whispered

Theo squeezed her lovingly in his arms "I love you, too, Lady Bug. Thank goodness I'm your man now. I'm sick of fighting off your stalkers," Theo teased. "Now, let's go to sleep."

FORTY

SINCE THE August heat sweltered to temperatures in the high nineties, Lillie decided to pick up CoCo and spend her Friday evening lounging at Theo's pool. Theo lived on historic Riverside Drive in a retro home, high on the hill, which rose directly behind the river. He had several acres of land and all the amenities you could ever need. Ready to shake off the dust of the workweek, she dived into the deep section of the pool and swam several laps. Once she finished her workout, it was time to relax, so she lounged on an oversized float while listening to some mellow music. Lillie decided to surprise Theo with a light dinner. She rummaged through the custom designed kitchen to determine what the king would feast on tonight.

Since Theo spent most of his time at work, Flow, or Lillie's place, he rarely used the stainless steel appliances and subzero freezer. Yet, they were always full of yummy food. She sliced some Yukon Gold potatoes on a cutting board to protect the beautiful granite countertops. Next, she shook a few drops of olive oil on the tubers then seasoned them with rosemary, sea salt, cracked pepper, and JuvaSpice. While the potatoes baked, Lillie spiced up a few tilapia filets and placed them on the hot grill on the deck with several broccolini stalks. To top it off, she made a pitcher of Theo's favorite mango green tea. When she finished preparing the meal, she set it up inside of the gazebo and lit a few candles.

"What smells so good out here?" Theo asked as he greeted Lillie with a kiss. His touch set Lillie on fire, making her weak in the knees.

"Something special for a certain hard working attorney."

Lillie's gleeful response was so contagious; Theo smiled from ear to ear.

"I'm going to freshen up and join you in a minute." Theo turned to walk back in the house. Lillie couldn't help but admire how distinguished he looked in his tailored suit. He returned a few moments later in shorts and a fitted T-shirt that revealed each ripple of his chest and abdomen muscles.

"Lady Bug, you did all of this for me?"

"Yes, just for you," Lillie said as she caressed his massive arm muscles.

Theo took a seat and gazed into Lillie's eyes as he partook in the meal. Theo told her about the events of his day and she shared her own. When the work conversation died off, Lillie started a conversation about their weekend plans.

"Hey handsome," Lillie cajoled Theo. "Let's have a cookout here tomorrow."

"Sure. What's the occasion?"

"I just feel like celebrating having you in my life. Plus, you have the pool in your backyard."

"Oh, so the truth comes out. It's not about me, it's about my pool."

"No. It's about you and the pool," Lillie responded.

"Of course, I expect a huge breakfast with all of my favorites on Sunday, since it's about me and my pool," Theo teased.

"As you like, my king," Lillie responded in a fake English accent, causing Theo to blush.

They invited Lisa, Elaina, Grace, Masseri, Bianca, Todd, and Dave, Theo's friend from work. Dave was an attorney in his early fifties. Fifteen years ago, his wife died in a horrible car accident, and he'd remained single. Now, he was ready to date and find another woman to make his wife.

"I'm so glad we introduced Dave and Elaina. They seem to really be hitting it off."

"Yeah, Theo. They're a regular item now." Lillie and Theo slapped a high five as they sat back and grinned like two Cheshire cats.

෨ ෬

The mouthwatering spread in Theo's kitchen emitted an aroma that beckoned hungry people to take their fill. Laughter flooded the kitchen as friends broke bread and enjoyed one another's company. Lillie couldn't help but notice Elaina's discomfort with Grace and Masseri. She kept staring at them as they fed each other.

When she couldn't take it anymore, Elaina pulled Lillie into the dining room and said, "I know I'm older than all of you and set in my ways, but I don't know how you can tolerate all of that mess. Back in my day, people hid that kind of lifestyle. Not these two! They're walking around with an unnatural pride that makes me uncomfortable. I respect their choice, but I've got to say something."

"Now, Elaina, times have changed. I don't agree with their decision, but what they're doing is no different than what Adam and I were doing."

Elaina cocked her hip to the side and planted her hand on it with authority. "You're darn right, Lillie. That's why I told you about your fast tail, too. Don't think I'm holding my tongue, either. You young people think tolerance means acceptance, and it doesn't." She took a deep breath, shook her head, and stomped out of the room. Lillie couldn't help but follow her to see what she was going to do.

"Excuse me," Elaina said as she walked in the living room. Everyone turned their attention to her direction. "There's an elephant in this room that we're all ignoring, and I can't take it any longer." Silence permeated the room, inviting in a pregnant pause.

After a few moments passed, Masseri stepped forward to speak. "I guess Grace and I are the elephants. So let's get it over with and hear what you've got to say."

Elaina pierced her eyes at Masseri. "According to the Bible, we shouldn't even be hanging out with you and Grace since you're both living in sin."

Grace's face turned beet red and she buried it in her hands. Sensing her lover's discomfort, Masseri jumped to their defense. "With all the sin going on at Radical Faith, none of you know real love when you see it. Grace and I are committed to one another, while all these married folks are running around cheating. To make matters worse, half of the cheaters are elders, ministers, and deacons. Supposed to be men of God, humph!"

Theo laughed loudly and said, "Yeah, that's true, yet it doesn't justify your relationship with Grace."

Grace chimed in, "I guess, you can't help who you love, right?"

Lisa stood up and pointed in Grace's direction. "Oh, heck no! You just wait a dang on minute. You can help who you love. Lillie loved Adam and he wasn't right for her. You and Masseri love one another, but that type of affection is unnatural. Guess what? That means you're not right for one another. The fact that you both drool whenever a handsome man walks in a room lets me know you're not committed to this. You need to break it off." The silence in the room was as thick as molasses.

"Don't you want to be right with God?" Elaina pleaded.

Masseri stood up and declared, "Your God? The one who does nothing but condemn people to hell. I don't think so."

Grace stood by her lover's side. "Yeah! Closed-minded men who were too barbaric to know anything about love wrote the book you follow. What do they know? Why do we even adhere to those ancient principles, anyway?"

Elaina walked over to Masseri and looked her dead in the face.

"Now, Elaina, leave these young people alone. If they want to bust hell wide open, all you can do is pray." Dave flashed Elaina a grin.

His statement appalled Lillie. He might be entitled to his own opinion, but he doesn't know us like that, she thought.

Despite his request, Elaina didn't relent. Instead, she answered Masseri's question with power and authority. "That's the problem with this generation. You do whatever you think you're big and bad enough to do and have no respect for the spirit realm. Whether you believe a biblical principle or not doesn't change the fact that God is real and he has standards of obedience. What gives you the right to question the one who created you?"

Masseri responded, "I believe in God, and I'm not questioning him. I'm questioning man. Why are we so focused on my so-called sin?" Masseri asked. "What about Lillie's abortion."

Those who knew about the abortion refused to make eye contact with the others, who gawked in surprise. Maserri's intentional deflection worked like a charm. Theo immediately jumped to Lillie's defense.

"Masseri, that was a low blow, and you're deflecting the attention from you and Grace when you could have chosen not to engage. We're not going to talk about this here unless Lillie is okay with that."

Masseri sneered at Theo and rolled her eyes.

Lillie spoke up. "It's okay. I'm still struggling, but I'm not afraid to face my mistake."

"You didn't have to go that route. We would have helped you," Lisa pleaded. "That baby was a gift from God, no matter what the circumstances may have been. It wasn't yours to take away. I'm not chastising you, just not sure what you were thinking."

"It sounds like a chastisement to me," Lillie chided.

"Do you know what you opened up in the spirit realm when you decided to end your child's life?"

Lillie squirmed in her seat as she contemplated the answer to Elaina's question. She'd never thought about the consequences in the spirit realm. The only thing that mattered was getting rid of Adam's seed. Especially after how foolish she'd been.

As if she'd read Lillie's mind, Lisa inserted her two cents, "Every woman plays a fool at some point in her life. The beauty of it all is that you don't have to dwell on your mistakes, you're free to move on."

"I know that's right, Lisa. Tell it," Elaina chimed in, turning her attention to Lillie. "Now, let me tell you what doors you've opened and how we're going to close them."

∞ ☾

As Elaina shared the spiritual origin and implications of abortion, everyone was enthralled. "In Kaballah, the religion of Jewish mysticism, there's this myth that says Adam had a wife before Eve, named Lilith,"

"Oh, no. Her name is too close to mine," Lillie exclaimed.

Theo, the Bible scholar, couldn't let Elaina's statement slide. "No disrespect, Elaina, but I really want to hear this from the biblical perspective. I'm not concerned about any other religion."

"Hush, boy, and take the time to listen to the wisdom of seasoned saints," Lisa scolded Theo obeyed her directive. "Go on, Elaina."

"Thank you." Elaina winked her eye at Lisa. "So, anyway, Lilith was what we'd call a domineering wife. She emasculated Adam by constantly putting herself in dominating sexual positions. If she couldn't be on top, then they weren't having sex. It was on her terms or not at all."

Dave spoke up, "Now, Elaina, when we get married, you being on top is cool with me, as long as you're open to other positions." Everyone in the room cracked up laughing. Theo and Todd gave Dave high fives to show their support of his statement and their solidarity. Masseri rolled her eyes in disgust.

Elaina smiled brightly, shook her head at Dave, and continued sharing. "As you can imagine, she also wasn't a faithful wife.

Tradition says that she left Adam and mated with demons, and as a result, produced evil offspring. God wasn't pleased with her behavior, so he killed all of her demon babies. This sent Lilith on a rampage to kill the children that Adam would have with Eve."

"I guess the old saying about a woman scorned is true." Theo laughed.

Elaina ignored his snide remark and continued her story. "Even though this is a myth, the Bible says that the enemy is out to kill, steal, and destroy you. Abortion is just one of the many ways that the enemy tries to take out our children."

Grace drew her head back and squinted her eyes at Masseri.

"What's wrong, Grace," Masseri asked.

"When I was sixteen, I was raped. I ended up pregnant, and my adopted mother forced me to get an abortion." Tears streamed down her face as she shared the secret that had been gnawing away at her for years.

Lillie related to Grace's pain, so she sat next to her to offer support. "I never knew. We have more in common than I thought." Lillie hugged Grace and wiped away her tears.

"So, why is the enemy so concerned with our children?" Theo asked. "I need to understand this because Lillie and I plan to have at least three."

Glad to share her knowledge, Elaina responded with joy. "The enemy wants to kill you because he hates God, and he's jealous of God's creation. What better way to kill someone than from the womb? The scriptures tell us the Lord knew us before we were in our mothers' wombs. If Satan can bump you off before you're even born, there's no opportunity to fulfill your destiny, right?"

Masseri nodded her head in agreement. "Elaina, this is some good stuff. Why don't they teach this at church?"

"Good question. Maybe I should talk to the women's group leader about this. The point I want to make here is that the enemy is all about death. He sends a spirit of death to attack some people."

Lillie suddenly remembered the psychic in California telling her that the spirit of death was all around her.

"It manifests in the natural realm through miscarriages, abortion, infant death, and difficult pregnancies. It can also show up through shattered hopes and dreams, causing people not to fulfill their destinies."

Lillie opened up to hear more about what Elaina had to share. She liked Elaina's straight-forward style and the fact that she didn't sound all preachy.

"Back to Lilith," Elaina said. "Even though we know Lilith's story is a myth, her spirit is alive and real. Almost every fertility problem today is related to this spirit or people not properly caring for their bodies."

"What about heredity?" Masseri asked.

Elaina chuckled and answered. "If my parents have diabetes, I'm only prone because I'm probably eating the same diet as them or they passed their defective genes to me. If I eat to live, diabetes will most likely not be an issue for me."

For the rest of the night, Elaina and Dave ministered to each person's individual need. Prayer and deliverance took place on that evening. When it was over, Lillie felt like a heavy load lifted off her shoulders. Her mind was clear and she loved that state of clarity.

Lillie noticed Grace was pacing the floor in Theo's kitchen.

"Grace, girl. Please have a seat. You're making me nervous with all that pacing." Lillie playfully punched her in the arm.

"Lillie, you were right. Even though I do love Masseri, it's not the same type of love that I have for a man. This was more of an experiment for me," Grace admitted.

"I wasn't trying to be funny, Grace. I just know the difference between curiosity and being a lesbian," Lillie said.

"Excuse me. Am I interrupting something special?" Masseri peeked around the corner, seeking permission to enter the kitchen.

"Um—" Grace started to respond.

"No need to explain, Grace. I heard you. This hurts, because I do love you, Grace, but I really want to try to make things work with Alvin."

"Really?" Grace asked with a look of relief on her face.

"Yes, really. Can we still be friends?" Masseri asked.

"We'll always be friends, Masseri. Plus, we're business partners. We shouldn't have mixed business with pleasure anyway." Grace and Masseri shared a plutonic hug.

When the festivities ended, Lillie and Theo washed dishes and cleaned the kitchen. Theo popped a movie in the DVD player and Lillie wrote in her journal.

Healing Rain

Healing rain pours into my soul
Cleansing rain making me whole
Drip drop, drip drop
Drip drop, drip drop
Sweet mesmerizing, watery sound
Keep on falling down, down, down
Pitter pitter, patter patter
Patter patter, pitter pitter
Cleaning, renewal, refreshing
A heavenly portal connection
Splish splash, splish splash
Splish splish, splash splash
Cisterns of the deep replenished
You're healed now—It is finished

As beautiful as the words were on paper, Lillie didn't feel them in her heart. Healing was so far from her reach. She would go days feeling great, then she'd start having nightmares again. This frustration gave her the drive to finish the poem, so she started writing again. Then, the piercing ring of her cell phone interrupted her flow. Theo grabbed the phone off the coffee table and tossed it to Lillie.

"Hello?"

"Hi, Lillie. This is Gabrielle Warren Johnson."

"Umm . . . Hello. How are you?"

"Not too good. I wanted to talk with you about what happened with Adam. Do you have a moment?"

Gabrielle told Lillie that she had a run in with Brandi from Nirvana. Doing what Brandi does best, she told Adam's bride about his relationships with Dena, the club owner, Mallory, and Lillie. During the conversation, she'd ascertained Gabrielle's eloquent and peaceful spirit. A far cry from any of Adam's other conquests. She almost felt remorse in confirming the stories from Brandi's gossip fest were the truth. As much as Lillie wanted to help Gabrielle, she had her own issues. Ever since her secret trip to the women's clinic, she'd fallen victim to more horrific nightmares. Just last night, she dreamed that a fetus jumped out of the disposal receptacle and asked sweetly, "Mommy, why'd you kill me? Didn't you want me? Didn't you love me?"

Theo's laughter brought her back to reality. Lillie hadn't paid much attention to the movie yet Theo was engrossed. She decided to kick back and watch the rest of it in the comfort of his arms.

"Babe. I've been thinking." Theo stated. "Can your new consultant work your accounts next week? You know, it was a great idea to groom her to take over your role."

"Yes. In fact, we hired another consultant who starts today. She comes from a similar firm so her ramp up time will be short. So, in other words, yes, I can," Lillie answered with excitement in her voice.

"Whew! I'm so glad you said 'yes.' I took a chance to surprise you." Theo reached under the seat cushion and handed Lillie an envelope.

She opened it and started screaming with excitement. "California, here we come!"

FORTY-ONE

ILLIE WOKE up early in the morning to go for a run in the San Diego state park. Her spirit connected with the universe as she breathed in that ocean air and received the sound of the crashing waves. The breath taking scenery exemplified the beauty of God's creation. When she'd left the suite, she peeped in Theo's room to see him as he slept peacefully in a ball on the floor. They spent the previous evening in the Gas Lamp District and he was exhausted. Always the perfect gentleman, he insisted they stay in different rooms to protect one another's virtue. Theo's travel agent solved the dilemma when she found a two-bedroom suite with a common living room and kitchenette.

Lillie stopped to hydrate when she noticed a flock of seagulls flying through the air. She couldn't help but admire the avian understanding of purpose. Without inhibition, they flew to and from water-filled destinations. She stopped and sat on a bench to observe their activities while sipping from her water bottle. With no warning, Lillie felt like her spirit was separated from her body, like she was hovering over the park. In tune with the spirit realm, she heard the voice of the Lord speak.

"Lillie, you're a beautiful flower, and it's time for you to bloom. Like the seagulls, you are free to fly." Overwhelmed by the experience, Lillie's face muscles quivered and tears fell from her eyes. At that moment, a sense of freedom overtook her. Lillie felt as light as a feather, enjoying the peace and serenity. She now understood why Jesus went to the mountain to connect with his Father. Without warning, the enemy came to steal her newfound peace. Lillie heard a voice that sounded like her own. "You're not worthy. There's no freedom for sinners like you."

Lillie shook her head because she wasn't sure why she heard her own voice even though she wasn't speaking. If she wasn't sure the first time, the voice that sounded like her own spoke again.

"God really didn't forgive you, you baby killer!" The spirit of fear had returned, and Lillie bought into it, allowing it back into her life.

"Hey, Lillie. Why didn't you wake me up? I wanted to run with you." Theo ran up to her, wearing workout gear that showed every ripple and muscle on his body. The morning heat caused him to break a sweat that glistened all over his body. Perfectly groomed locks added flair to his swag that made Lillie woozy in love.

"Good morning, sunshine." She hugged Theo and feigned a smile.

He's such a good man. He doesn't deserve someone like me.

In her state of confusion and negative, Lillie began to disconnect from him mentally.

"Lady Bug, what's wrong?" Theo asked.

"Nothing," she lied.

"Come here and sit down on this bench." As Theo gave Lillie the directive, three men appeared and set up a blanket on the beach. One of the gentlemen carried a wicker basket, and when he opened it, the aroma of delicious cuisine filled the air.

"Lillie, I wanted our last day here to be special. We have a flight to catch this afternoon, and I needed to make sure that we did this right."

"This is wonderful." Lillie feigned excitement. As much as she wanted to accept what Theo was offering, the negative thoughts filled her mind.

He doesn't really love you. You know what happened with Adam. He pretended to be a man of God and turned out to be the enemy's best friend . . .

Lillie was so spiritually weak she couldn't even silence the negative thoughts.

They enjoyed their breakfast in a beautiful, yet eerie silence as they took in the awesome scenery. Lillie was most fascinated with the view of the Pacific Ocean in one direction and mountains in the other. God's indescribable creation consumed her everywhere her eyes could see. Even still, the spirit of fear had full reign in Lillie's being, causing her to redirect her focus.

Theo made Lillie a virgin mimosa, one of her favorite drinks. It consisted of non-alcoholic champagne, orange juice, and a straw-berry. When she turned up the flute, she noticed a glimmer of the little girl in the dirty gingham dress from the psychic's home she and Grace visited on their trip to California so many years ago. To no avail, she tried to ignore the tormenting spirit.

"You can't get rid of me, no matter how hard you try." Lillie heard the spirit speak as clear as day.

"Theo. Did you hear that?"

"Hear what?"

"That little girl."

"What little girl?"

"The one in the gl—" Determined not to make a fool of herself, she decided against sharing with Theo. In her mind, she willed the vision to go away over and over again. Eventually, her desires came to pass and she was back to normal. As she went to take another swig from the champagne float, she realized what the glimmer really was.

"Oh, my God! Oh, my God!" Lillie was so excited that she couldn't breathe.

Theo cocked his head at Lillie and licked his lips. Seduction exuded from his swag and she thoroughly enjoyed his display. It sent chills down her spine every time. With ease, he got on one knee, took the ring out of the flute, and said, "I have loved you since we were ten-years-old, and I have dreamt of this special day forever. Lillian Michelle Corven, will you marry me?"

Without hesitation, Lillie screamed, "Yes!" Tears streamed down her face and she was full of joy. Then, as quickly as she'd dismissed them, the negative voices were back. Lillie's hesitation in response was confusing to Theo, yet he waited patiently in anticipation of an affirmative response.

After what seemed like hours, Lillie finally responded. "No. I can't marry you."

Theo's mouth dropped open and his eyes widen. Lillie sensed his disbelief; however, he didn't utter one word. "You're such a wonderful man. I don't deserve someone like you."

Holding back his anger and disappointment, Theo remained rationale despite the circumstances. "Lillie. I've loved you since fifth grade, and I know you love me."

"That's just it. You can't still possibly want me after everything I've done with Adam." Lillie quivered and shook as she completed her statement. Theo reached out to embrace her and soothe her pain.

"I don't hold that against you, Lady Bug. According to the marriage vows I want to take with you, I'm making a covenant with you and the Lord, to love you in sickness and in health, for richer or for poorer, for better or for worse. If I can't love you like that before we're one, then I shouldn't be seeking your hand in marriage."

Listening to Theo's declaration of unconditional love broke Lillie's heart when she knew she couldn't give the same in return. Lillie cried excessively, and even though Theo was hurting, he tried to comfort the love of his life.

"You're always the gentleman. After I just refused your marriage proposal, you have every right to leave me right here on this beach, but you would never do something like that to me. I've rejected you repeatedly due to my own issues and idiosyncrasies. This is exactly why I don't deserve you." Lillie bared her heart to her suitor, with all the candor she could muster.

"Let's get to the core of this issue. What's really going on?"

Lillie knew she could trust Theo with her life, but she struggled to tell him about her dreams and the negative voices in her head.

"I'm looking past your words and I see the fear in your heart. Come on. Tell me."

"Well, do you remember the last time I was here in California?"

"Yes. Your trip with Grace, right?"

"Right. Well, we visited a psychic."

"I remember. And?"

"Well, the funny thing is her daughter saw me and freaked out in the middle of my reading. When I asked Sage to explain her reaction, she revealed that her daughter saw the spirit of death all around me."

"You know those people are crazy, so why did you let that bother you?"

"That's just it, if she's crazy, then explain why I saw the same little girl in a vision when I was at the . . . um . . . women's clinic and just now, right here on the beach with you? I can even hear the stupid song she was singing."

Theo was speechless, so Lillie took this as her opportunity to continue.

"Well, that's not the only issue. I keep having another dream about the baby. In this one, the baby actually speaks, asking me why I killed it. Theo, it's so real and I can't get those images out of my head. To make matters even worse, there are these . . . voices that, um . . . speak negative thoughts into my mind."

Without hesitation, Theo reached for Lillie's hand and pulled her close to him. The warmth of his body was like the heat from a cozy fireplace on a cold winter night. His sweet actions brought Lillie the peace and assurance she'd been craving. She melted in his embrace as he squeezed her tight like a cocoon encasing a caterpillar. As his tears started to flow, Lillie couldn't mistake Theo's compassion.

"I want you to know there's nothing we can't work through together. I'm here for your, baby, and I'll make sure you get the help you need."

"Why do you want me with all my flaws and baggage? How can you continue to love me?"

Lillie looked down at the ground, not wanting to make eye contact with her beau.

Refusing to give into her fear, he kissed her forehead and with his forefinger, titled her chin towards him.

"God forgave you and that's all that matters."

Lillie closed her eyes to savor the gourmet words her lover spoke so eloquently. She wanted to believe him, but the voices told her differently.

"He doesn't love you!"

"It's just a trick!"

"He'll break your heart into a million pieces, just like Adam did."

"Don't trust him, girl! He's a man."

Just when Lillie couldn't take it anymore, she broke free from Theo's embrace and swung at the air like a mad woman. Then, she screamed, "Shut up! Shut up! Shut up!"

"Huh?" Confused by her reaction, Theo stepped away for his safety.

Lillie fell into a heap of sand on the beach and cried like she was losing a lung. Her face turned beet red as she choked on her own saliva. Ashamed and embarrassed, she buried her face in her lap to avoid looking at Theo.

"Babe. You've got to talk to me."

When she didn't respond, he kneeled next to her and stroked her hair as she continued to cry her heart out. Finally, she lifted her head to reveal a tear stained face and a runny nose. Anticipating her every need, Theo handed her his handkerchief.

"As much as I love you, Theo, I can't let you ruin your life by marrying someone as tainted as me."

Lillie knew that she'd just made a major mistake.

"Don't run away from our love, Lillie. It's real. It's been real since fifth grade. Fifth grade, baby."

"Running sounds good right now. In fact, I think I will. Literally."

Before Theo could respond, Lillie jumped up from her heaped position and took off running with no abandon. The more she ran, the more she cried. Before she realized it, she ran almost five miles. Unfortunately, no matter how fast or far she ran, she couldn't escape the pain.

FORTY-TWO

GIRL, ARE you crazy? You mean to tell me that you turned down a marriage proposal from a perfectly good man who loves and cherishes you. One who wants to keep your virtue intact? Yet, not too long ago, you accepted a bogus proposal from that jerk Adam. I can't believe you!"

Lisa was livid and didn't hold back her feelings about Lillie's proposal drama.

"This isn't your life, Lisa. If Lillie wants to turn down a perfectly good man who wants to do nothing but love her, then let her."

Bianca had fooled Lillie, because she initially sounded supportive. Now, she was just being plain old sarcastic.

"I'm not going to let either one of you guilt me into feeling worse than I already do about this. As I've told you a hundred times, this is my life. I got this!"

Whipping her head to the other side and turning up her nose, Lillie's pompous attitude showed through and through.

"I'm not sure you really feel that way in your spirit," Lisa said. "In fact, I think you're confused." Lisa shot Lillie a scowl, daring her to disagree.

"That's the problem, Lisa. You think you know everything, and you act like you're perfect," Lillie snapped back.

"You haven't dealt with the residual effects of the abortion. In fact, I bet you're still having those nightmares," Bianca challenged.

Lillie looked away from her to avoid eye contact, and Bianca arched her eyebrow in disapproval.

"Bee, you're not my psychologist nor are you my moral compass, so stop it."

Ignoring Lillie's outburst, Bianca continued to share her perspective. "We know your emotions are all out of whack, causing you to make some dumb decisions. Mark my words, Theo won't always be there if you keep doing things like this."

"Dumb decisions? Dumb decisions? Bee, you know you can't talk about anyone making dumb decisions. Don't get me started on you," Lillie yelled.

Bianca retreated. "Okay, Lillie, I apologize. Maybe that was too harsh."

"Yeah, Bianca, that was harsh. Even I wouldn't have said it like that. Dang, girl." Lisa gave Bianca a high five and chuckled. "I know, girl, you were just keeping it one hundred." Lisa paused for a moment to reflect. She gave Lillie a sisterly embrace and asked, "Are you going to let a mistake with Adam ruin your future with Theo?"

"This is not about Adam. It's about Theo deserving someone better."

"Adam made you feel good, but Theo is good. For all you know, Theo can make you feel real good, too, once you marry." Bianca rationalized the situation. "Girl, I'm speaking from personal experience. I almost lost my marriage over lust."

Lillie was surprised that Bianca was walking such a thin line of transparency in front of Lisa, who just shrugged her shoulders and didn't ask any clarifying questions. Lisa's doorbell rang and she sauntered into the hallway to answer it. Lillie heard a familiar voice that caused the hair on her arms to rise. Theo and Elaina entered the room with smoothies and veggie chips in hand.

"Oh yeah, I forgot to mention Theo was coming over to take some hair products to the shop." Lillie noticed that Lisa winked at Bianca and Elaina.

"Hey, Elaina."

Lillie greeted her with a hug.

"Hi, Theo."

Lillie quickly waved and turned her attention back to Bianca. Theo was determined not to be ignored, so he walked over to where Lillie was sitting.

"It's no secret we didn't end on the best of terms, but can I have a hug from my childhood best friend?"

Sensing the tension, Lisa decided to intervene. "You know what? Why don't you have a seat next to Lillie. The rest of us will go organize the boxes, and you can get them when we're finished."

"Lisa, I know what you're trying to do and it's obvious these two are helping you." Theo pointed at Bianca and Elaina. "I appreciate it; however, it seems that Lady Bug is not happy to see me."

"I'm always happy to see you," Lillie responded sarcastically as Lisa, Elaina, and Bianca walked out of the room.

"Since our friends took the time to make sure we're in the same room, then I guess I should drop the bomb." Theo's lightly roasted skin shined as he removed his hat to reveal newly groomed dreads. The new style added an exotic flavor to his already handsome appearance. "I just want you to know that my offer is still on the table."

"Theo, I—"

Before Lillie could protest any further, Theo cut her off with a juicy kiss. She couldn't help but respond as the passion in her heart poured out of her lips. Even in Theo's loving embrace, she couldn't escape. Just last night, she'd had another horrific nightmare.

This time, the baby not only asked, "Mama, why'd you kill me?" it disintegrated into a pool of blood and then, out of nowhere

Doctor Samuelson appeared with his intern.

"Lillie, people do this all the time. What's your problem?" Doctor Samuelson asked with a sinister grin plastered on his distorted face.

Right before Lillie's eyes, the enchanted doctor turned into a cackling witch, while his accomplice intern morphed into a hideous black cat, hissing incessantly. The sorcerer took the pool of blood that was once Lillie's baby and mixed the contents into a huge black cauldron. While he stirred the concoction, little babies jumped out of the receptacle chanting, "Baby killer! Baby killer! Baby killer!"

The torment was too great for Lillie to bear, so she placed her hand over her ears and let out a boisterous scream. She must have been screeching in the natural realm too, because she jarred herself awake, grateful to see her friends at the foot of the bed praying in the spirit. Unfortunately, the condemning voices in her head were much louder to Lillie than the spirit filled prayers.

Theo stroked Lillie's hair and said, "God has forgiven you, now it's time to forgive yourself."

"I don't know how, Theo," Lillie admitted.

"Pray what's on your heart until you get a breakthrough. You know we'll stay here with you for as long as it takes."

Lillie prayed so hard that she fell asleep in a kneeing position. When Lillie awoke, she was at Theo's house in the guest room. When her eyes adjusted to the darkness, she found a decorative jar full of a thick amber-hued substance at the edge of the bed. Recalling Masseri's story about the honey church and her eerie dream, she twisted the cap off the jar and dipped her finger in the sweet, sticky liquid, ran it across her tongue. Lillie savored the pure taste of the honey and knew it was symbolic of her healing. Finally, she was free! But where did the honey come from?

"Ah. I see you found my treat. Babe, we need to talk."

"Yes, we do. I want to start by talking about our church life. All of the things that have happened have me questioning organized religion."

"We're definitely meant to be together because so am I. Tell me what you're thinking."

FORTY-THREE

S IX MONTHS had passed since Lillie's deliverance and freedom rang in her spirit. She blossomed like a spring flower full of rain and sunshine. As she and Theo strolled into Flow, the place was standing room only. The crowd was so thick that Lillie's normal table wasn't available.

"Hey, Elaina. What's the occasion in here?"

"Girl, after your Mr. Caramel Latte Dream went to jail and I hired that new guy, my business grew exponentially."

"Check out your man, all excited about his poetry," Elaina teased. Theo took the stage along with his typical musicians and artists. Lillie loved to hear him flow and waited in anticipation for his latest creation.

"Many of you may recall the piece I read quite frequently, 'My Lady in Waiting.'"

A number of "yeahs" and "uh huhs" floated through the crowd.

"As you know, I am no longer a hot commodity on the market."

Many of the ladies in the crowd expressed their disappointment.

"My lady in waiting finally came around, and she's here with me tonight. This poem is dedicated to the love of my life, Lillie Michelle Corven."

The crowd applauded and acknowledged Lillie with smiles and waves. "Lady Bug. I'd like you to come up here and receive what I have for you."

Lillie practically ran to the stage to be with her love. She loved when Theo gave her the special attention she craved. He knew how to make her feel good without one touch. Lillie sat on the chair Theo provided for her and she crossed her legs in anticipation of what he had to say.

Becoming One

As I gaze into your eyes, I see the mirror to my soul
So succulently virtuous, once my lady in waiting
Now that we're dating
We're connected in the spirit realm
The cosmos are aligned and our hearts are in tune
I live for you, I'm excited about providing for you
I'm willing to die for you
Can't stop thinking about you
Overjoyed every time I lay my eyes on you
Nothing matters but this moment in time
I appreciate how you keep it tight, making sure it's right
For the moment we unite, in holy matrimony
As we take the steps that prepare us to become one
I hear you, see you, smell you, feel you. I love you
Thanking the Lord for you each time I set eyes on your beautiful face
A wonderful abode for your beauty and grace
No longer my lady in waiting
I'm just saying …
Let's unite in holy matrimony, so the two shall become one

Theo bent down on one knee and pulled a purple velvet ring box out of his pocket.

"Lady Bug. We tried this before in California and it didn't work out. Since then, we've both grown and changed for the better. Our growth just adds to the many reasons I want you for my wife. So, with no further ado, I have an important question to ask you. Lillian Michelle Corven, will you marry me?"

Everyone waited in anticipation of Lillie's response.

She started screaming words of joy, and her elevated level of happiness was apparent to everyone. "Yes! Yes! Yes! Yes, a trillion times!" Lillie shouted with joy. "I love you, Theo Aaron Smith."

He removed the ring from the box and placed it on her finger. Then he replaced the Tiffany bracelet on her wrist that she'd given back to him when he and Sharon announced they were dating. The crowd went wild and started running up to the stage. Theo picked Lillie up off the chair and swung her around in circles, then he kissed her passionately. Elaina grabbed the mic and sang a prophetic song to Lillie and Theo. Just as she ended the song, both Lillie and Theo's parents came to the stage with flowers and gifts. At that moment, Lillie realized Theo planned this proposal. That was the real reason the place was packed beyond capacity.

Elaina announced, "As you can see, this is a special moment. We planned this engagement party with the anticipation that Lillie would accept Theo's proposal, and of course, she did." The crowd applauded and shouted words of joy. "Please make sure you greet them and their parents. Thanks for helping us keep this a secret from Lillie and making this a great surprise." Elaina passed the mic to the next poet and escorted Lillie and her entourage to a private area with chocolate brown couches full of large, fluffy green throw pillows. She served them one of Lillie's favorite beverages, non-alcoholic mimosas with huge strawberries along with a spread of hors d'oeuvres. Semaj, the resident artist, was the first to greet them. His gift was the print he sketched of Theo proposing to Lillie. In anticipation of a "yes," he'd purchased a special frame for the picture.

"Oh, Semaj, this is absolutely beautiful. If we have a mantel piece in our new home, this will definitely be hanging above it," Lillie said.

"So when's the big day?" Lillie jumped out of her seat when she heard that deep, baritone voice bouncing off the walls. Before she laid eyes on him, she knew it was Alvin.

"Alvin!" Lillie jumped into his arms and he held her tightly. Tears poured from both of their eyes as they knew without speaking that coming to Ohio was a big step for him. Lillie parents embraced their godson while Theo, Grace, and Masseri joined in. They hugged for so long, Lillie was almost oblivious to the round of applause from the audience. They may not have known why this was such a big deal, but they could tell this was a family reunion unlike any other.

"Mama Sophia told me everything."

"It figures," Sam chimed in. Lillie thanked her lucky stars that he wasn't high for once. He typically saved that pleasure for his own home.

"I heard I have a little brother that I need to meet."

Without any ado, Lillie grabbed her cell phone from her purse and called Adam. When he answered, she handed the phone to Alvin. He took a deep breath and said, "Hello, brother. I've been waiting to meet you my entire life." Alvin looked up into the sky and whispered a thank you to God as he walked towards the foyer to continue his conversation with Adam.

"So, just like Alvin asked, when is the big day?" Sophia Corven chimed in.

"Good question, Mom," Theo responded. "If it was up to me, we could get married as soon as the license is signed. Right then and there. I'm going to defer to my bride to pick the first day of the rest of our lives." He smiled at Lillie, anxiously anticipating her response.

"Baby, I'm in agreement with you. Let's get married as soon as possible. We've only been in each other's lives since we were ten-years-old, so no need to hold up our big day any longer, right?"

"Lady Bug, that's music to my ears." Theo kissed Lillie passionately and she returned the gesture. Both of their parents and the onlookers cheered, while they continued to kiss and embrace. To Lillie, the world had stopped for this one moment and she wanted to cherish it for as long as possible. They continued to embrace one another throughout the rest of the evening.

Theo's dad playfully punched him in the arm and said, "Son, are you going to let the girl go so she can breathe and mingle with her friends?"

Chuckling, Theo responded to his father. "I let her get away from me once, and it will never happen again. So excuse me if I hold my bride to be while the rest of you enjoy the evening."

"My, my my, son. I know you found yourself a good thing. Just like I found in your mother. So, I'm going to get some of that delicious cake and let you young people do your love thing." Theo's dad kissed Lillie on the cheek and headed to the cake table just as he promised.

"Theo, you never have to worry about me running ever again. I love you and I need you in my life. I've denied it for years, and I can't lie to myself any longer." They kissed passionately while Flow celebration continued to go full force.

Lillie knew she was making the right decision this time. There was a peace in her spirit that words couldn't explain. She felt safe in the arms of her lover, as if it was where she had always belonged.

FORTY-FOUR

LISA KEYES was running the show in the dressing room. Her morning was quite busy since she and her crew were responsible for styling each bridesmaid's hair in the wedding party. Theo's client volunteered his estate for the wedding. It was a beautiful mansion on 20 acres of land near the Columbus Zoo. The dressing room décor was funky and eclectic, perfect for a memorable wedding day.

As Lisa finished Lillie's hair, she asked, "So Lillie, have you and Theo found a new church home yet?" Lisa asked.

"No. We no longer subscribe to the tenets of organized religion. We've been going to a home study that we love," Lillie responded.

"That's different. Darn it! I forgot the tiara in my car. Hold tight while I grab it."

While waiting for Lisa, Lillie sat in front of the mirror admiring her up do, which was styled to perfection. She couldn't wait to see how the veiled tiara would complete the ensemble. Lisa ran back into the dressing room with the tiara in hand.

"Girl, I'm so glad you decided to have your cousins serve as junior bridesmaids. They went out to my car and got the tiara in a flash." Lisa laughed heartily. As she placed the veil on Lillie's head, the perfection Lillie sought in the ensemble came to light. Just then, her mother entered the room, flustering around, telling everyone what to do. When she saw her beautiful daughter, she stopped in her tracks and her jaw dropped in awe.

"I'm so glad to be here sharing this day with you, daughter. I've dreamt of this ever since the day Theo walked you home from the fifth grade dance in the gym."

"Come on, Mom. How could you have known way back then?"

"Some people call it a mother's intuition."

"Well, alright," Lisa signified as she closed her eyes and waved her hands in the air.

"Now, you know I'm not into all that tradition and wedding bru ha ha about something old, something new, something borrowed, and something blue. Instead, I want to offer you some womanly advice."

"What is it, Mama?" Lillie was all ears, anticipating her mother's words of wisdom about a successful marriage.

"Always be fresh for your husband. This ensures spontaneity without complications."

Lisa snickered, covering her mouth to hide from Sophia. Disappointed in her mother's simplistic advice, Lillie sighed so loudly that the sound echoed in the room.

"You can't be serious, Mama. I mean, being fresh is important but, certainly, it can't be the most important thing you should tell me on my wedding day."

"Lisa, does James act better when he's satisfied?"

"Now that you mention it, Mama Corven, yes, he does."

"There you have it, Lillie," Sophia said, shaking her head with confidence. "Another happily married woman is cosigning. I'm not saying it's the most important thing, but I am saying if you get that part right, it makes the other stuff much easier."

Lillie giggled at her mother's graceful candor. Then decided to chime in with some thoughts of her own.

"Humph! I hope his father is telling him to keep it fresh for me too."

Lisa and Sophia give Lillie high fives and they all burst out laughing hysterically.

"With that, I'm ready to become Mrs. Theodore Aaron Smith. Let's get this show on the road, Lisa Keyes!"

Lillie's father was waiting at the door to escort her down the aisle. As the wedding march played, her dad whispered in her ear, "You finally did it, baby girl!" He kissed Lillie on the cheek and pulled her close. "I even decided to give up that Mary Jane just for your wedding day!"

Lillie was elated with her dad's announcement. As he began to walk her down the aisle, she was ready to conquer the world and become Mrs. Theodore Smith. All she wanted to do was have him, hold him, and cherish him for the rest of their lives. Lillie couldn't take her eyes off him as they walked. His locks were groomed to perfection and his choice of tuxedo worked perfectly for his muscular build. Her entire family showed up for the event and to her surprise, Adam and Gabrielle sat right next to Alvin and Masseri who he flew in from Hawaii for the occasion. Grace cuddled up next to the Caribbean man she'd met at Flow who taught her how to cook all those exotic dishes. She even saw people she hadn't laid eyes on since her high school graduation. Theo's family showed up in mass numbers, too.

When she met Theo under the gazebo arch, she noticed the plethora of calla lilies, her favorite flowers. She batted her eyes at Theo and smiled sweetly. At that moment, she felt a sense of oneness with him that was comforting and ethereal. Today would be the first day of the rest of her life, and she would spend it with Theodore Aaron Smith. She turned towards him to take him in, and he slowly licked his lips, oozing seduction from his pores. She couldn't help but think of the letters he'd written her about what their wedding night would be like. Theo was a man of his word, so Lillie knew they would have an exciting and fulfilling evening. They planned to honeymoon in Tuscany, Italy. When they were in high school, they'd collaborated to complete a report on Italy. Lillie and Theo would gaze at the stars at night and discuss how they would visit the country one day. Lillie was amazed that he'd remembered.

Pastor Kendall began the ceremony, and when it was time for the vows, Lillie's temperature rose.

"Theodore, will you take Lillian as your wife? Please affirm by saying, 'I will.'"

"I will," Theo said with excitement.

"Lillian, will you take Theodore as your husband? Please affirm by saying, 'I will.'"

"I will," Lillie said confidently as tears rolled down her rosy cheeks.

The pastor cued them to pull out their rings. "Your wedding rings are an emblem of eternity. In the natural realm, gold rings tarnish the least and endure the most. In the spiritual realm, your rings are symbolic of the lasting and imperishable covenant the two of you are making with God and one another. For what God has joined together, let no one put asunder."

"Lillian, please take Theodore's hand and repeat after me." The pastor waited for Lillie and Theo to make the adjustment and then shared the words. "Theodore, as a pledge and a token of the vows made between us, with this ring, I thee wed." Lillie repeated these words with care and compassion in her voice.

"Now, Theodore, take Lillian's hand and repeat after me." Theo radiated a smile that could light up the entire city. As he held Lillie's hand, he stroked it gently.

"Lillian, as a pledge and token of the vows made between us, with this ring, I thee wed." Theo gazed steadily and intently into Lillie's eyes, the gleam showing his love for her, as he repeated his vows with an intense passion.

"By the power vested in me by God and the state of Ohio, I now pronounce you husband and wife. Theo, you may salute your bride."

Theo and Lillie kissed passionately for longer than the customary time. Their family and friends cheered them on and snapped picture after picture.

The pastor chuckled and said, "I bet you two are in for a long night." The wedding guests laughed heartily. "I now present to you, Theodore and Lillian Smith."

Lillie was the happiest woman in the world. Finally, she was married to a man who loved her and treated her with the utmost level of respect. She intuitively knew it wasn't happenstance that he was powerful and influential. The California psychic words rang true in Lillie's spirit.

Tonight will be wonderful, if we make it 'til tonight.

Lillie was already planning to convince her new husband to make a pit stop in her dressing room before the reception. In holy matrimony, Lillie could really feel the heat she had for Theo. It was hot. Hot, like fire. And this time, the heat would last forever.

Book Club Study Guide

1. What are your thoughts on Lillie's diverse group of friends? How do they impact her life?

2. All of Lillie's friends were successful entrepreneurs. How did she end up with someone like Adam?

3. How did Lillie's relationship with her parents impact her love life?

4. Do you believe that Lillie's godmother's spirit had a hold on her? Why or why not?

5. What is the connection between the psychic and Christian worlds, if any?

6. Grace and Masseri clearly weren't in agreement with the teachings of the church. Why do you think they attend Radical Faith?

7. What are your thoughts on Masseri's perspective of pastoral worship versus getting to know God for yourself?

8. Every church has a Ms. Blakey. How do the Ms. Blakey's of the world add value or not?

9. From your perspective, why did Adam have so many issues?

10. How did Adam's issue affect his relevancy in the ministry?

11. How did you feel about Lillie's decision to terminate her pregnancy?

12. Considering the Kaballah myth about Lilith, how do you feel about protecting the seed of mankind?

13. Should Bianca have supported Lillie by taking her to the appointment and keeping her secret?

14. What are your thoughts about Grace and Masseri's relationship?

15. Should Alvin have been so nonchalant about Masseri's relationship with Grace? Why or why not?

16. What impact do gay and lesbian relationships have on the traditional family unit, if any?

17. How do you feel about the fact that Alvin and Masseri ended up together?

18. Do you think Lillie should have made the decision to marry Theo? Why or why not?

19. Will their relationship last? Why or why not?

20. What are your thoughts on their choice to forgo organized religion and to get to know God for themselves?

ABOUT THE AUTHOR

Sherrice Thomas tells inspirational stories with elements of love, deception, and a twist of taboo. She also an experienced motivational speaker and workshop facilitator. Sherrice is married and the mother of three handsome young men. She enjoys meditation, yoga, and free-spirited dancing. She's also the author of the inspirational book The Balance Finder. Stay tuned for more great things from Sherrice Thomas in the literary realm.

www.ingramcontent.com/pod-product-compliance
Lightning Source LLC
Chambersburg PA
CBHW020231180626
46810CB00006B/2136